I0688211

Eden St. Leonards

Oberon Spell

Vol. 1

Eden St. Leonards

Eden St. Leonards

Oberon Spell
Vol. 1

ISBN/EAN: 9783337348182

Printed in Europe, USA, Canada, Australia, Japan

Cover: Foto ©Andreas Hilbeck / pixelio.de

More available books at **www.hansebooks.com**

OBERON SPELL.

A Novel.

BY

EDEN ST. LEONARDS.

IN THREE VOLUMES.

VOL. I.

LONDON:
TINSLEY BROTHERS, 18, CATHERINE STREET, STRAND.
1869.

[*All rights of Translation and Reproduction are reserved.*]

LONDON
SAVILL, EDWARDS AND CO., PRINTERS, CHANDOS STREET,
COVENT GARDEN.

PREFACE.

Some few years have passed since this story was written; but the author believes that it matches well with the current time. The characters introduced are all purely fictitious; no real person is depicted in these pages. The tale unfolds itself as it proceeds. A formal introduction would be, therefore, superfluous.

CONTENTS

OF

THE FIRST VOLUME.

OBERON SPELL.

"Who can control his fate?"
"There's a divinity which shapes our ends,
Rough hew them how we will."

CHAPTER I.

FORESHADOWINGS.

TWO boys sat on a door-step in the shattered and neglected village of Edelstone. The railways had been some years at their work of modern change and innovation. The high road which had fed the hamlet for ages with gossip and business, was now itself shelved and almost forgotten. The old stage coaches were huddled away in the back sheds, or turned into firewood, or other more profitable and useful material. The horses—those wondrous animals which did their regular ten miles an hour, were gone, no one knew whither—to the cab, to the cart, to the plough, to the knacker's. They were off the road, and had lost their individuality. With their emigration, or transfer, arose a new order of things. The stage-coach world had passed away, and the railway train had begun to run. As to coachee and guard, they were either landlords of the wayside inn, telling over bygone experiences, or had got among the betting cribs, or into the workhouse, or to the dogs at last. The steam was up, the earth was changed, and the men and women on it. Expedition was the order of the day — expedition and success. Do it quickly and do it well, or lag behind for ever.

It was a summer evening, and the two boys, Oberon Spell and Hugh Graff, as they sat on the worn stone, heeded little the faded glories of their birth-place. They did not seem to remember them. The village, to their eyes, looked, as it always had looked, a shrunken, shabby, out-of-the way corner; and yet a pleasant haunt, filled with everything they cherished. Their contemplation now was of the world above them.

" There is nothing like a setting sun, Oberon. Is not that fine ?"

" Glorious. Yet, Hugh, 'tis only smoke, after all, and the decomposition of the solar rays."

" Smoke ?"

" Smoke, or something like it. The bed-curtain of the sun. A toy to please God's children. The world is full of false appearances. There is illusion in everything. We live in dreamland."

" But to me, Oberon, that sky looks real. Is not yon figure like a lion with a horse under his paws ? —that, a goat ?—that, a whale ?"

" Very like a whale. You remember the play ?"

" Yes, but Hamlet was in jest; I am in earnest."

" And yet, he may not have been in mere sport to Polonius. He may have pointed to a picture as striking as that; for he gazed, like you, at the clouds."

" I wish I could take that bit in my sketch-book. Ah ! 'tis altered now."

" And will soon have faded. 'Tis but an evanescence. The painter fixes their spirit."

" I wish I were a painter, Oberon. But, when I look up, I despair."

" Then look down, and be hopeful and succeed. Nature was given us for inspiration, not to copy. Get any old picture or engraving; try and imitate that. It will not, if you have the right mettle, discourage or disappoint you. Art is not topography, but the heart and soul of things embodied and expressed."

" I wish I could think and talk like you, Oberon. I see things as they are; you see inside and beyond them."

" I am older than you."

" Only by a year."

" But that is a great start in a short life like ours. Besides, while you have been looking at and about, I have been looking within."

" One cannot think upon nothing; at least, I cannot. And the power of books you read would drive me crazy. I do not want to be learned, only to paint a picture and to get money by my art. Ah ! Iris, hold off. I know it is you; you are blinding me. Do, there's a good girl. I have nothing but my eyes."

These hurried words were addressed to Iris Dove, a lovely girl about fourteen years old, some two years the junior of Oberon Spell, and one year of his companion, Hugh Graff. She had glided noiselessly from the house along the middle walk, and, stealing behind the two friends, suddenly blindfolded the cloud-gazer. She did not, however, keep him long in darkness; but, laughing merrily, withdrew her hands, and took the seat opened for her between the two.

"Now, what were you talking about? I have interrupted you."

"Not disagreeably," said Oberon. "I am glad you have come. We were growing prosy and dull. But what have you here?"

"Why, my doll's quilt, to be sure. Women, as mamma says, can talk and work."

"Women!—Great baby! with a doll! You ought to be beyond that, Iris," said Hugh, rubbing his eyes, and at the same time looking through the lids admiringly on the tiny patchwork.

"When I am beyond dolls, Hugh, I fear I shall be very old."

"You will, indeed," said Oberon. "But why did you not blindfold me? My eyes are not so valuable as Hugh's."

"I don't know. Somehow it is different, and I didn't like. But, Oberon, I have learnt that pretty poem, 'A Family Picture,' by heart. Papa taught it me, word by word, line by line."

"He did?" said Hugh. "He is a good fellow, is your father, Iris. I do so love those verses.

Ah! Oberon, I wish I could compose that picture."

" 'Tis a gift, Hugh, a gift. I have mine; you have yours."

" And I?" said Iris

" Have yours also."

" Oh! what is it? Do tell me, Oberon. I thought I had nothing. Mamma says I am a useless lump of clay."

" Well moulded," said Oberon, almost to himself.

" Not so, Iris," said Hugh, " not so. I could not do that out of nothing, or a lump of clay." And he drew from his breast a fold of tissue-paper, enclosing a full-length portrait in crayon of Iris.

" Why, that is me. Oh! how charming! Thanks, thanks, dear Hugh. Is it to be mine? Am I to keep it?"

" I did it for you, as a small keepsake. What do you think of it, Oberon?"

" Let me look at it!—Nay, in my own hands, young lady. 'Tis very true, very living, very clever. Hugh Graff, you are a painter."

" Oh, good-bye! I must run and show it to mamma. I am not a lump of clay, after all."

" But, Iris, you forget 'The Family Picture,' Oberon's poem; I thought you were going to repeat it."

" And so I was. Stupid that I am! But how could I help but forget with this nice present in my hand? I am sure I laboured hard enough at my task last night. Papa hammered at it so. But I know Oberon will excuse me."

Oberon was thoughtful and silent.

"Come, Iris dear, you must begin," said Hugh; "I long to hear that pretty story from your lips, and in the way your father taught it you."

"Well, let me take care of my picture first." And, wrapping the portrait in the tissue paper, then in her doll's quilt, she placed it near her heart; then, still seated, she drew herself up, hemmed two or three times, and after a little puzzling thought, said,—

"Let me see, where does it commence? Ah, yes: I have it.

'A FAMILY PICTURE.

BY MASTER OBERON SPELL.

' Beside a cheerful fire in a low room
  A youthful mother sat. Her face was fair,
  A crystal mirror of chaste thoughts and sweet
  Imaginings, as if a seraph's hand
  Had moulded it in meekness and in love.
  You gaz'd, and instant felt 'twas religion,
  Even of the sanctuary, the consecrate of heaven.
    Pressed on the yielding damask of her cheek,
  Where smiled contentment's rosy light, a babe
  Unconscious slept; his little, listless limbs
  Spread heavily athwart the milky bulbs
  Of infant nurture: and his small plump arms,
  Dimpling like cherub's, o'er the soft white neck,
  Affection's clutch and anchor—rested there,
  As on the yearning hold 'twixt brain and heart,
  Unknit, yet graceful, while his sunny locks,
  Like corruscations from au angel's brow,
  Shower'd o'er her laughing love-kiss'd forehead, full
  And wild, as summer hay-sheaves newly mown.
  They were twin forms, but one expression, one
  Quaint portrait of infantile trust, and deep

Maternal cherishing.   She grew to him,
And he to her, till both their features blent
In grotesque union, incarnation pure
Of child and mother; a heart argument,
A bosom revelation, of the good
Pervading all this wondrous frame of things.
　　Her large blue eyes suffus'd in lum'nous love,
Were fix'd with soul-orb'd fulness on the hearth.
Beside it sat her husband—homestead word,
Whose echo lives not in strange language—bond
Which centres house and hopes, the earthly all
A gentle woman's fond ambition craves.
The sturdy, direct presence of a man
Whose limbs were ribb'd on Nature's highway, ward
And watch kept there.   The milk of liberty
Had pour'd its wealth of nurture thro' his blood,
And o'er his noble countenance diffus'd
The conscious purpose of heroic deed,
And magnanimity of dauntless truth.
The light of sanctity was on his brow,
A plenary globe of intellect and power,
For by his sinewy knees his daughter pray'd.
　　The unlearn'd, unreason'd, hearty, trusting faith
Of full-believing childhood, meeting God
In prayer, gave earnest and demure repose
To features sunn'd all o'er with rosy smiles
And laughing beauty; while the low, sweet voice,
In falling murmurs meek and monotone,
Thro' solemn, listening air ascended heaven.
A mystic, reverent sympathy attun'd
The sealèd index hands, devout and serious lips,
Unseeing, open eyes, and forehead pearl'd
With lum'nous vision of beatitude;
As if OUR FATHER were incarnate there,
And awful communing transfix'd the limbs,
Lissome and restless, of the kneeling child.' "

　　" Bravo," said Hugh; "a charming piece, and
charmingly recited."

"And you think I did it well?"

"Admirably."

"I am glad of that. It was such a bore to learn. But, Oberon, why will you waste so much paper? Mamma says she could do it on the quarter of what you use."

"Your mamma's name ought to be Thrift, Iris. She is a model of small economy."

"She is indeed. But I must hurry in and show my treasure. I will run out this evening again, if you are here. Good-bye, Hugh dear. Good-bye, Oberon."

"She recited your poem splendidly," said Hugh.

"But she ran off in raptures with your picture of herself."

"Ah, Oberon, a liking for poetry is not given to everybody. I know I learn more from your verses and conversation than from books and teachers. You always set me a thinking. Is it true that Miss Wheatley is to be at the next Exhibition?"

"I understand that Sir Roger is to present the prizes, and I believe Lady Wheatley and their daughter will accompany them."

"Do you remember, Oberon, what a rare Tom-boy she used to be a few years ago when playing in the park with you?"

"All that, no doubt, has long been forgotten on both sides."

"But then she was so fond of you, her brown-haired boy and husband, as she used to call you."

"She was a mere infant then."

"Scarcely an infant; a child of some seven or

eight years old. Everybody used to say you would have the heiress yet. She will be very rich, Oberon, and she is as pretty as Iris."

"Iris is not pretty. We must not talk now, Hugh, of what passed in Priory Park when Miss Wheatley and I were very young children."

"But you were much the older. Let me see, I think she is four years younger than you, and must now be about twelve. I understand she has grown very beautiful. I hope you like that word. We may talk, Oberon; and it would be a fine thing for you and for us all, if you were one day the master of the Ravines and Priory."

"We ought not to talk of these things, Hugh. I must to work. I have my lessons to prepare for to-morrow, and some cramming to do for the exhibition, besides some private scribbling and reading of my own. I shall not be out again to-night."

"If Iris comes, then, she will not find you."

"That will not break her heart."

"It will make her cross, though. She is quite different before your face and behind your back. I don't think you understand her."

"Oh, yes, I do. Good-bye, Hugh."

"Good-bye, old fellow." And the two friends parted.

Oberon Spell and Hugh Graff were quite dissimilar in appearance and character. The former was a decidedly handsome boy. Well knit and symmetrical, he yet had the growing look of a stripling. There was nothing set about his limbs. The build was for development throughout. Though

only sixteen years old, he was tall for his age, and
promised to be a lofty stalwart man. Already there
was much of the expressiveness and power of man-
hood in his countenance, and when seen in conversation, animated by his subject, one forgot the lad
in his first teens who was speaking, and listened as
if to a person of riper maturity and more confirmed
knowledge and judgment. His head was large, but
not out of proportion to his body, which, as we
intimated, presented the broad, muscular front of a
future strong man. The very ample forehead
formed one-half the face, and convexed rather heavily
over a pair of full and well-set blue eyes. The nose
was straight; the nostrils open and magnanimous.
The mouth exquisitely chiselled, with speaking lips,
and adorned with a case of bold ivory teeth; the
whole terminating in a chin of breadth and firmness
sufficient to sustain the general force of character
evinced in his countenance. He had a profusion of
auburn hair, which, folding in natural ripples, was
easily kept in order, and never wore the appearance
of slovenliness. Added to these personal endow-
ments, he was well dressed, quite in the costume of
a boy, and with a refreshing display of neat, white
linen to match the delicately transparent skin, whose
scrupulous purity seemed to indicate a habit of
interior fastidiousness and decorum.

Hugh Graff, his companion and *protegé*, was
somewhat short for his age. His hair, of a sandy
colour, was coarse in texture, and required much
brushing and skill to keep it from falling about his
face in straggling lines. The eyes were of a very

light china blue, but full of intelligence and observation. His other features were pleasing and regular, although one might object that the mouth was rather animal and the chin weak and submissive. The principal charm of Graff was his low, gentle voice, always distinct but never loud, vulgar, or rude. This, added to a face rather pale and even sickly, subject to hectic flushes at times, made him appear, as he really was, the most quiet and inoffensive of mortals. But Hugh Graff, when tried, was found to be dexterous and active. He performed every manual operation with an address and skill not given to his more intellectual companion. But on the whole he must be taken as of humbler nature and origin than Oberon Spell, and his costume by no means suggested easy and careful circumstances at home.

Iris Dove was a contrast in herself, of child-like disposition, yet bold and decided withal. Her appearance was brilliant and showy. She was very fair, very innocent, graceful and beautiful, with a harvest of sunny locks set off to the best advantage by her mother, and light, aerial carriage and motion, which at once reminded the beholder of the inhabitants of a higher and brighter world. She was not richly dressed; on the contrary, her frock was of the cheapest materials, but well made, and put on and worn with an eye to effect, while her pretty shoes and white stockings, sandalled with black ribbon, exhibited a perfect specimen of the feminine foot, small, arched, springing, and fastened, as it were, to two of the neatest love-knots of

ankles. Iris was a lovely girl, with a clear, ringing
voice and a remarkably fine elocution—a gift she
derived from nature, but which the diligent care of
her father had studiously watched and cultivated.
But though still a child, and with its freshness and
innocency, there was perceptible in her an absence,
so to speak, of that exquisite and unattainable refinement which constitutes the natural lady. She
was the daughter of a man of outside display, and
she bore much of this character in her language,
manners, appearance and motions. She had, however, a strong mind and stronger will lodged in a
thoroughly sound and healthy body, and capable of
large and solid improvement. Like Oberon Spell,
she manifested no forced precocity.

CHAPTER II.

THE village of Edelstone contained some good old houses; but we are not about to enter any one of them now. The personages of our drama already introduced were at best only of moderate means. Their dwellings were quite in character with their middling position.

Oberon Spell was the only child of a still youthful widow. He had never seen his father, as he was born some months after his death. The bereaved mother was not left unprovided for by her husband, who had made her sole executrix of his will. She found enough, when all debts were paid off, to realize from Consols a little over five hundred a year. She thus had no encumbrances to begin with. The world was all before her. Her house was well furnished, and the plate, trinkets, and jewels of considerable value. She was an educated woman, of methodical habits and sober, respectable bearing, and never thought of living beyond her means, or aping the finery of her wealthier or more pretentious neighbours. So that three hundred a year was ample for her regular and limited household. The surplus she invested in shares under direction, in order to make a quiet provision for her son when he should come of age. She herself would then be only in her prime, if she lived so long, as she had married at eighteen, and was a mother before her twentieth year. She never entertained an idea of changing her state of widowhoood. To her thinking it would be an act of impurity; and her sentiments becoming quietly perceptible, no one approached her with a notion of suggesting, much less of offering, a second marriage, or disturbing in any degree the fond and sacred relations which existed between the relict and her departed husband, and the noble pledge left of their heart-sprung affection. As there is something in the truly virtuous wife which protects her from even the evil thought or look of designing vice, the same happens to the woman who is a widow indeed. She must first trample on the memory of the dead—forget her virgin love, prior to encouraging even the boldest man to draw near her with the ideas, the feelings, or the conduct of a suitor. Martha Spell was very beautiful, she also mingled agreeably in society, and had little of the recluse in her character; but, as we have said, there was that about her which plainly forbade any kind of allusion to a second union. As her son grew up and almost took the place of a husband in the household, even in his boyhood years, the chances that she would ever alter her condition and nature, and begin to angle for a lover, became more and more an improbability.

The house mother and son resided in was small, but in the neighbourhood of respectable mansions, and was itself a model of neatness and order. Once a year the painter renovated the exterior for a moderate contract price, and the same signs of lively reparation took place in the interior every lustrum. It was the home to which her beloved husband had led her when a bride; it was the scene of his premature death; it was the birth-place of her son; and she resolved, should heaven so will it, that in the same abode she would grow old and end her mortal career, leaving to her child a larger span and a more ambitious destiny, suited to his superior powers, if such should be the decree of that controlling Providence to whom she submitted all her aspirations.

Mrs. Spell's house possessed every convenience and modern improvement that did not involve an outlay opposed to a systematic economy. The furniture was, in truth, what may be termed the best —a luxury not always to be had for money, or known even in the costliest mansions. The materials were good, thoroughly well put together, and of artistic pattern. The same soundness and decorative form characterized the whole of the fittings and apparatus down to the meanest articles of the kitchen.

The servant who blessed this happy home was one who had grown up with a kind of reverence for the property confided to her care. It was the selection of Deborah's deceased master, and the prize and store of the kindest, the most considerate, and the worthiest of mistresses. The home had been her own for many years. She had no wish on earth but to labour in it, and die in it, leaving every article there, as whole and perfect as possible, to the dear child she had welcomed at his birth, rocked in his cradle, and nursed, fostered, and tended to that boyhood which she now beheld with almost parental pride springing forward with large promise of a noble career as a man.

The entire hamlet was only a five minutes' run. You could compass every corner of what may be called the old town and new town in a quarter of an hour. But, then, there was the grand road adorned in separate patches by handsome modern villas, whose number yearly increased, and promised at length to stretch up to the Priory, or Edelstone Park, the seat of Sir Roger Wheatley, one of the county members and formerly a cabinet minister. This gave the whole place importance; and its proximity to London, being only eight miles distant, made the village, or rather its new adjuncts, a convenient suburban residence.

At the western or extreme end of the abode of Mrs. Spell, was the compact house in which the Graffs resided. This was a crowded nursery; every one of the twelve rooms of the cottage was crammed with children. Mr. Graff had been married before, and left a widower with a large family when he became the husband of his present partner, who also blessed him with another numerous and thriving flock. The whole group lived in the village, and as none of them were settled out in life, the wonder was how such a collection—sixteen in all— could stow away in so small a tenement. But they did manage; what with double-bedded rooms, press bedsteads, turn-up stumps, sofas, ottomans, and other ingenious contrivances to make day space and night accommodation, the entire family were comfortably and properly lodged.

Zadok Graff was a carpenter by trade, in a small way of business for himself, creeping on by slow degrees to a forward position. It would be hard to go into particulars as to his household, where the children were like steps of stairs, from the infant at the breast, to the great man whom his father had made a blacksmith, and where the whole round had to be provided with board and lodging. There was little distinguishable in the routine, but eating, drinking, sleeping, washing, mending, making and cleaning—the ordinary life of English families in their neat orderly dwellings, where there is seldom a thought beyond this world as a habitation, or of anything but home for real comfort and enjoyment. The house was Zadok's own freehold, and he managed with his sons to make a small garden productive. But at the year's end there was nothing to spare, and not a sixpence went into the savings bank. In this higgledy-piggledy, but plentiful, busy and moral home, Hugh Graff commenced his career as a painter. His beginnings were very humble; a rather lame attempt to sketch the bedpost or looking-glass of the little room where he worked, and this only after school hours, and when he had conned his tasks for the morrow. The young artist met with no encouragement at home. His father's utmost ambition was to see him a clever grainer or letterer, never soaring beyond mechanical trade. Hugh had to learn art as he best could, to make a way for himself and earn his reputation.

Iris Dove was born and reared in quite a different description of home. There everything was larger, looser, and more dilapidated. It would have taken a small fortune to keep Proscenium Villa in repair. This the proprietor could not afford, and so house and grounds went to ruin. Mr. Dove was a needy man. Nobody knew how he lived, and perhaps he did not always know himself. He managed to exist by that domestic legerdemain—shifting, and as the changes and contrivances were various and .never-ending, it was hardly worth the trouble to note or observe them. Mr. Dove, it was believed, did the business of a commission agent and promoter of public companies in London. Certain it is that he went to town daily, and spent half his time in journeying to and fro on the rail. He was subject to fitful gusts of fortune; now up, now down in the world. He had gained wealth and fame by the railways, and lost both by the same kind of speculation.

Through all his vicissitudes, Mr. Dove comported himself with the most placid equanimity. He had either been born in a sea of troubles, or had grown used to the storm by many a rough passage. Care sat lightly on his heart, and his fair, sunny face seldom gave indications of the embarrassments and difficulties which tracked his career. Whatever turned up or turned out, he drank his two glasses of stiff brandy-and-water every night in the select

parlour of the Merrythought, the principal inn of
the village.   It was in this genial seat that the
celebrated Planet Club held its meetings; of the
distinguished *réunion* Hilary Dove was president
or central luminary.   Here his authority was well
maintained; for betide what might, he always managed to pay his tavern bills.   This was the only
account which met with so exceptional a stroke of
favour.   The rest were relegated to the limbo of
embryons and shadowy existences which might
never know substantial realization.

A house conducted on the versatile principles of
Hilary Dove, could not be very snug, comfortable,
or flourishing.   There was a bareness and shabbiness
about the interior.   Some of the seizures had left
the best rooms without a vestige of furniture, or
only fitted up with odds and ends and incongruous
spoils from the other apartments.   Mr. Dove was
a persuasive and even an eloquent man, but he
could never talk the upholsterers or brokers into
garnishing the desolate chambers of Proscenium
Villa.

Mrs. Dove bore her troubles quietly.   She never
murmured.   She was a silent woman, almost a mute,
and very submissive to her husband.   In her heart
Keziah was a miser; if she could, she would live
upon nothing; but as she never dreamed of con-
tradicting her liege lord, she joined his extravagances
and shared with him a life of broils and hot water.

The commission agent deemed himself a statesman.   He only wanted an empire to display his art
of governing.   The absence of this alone spoilt

great natural powers. He always thought he would
have made a capital Chancellor of the Exchequer, and
treated debts and duns as so many affairs for the management of a financier. In this spirit he made the
most of Proscenium Villa, and was proud of it,
albeit a bare and rickety tenement. How many
kingdoms were there not in the same condition ?

He beheld in Oberon Spell, the young poet and
scholar, a prodigy—a being to be protected and pa-
tronized—perhaps one day brought within the genial
circle of his own family. His wife, when consulted,
did not second his views here. She thought match-
making for children in itself a child's game. Besides,
in her heart Mrs. Dove did not like the youthful
genius, his name, or pursuits. She may have had
her secret reasons, but she could not comprehend
intellect. She cordially despised learning, and
thought that people got on just as well who had
none. Her opinions, it is true, were mainly locked
up in her own breast, or communicated at rare intervals to her daughter. But Mrs. Dove, like other
silent persons, had a way of conveying a lasting
impression. This she always exerted in favour of
little Hugh Graff, and to the disadvantage of his
friend, Oberon Spell.

CHAPTER III.

THE GREAT DAY AT CRAMTON HALL.

DR. ISAIAH FLOWERS, the proprietor and principal of Cramton Hall, was certainly the greatest schoolmaster in the country. According to his own boast, made to a private friend, he could go into any neighbourhood as a mere stranger, and fill a school there in three months. And yet the Doctor knew nothing. It may be truly said that on no one subject could he stand the mildest examination. He was, nevertheless, the successful and flourishing master of a Collegiate school, wherein was taught the usual curriculum of languages and sciences. Dr. Flowers did not trouble himself about his own proficiency in these matters. There was no one to question him; no diploma was required; and his assurance was unbounded; unbounded too was his thorough contempt of every pursuit that did not bring in actual money. He kept good masters, whom he could effectually rule. They were machines in his hands to grind gold out of parents' pockets. If at the same time they could grind learning into the brains of the pupils, so much the better. He was Dr. Flowers. No one knew whence the title originally came; it was either Scotch or foreign, or might have come from the clouds. He had been twenty years in Edelstone, had turned out some excellent scholars, whose natural abilities were set down to his account, and whole scores of dunces who had to bear the weight of their own dulness.

Cramton Hall comprehended a very wide range of education in more ways than one. It was the only school of any note in the neighbourhood, and was the recipient of scholars from every class of inhabitants able to pay the regular quarter's bill. The boarders were understood to be more select, as a higher charge was made for them. The sole object of the educational luminary being to fill his purse; and for this the poor man's shilling was just as good as the same coin from the rich man's treasury; social distinctions they could manage out of doors. With him education was catholic. Dr. Flowers was a fortunate man—*a vir felix*—and nature as well as art seemed to take a delight in raising his academy. He had always one clever youth or other to give Cramton Hall a reputation. Oberon Spell, with his great mental gifts and handsome person, was a mighty acquisition. As to Hugh Graff, the way he got into the school was this: his father happened to have an inconvenient demand on the Doctor for work done, and he was advised to pick out a son from his family for special enlightenment in the academy. In this way the liquidation could be effected.

It was a grand day at Cramton Hall, the commencement of the schoolboys' long vacation. There was a crowded attendance, and to amuse them there was a profusion of maps, plans, drawings, and other attractive paraphernalia hung about and displayed, some of them the real productions of the scholars, many the decorated and reparatory works of the teachers, and not a few exotic interpolations, into whose history nobody was disposed to inquire too curiously.

Precisely at twelve o'clock Sir Roger Wheatley entered from the house, accompanied by his wife and daughter, and attended by Dr. Flowers, Mrs. Flowers, and a large tribe of female Flowers—all the children of the Doctor being of the gentler sex. There was a goodly gathering of the respectability of Edelstone, among whom the portly figure of the Vicar, a quiet, sensible man, was conspicuous. The Cramton Hall boys parading every Sunday to the regular services constituted one of the attractive features of the church; and whenever the bishop visited for confirmation, Dr. Flowers' scholars were sure to form the most imposing band in that gala ceremony.

The parents and friends of the scholars were likewise in full force at the present examination. Of the latter body Mr. Hilary Dove was a prominent personage. Iris sat, gaily dressed, between him and her mother, and the whole family of the Graffs were in the vicinity.

Sir Roger Wheatley was deservedly popular. A Tory in politics, he was the consistent advocate and promoter of every movement tending to improve and strengthen the rational liberty enjoyed by Englishmen. He was a practical friend of the poor, adopted and encouraged an enlightened system of agriculture, and steadily aimed at ameliorating the

condition of the labourer. Not an institution in
the country calculated to advance the moral, intellectual, or social status of the people, but experienced
in him an active supporter or dignified and influential
patron. He really believed Dr. Flowers to be a
hard-working, zealous schoolmaster, of great advantage to the neighbourhood, and he expressed his
approval of a well-established career by his countenance and presence on this occasion.

But though not quite aware of this himself, there
was another and a more interesting cause for his
courtesy and condescension. His beloved only child,
not long returned to the Priory, had expressed a
desire to be present at the exhibition, and principally,
though almost unconsciously, to gratify her wish,
the requisition of Dr. Flowers was accepted.

Ernestine Wheatley was born in the Priory. She
had passed her infancy and early childhood at Edelstone, and was much attached to the spot; but she
had now been absent some years, pursuing her
education at the Ravines, her father's Northumberland seat, and also on the Continent. Lady Wheatley herself undertook the superintendence of her
daughter's instruction, assisted by proper masters.
She had imbibed a prejudice against governesses, in
consequence of the negligence of a lady to whose
care Ernestine, when a very little girl, had been confided. The child had been indiscreetly allowed to
play and romp with some companions permitted the
entry of the park. Among these Oberon Spell
became her special favourite, and for months after
her removal from Edelstone she did not cease to

weep for her husband, as she used to call the handsome boy who often interrupted or postponed many a delicious contemplation in order to amuse the little *enfant gâté*. But Ernestine had now grown up a disciplined aristocratic young lady under her parents' judicious management. The unbecoming gambols in Edelstone Park had been long forgotten. The heiress was a beauty of a strictly classical type; she might have been a model for a Greek statue, so gracefully proportioned was her form and so chaste and exalted was the cast of her features. But there was little statuesque or cold in her character. Her eyes were restless and full of fire, and impulse and enthusiasm displayed themselves in all her actions and motions. She was still young, barely twelve years old, but in reality appeared the senior of Iris Dove, though born some two years after that important personage of our drama. If she had forgotten the tricks and sports of her childhood, she was careful to collect and conserve every possible memorial of Edelstone, among these, passages from the poems of Oberon Spell, appearing from time to time in the local newspapers and other journals, were especially treasured. She had not seen him since her return, and perhaps felt a natural curiosity to behold for herself the glorious being which everybody now described him. When not under the immediate charge of her mother, she was left to the society of Martin, a confidential maid, in whom the family justly reposed the greatest trust, aware, from many incidents and some years' experience, of her faithful, incorruptible, and discreet qualities. But

Ernestine was of a very active and inquiring mind,
and from the local organs, her maid, the other servants, visitors, and sometimes from her parents, she
gleaned intelligence of all that interested her in the
proceedings of her native village.   In this way the
approaching exhibition at Cramton Hall excited her
attention.

The old, decaying hamlet of Edelstone was not
the property of Sir Roger Wheatley, otherwise it
might have borne a far different appearance.   But
as the Priory was in the immediate vicinity, and he
was the acknowledged chief of the place, he took a
very lively interest in the affairs of the inhabitants.
His reception at Cramton Hall was, therefore, un-
equivocally cordial and popular.

However, the company had scarcely been seated,
and the baronet installed in the presidential chair,
and just as the regular business of the day was
about to commence, when up sprang Hilary Dove
in the centre of the room, and, standing on a form,
held something in his hand.

"One moment, honourable sir, one moment,
learned doctor.   Ladies and gentlemen, I crave
pardon, and ask a few minutes' indulgence.   The
interruption, I do assure you, is indispensable.   I
have found a brooch—some lady has lost a brooch.
What lady has lost a brooch?   I pause for a reply.
None?   Then no lady has lost a brooch."

"Will Mr. Dove," said Dr. Flowers, blandly,
"be good enough to hand the article up to me till
an owner be found?"

"With the most profound satisfaction, doctor,

only I do assure you I take a special interest in guarding such pretty feminine baubles. Hilary Dove, president of the Planet Club, is, I hope, known well enough here. The Dove of Proscenium Villa. I do trust I am sufficiently conservative, Sir Roger, to take care of the trifle. Ladies and gentlemen, I beg further to observe for your special information, that whoever has mislaid or lost this brooch, and will correctly describe it, may recover it any day by applying at Proscenium Villa, the residence of Hilary Dove, an old leaseholder and inhabitant of Edelstone. Mr. Chairman, ladies and gentlemen, I return you my most sincere and cordial thanks for the very kind indulgence you have displayed in listening to me with such marked attention while pleading the cause of right and honesty. But, as I perceive the meeting is naturally impatient for the speech of our worthy member and president on this interesting occasion, I will sit down."

And saying this, Mr. Dove did sit down, to the great relief of the persons present, at the same time pinning the brooch prominently to the front of his coat.

It cannot, however, be denied, that some of the audience, deeply impressed with Mr. Dove's oratorical powers, thought it a poor, flat affair, when Sir Roger Wheatley substituted for the deep, sonorous voice and graceful theatrical action of the tribune of the Merrythought, a quiet, common-sense style and manner, speaking rather to inform the mind than with the remotest intention of rivalling his eloquent neighbour.

The work of distributing the prizes did not occupy much time. Each happy victor was addressed by the president in a few appropriate words of praise and admonition. But when it came to Oberon Spell's turn to ascend the platform for the fourth time, Sir Roger Wheatley took the youth warmly by the hand, and giving way to his feelings, said with much emphasis—

"Mr. Spell, allow me to congratulate you, and to predict for you, as every one here must, a distinguished career, should you persevere in the same honourable and laborious course."

The handsome face of the youth was flushed with a becoming pride, and his elegant figure and graceful action in ascending and descending the platform, well sustained the lofty intellectual position he upheld that day in his school. Ernestine Wheatley, ever sensitive, was visibly moved, and more than once a tear stole from her eyes. She felt how many eyes were riveted on her, and by a powerful effort restrained her agitation. Nor was Iris Dove a tame spectator of the scene. A smile of ineffable pleasure overspread her countenance each time Oberon descended with a prize, and she joined all present in the clapping of hands and waving of handkerchiefs which followed Oberon as he took his place modestly by his mother's side in the body of the assembly, after Sir Roger Wheatley had expressed his final good wishes. He had many admirers both among fathers and mothers, many, too, among his own schoolfellows (Hugh Graff was the foremost), and many, it must not be concealed, among the gentle daughters present. His own mother, as befitted, felt most deeply, but was the least demonstrative. Now and then, however, and notwithstanding a severe internal struggle, an irrepressible tear would steal down her face and betray her emotion.

The best schoolboy recitations are but dull affairs to those not personally interested in the scene. These exhibitions are, as a matter of course, got up merely to display the learning of the seminary and the proficiency of the scholars. There was a Greek oration and a Latin essay, Greek Iambics and Latin Elegiacs; English composition, French composition, German composition, and Italian composition. How all this erudition was managed the masters knew best; but, undoubtedly, there was a show of genuine scholarship on the part of some of the pupils, of which Oberon Spell might fairly claim the lion's share. The only real hit was the performance of a laughable one-act farce which he wrote for the occasion, and which, in the spirit of the old Greek comedy, dealt broadly with the political characters of the time. The applause throughout was very cordial. Hilary Dove rose highest in praise. He never tired of " bravos," and always gave another when everybody else had done.

Order being restored, when the temporary excitement caused by the interlude was over, the business of cursorily surveying the objects displayed, commenced.

" And, pray, whose execution is this very clever portrait of a young lady I see present ?" said Sir

Roger Wheatley, as with his wife and daughter he passed through the room.

"Oh, that," said the doctor, "is from the pencil of a little fellow called Hugh Graff. His father, I believe, is a carpenter."

"Of course he received a prize ?"

"No doubt, no doubt, Sir Roger. But I leave these minor matters to the masters of the department." Dr. Flowers always put out his prizes to interest. They were so many sprats to catch salmon, as the common saying goes, and Hugh Graff was thought not to be worth the bait.

"'Tis a very charming sketch. I should like to see the artist."

Graff, who happened to be not far off, came forward.

"Well, sir, and so you executed this portrait ?"

"I did, sir." Hugh spoke in his calm sweet voice, looking mildly at his interrogator.

"'Tis very prettily framed," said Mrs. Flowers, by way of recommendation.

"The young folks are pressing on Lady Wheatley, I fear, Sir Roger," whispered the doctor. "The rogues want their tea and cakes ; besides, this is a day of liberty."

"We will enter the house, if you please, Dr. Flowers. And, young gentleman, what is your name ?"

"Hugh Graff, sir."

"Well, Hugh Graff, I shall be glad to examine your portfolio at the Priory, if you will call some morning."

Hugh bowed, looked ineffably grateful, and quietly retired.

"A very modest, well-behaved little lad," said Lady Wheatley, as she passed on to the house.

A few moments had only elapsed, when Mr. Hilary Dove was also invited in. He felt surprised and delighted at finding himself alone in a small room with Sir Roger Wheatley. His merits, he thought, were at last discovered and appreciated, and no doubt he was about to obtain some substantial reward from the hands of the county member. A cheque for a hundred pounds would perhaps, at that peculiar juncture, be the most convenient acknowledgment of past political services, and in particular of his exertions in favour of the baronet during the recent general election. But any convertible article, as a handsome gold watch, or even a prospective advantage, like the promise of an official post, with a good salary and not requiring close application, would be acceptable. He was not, however, long in ascertaining the cause of this sudden summons.

"I have sent for you, Mr. Dove, in order to thank you on the part of Lady Wheatley, for your care of that brooch. It belongs to my daughter. It was not immediately missed when you spoke, and when her loss was discovered her mamma very properly was unwilling to give rise to a scene on such an occasion; and presuming it was safe in your hands, preferred the quieter course I now adopt for its recovery. You have displaced it I see from your coat collar."

" My wife, Sir Roger, has taken the article home. I need not say, it is secure in her hands. Shall I send for it now ?"

" No: as it is a family relic, it had better remain in your wife's care. My daughter's maid will call for it with a proper description, rewarding you at the same time for your trouble."

" Sir, accept my profound acknowledgments. I am not so proud as to refuse a boon from a great man—a cheque, a present, a government appointment, are favours which one gentleman may receive from another without derogation, and, I trust, a member of the first assembly of gentlemen in the world will endorse that opinion. I am the president of the Planet Club, Sir Roger, as doubtless you know. Ours is only a social *réunion*—a gathering of choice spirits—the wits of Edelstone, the county cream, or milky way, as we are facetiously called. But, sir, we planets have our political influence and significance, I assure you. The orbs of night are a power, and have regulated the destiny of many a contested election, at the last moment, always at the last important moment."

" I have no doubt of it, Mr. Dove."

" With your gracious permission, Sir Roger, I would wait on you at the Priory, where I could fully explain matters. But I see you are pressed for time now, or I would seize the present occasion."

" I must not forget our worthy host, Mr. Dove," and the honourable member, without noticing his benefactor's self-invitation, politely bowed him out of the room.

The banquet in the house was a really elegant entertainment.   Mrs. Flowers was a woman of sense, and in this matter yielded the management to a couple of useful hangers-on of the family, a retired butler and housekeeper — husband and wife, who had passed their lives in noble mansions and in assisting at the preparations of the most splendid *fêtes* and entertainments.

Oberon Spell and his mother were present at this banquet.   They were assigned places at the third table, intended for the juniors and less important participators of the feast, the upper being reserved for the superior guests, comprising what was considered to be the aristocracy of Edelstone. Seated at the same table with the Spells was Jonathan Cubborn, an old antagonist and former fellow pupil of Oberon's.   He was two years his senior, and being the son of the leading solicitor of Edelstone, happened to be a marked favourite of Mrs. and Dr. Flowers.   During the previous two years this young spark had much increased his importance by taking a place in his father's office as articled clerk and mounting altogether the airs of an over-sharp, pettifogging attorney.   On this occasion he indulged too freely in wine, and being sore at the grand successes of Oberon Spell, he soon began to annoy him.

"I say, Spell, you don't mean to foist all that poetry stuff and nonsense on us as your own, do you?   As to the Iambics, Elegiacs, and all that, O'Kane and the other ushers can tell how they are done.   'Tis all very well to get a fellow like Dove, whom we lawyers have continually in our clutches, to puff you up; but mock auctions wont do in Edelstone. What is to hinder me, or anybody so disposed, from prigging a whole volume of rhymes out of old books or magazines, and palming them off as one's own? There's not a play produced nowadays but what's stolen. So are most of our poems and novels. What have you to say to this, my boy?"

Oberon raised his head, looked steadily at his maligner, who sat opposite, checked his anger, and remained silent. His mother answered for him in her usual quiet, decided manner—

"The natural abilities of my son render him superior to such mean and dishonest practices."

" Of course, since a mother takes up the cudgels for her son, I have done. I only thought Dr. Flowers too partial—not quite wide awake to the doings of authors, and all that. And as to that Irishman, O'Kane, he is a muff, or he would not be playing second fiddle at Cramton Hall."

" Mr. O'Kane is a gentleman and a scholar," said Dr. Flowers' second daughter, Emma, deeply blushing.

" I beg pardon, Miss Emma; I quite forgot that the usher is still a single man."

Miss Flowers once more blushed to the forehead, and then became deadly pale. She immediately rose from her seat and retired in company with her sister, Katharine, who was almost in tears; she was believed to nourish a girlish passion for Oberon Spell, her father's favourite pupil.

"I think, my dear, we had better withdraw too," said Mrs. Spell to her son; and they instantly quitted the room.

"I thought they couldn't stand the truth," said Cubborn, laughing aud chuckling aloud. Every one in the place was startled at this vulgar display; and a rather unmistakeable hint soon after from one of the servants compelled the disturber to leave the room. This he scarcely felt as a loss; for even he was satiated, and he felt cowed at his own insolence and unceremonious expulsion.

Thus ended for Oberon Spell and his enemy the great day at Cramton Hall.

CHAPTER IV.

THE CLOSE OF THE EXHIBITION DAY.

ONATHAN CUBBORN was only too
eager to join his ordinary companions,
and give his own version of the way he
had managed to get rid of the widow Spell and her
impostor of a son, as he still persisted in calling
Oberon. He was speedily abroad for an early stroll,
short pipe in mouth, as usual with him on his
rambles. Two or three of his chums came up to
him, and in the course of the evening he had quite
a bevy of mischievous youths as followers. As the
noisy gang approached a narrow side road with an
adjacent paddock, they were suddenly confronted
by Oberon Spell. He was alone, and deliberately
stood in wait for Cubborn, who, he conjectured,
would be likely to pass that way.

"Ha! Snob, is that you?" said the attorney's
clerk, halting. "What brings you here?"

"To chastise you," was the ready and firm
answer. "You see that field; turn in here and
meet me, or apologize for your rudeness at Dr.
Flowers' to-day!"

"Apologize with a good kick!" and saying this,
the young ruffian raised his foot to put his threat
in execution. That moment, quick as lightning,
the right arm of Oberon was flung forward in a

straight blow from the shoulder, and his assailant lay bleeding and sprawling on the ground.

"A ring! a ring!" cried the boys, lifting Cubborn to his feet, and wiping the blood as well as they could from his nose. "Come on to the paddock."

"Will one of you stand by me," said Spell, "and see fair play done?"

"I will," said one; "I will," said another; and second and bottle-holder were soon provided. Cubborn had quite a choice of grown youths for this purpose, so that the preliminaries were quickly arranged.

The spot was well chosen for a fight, being retired, and with the sod firm and level to the tread; the combatants, moreover, had the setting sun between them, as they stood due north and south, with their backs turned to the smaller sides of the paddock. They could not be said to be equally matched in age, for Cubborn was over eighteen, while his opponent was barely in his sixteenth year. But the elder of the two was a loose-limbed hobbledehoy; and Oberon, although two years his junior, was well boned, firm in muscle, of great vital force, of strength and power of endurance, of hard flesh and balanced proportion and symmetry. Neither could boast of any science in boxing beyond routine schoolboy skill; each had had some experience,—they had a general rough and ready idea of how to do the work, and the usual English knowledge, or instinct, of fair play. This sufficed for the occasion, and if always adhered to, would give earnestness and satisfaction in many a more pretentious pugilistic encounter.

Both of the young athletes stripped for the battle: a couple of cans of water were speedily procured by one of the more nimble of the gang from the nearest public-house, which happened to be not a great way off, and when everything was expedited and settled, the belligerents in due course were left to themselves to begin the first round.

From the beginning Cubborn laboured under a disadvantage in the conflict. The blood still continued to gush from his nostrils. This not only weakened him considerably, but made him savage and confused. Oberon, who was cool and confident, still plied his blows on the face, and quickly increasing the torrent from the nose, succeeded in planting a terrible stroke under the left eye, which cut open the flesh piteously. They had now been fighting a full quarter of an hour, still the first round was not finished. Oberon, as nimble as a cat, avoided closing with his savage adversary, and Cubborn thus early began to present signs of feebleness. His seconds, alarmed at his plight, asked him to give in, but he only swore at them and went on. Spell, continuing his tactics of caution, aimed blows where he could, then darted like an antelope away. At length Cubborn retired to his goal, washed and wiped the blood from his face as well as he could, gulped down the remainder of the can of water at one famishing pull, and jerking himself furiously from the grasp of his two friends, who entreated him to give over, rushed forward with a hideous and disgusting oath and seized his opponent, who was taken somewhat unawares. The ferocity and power of the attack brought Oberon suddenly to the earth, Cubborn upon him. Instantly the brute, bellowing and cursing, spread himself over his enemy, clawing him with his nails and literally gnawing off his ear.

" Hallo—hallo, this wont do!" cried the seconds on both sides, and all the boys. " Drag him off— he is biting him!—lug him away!—he will choke him!—pull him up by main force!—he will murder him!" and they strove in a crowd to tear them asunder, but could not. The enraged cannibal had resolved not to quit his savage grip of his victim till he had eaten or strangled him. Just at the moment some men who were passing the high road, attracted by the shouts which now came fast and loud, hurried to the rescue, or Oberon Spell might never have quitted that field of battle alive. Two or three strokes of a blackthorn across the prominent back of the assassin made him shriek with agony and drop his hold. He rolled off, and lay on the ground a horrible spectacle, blubbering and yelling the most outrageous blasphemies, and presenting to the eye a mass of bumps, bruises, raw flesh, and oozing gore.

Spell was awkwardly scratched about the face and neck, had a black eye, and a pendant ear. But his wounds, not given in fair fight, were far less serious than those of his brutal adversary.

The police soon made their appearance, and both pugilists were marched off summarily to the station, which was not far distant. Here it was found to be necessary to summon the aid of a surgeon, who, as it happened, lived only a few doors off. This gentleman, a new comer in the neighbourhood, made short work of joining the bitten ear. He was not so felicitous in his treatment of Cubborn. He attempted an offhand remedy for the battered nose, causing the sufferer to howl like a demon, and was obliged to leave the feature far more disfigured and impaired than he had found it. The other wounds, requiring no great professional skill, he soon doctored. But at length, worn out from pain and loss of blood, Cubborn fainted, and he had to be conveyed, strapped down, on a stretcher to his mansion.

The hero of Cramton Hall, and the cynosure of so many observers and admirers, still bleeding from his flesh wounds, covered with dust and gore, and surrounded by a posse of boys and men, beside a policeman, walked to Myrtle Cottage. In this condition he was delivered into the hands of his mother. It would be useless denying that Mrs. Spell was more than shocked at her son's appearance. There arose in her mind a sudden and unaccountable superstition and fear, and she regarded this untoward occurrence as of evil omen. It recalled another frightful memory. Once before she saw a mangled form borne to that home, and accompanied, as it turned out, by the same policeman. It is true, when she found that the wounds were not serious, and had learnt the full tale in all its particulars, although no word of commendation or approval escaped her lips, in the bottom of her heart she was glad of the gallant and manly part her son had played in an affray otherwise deplorable.   She began no lecture or admonition.   She knew that her boy wanted rest.   That day had been one of continual and fearful excitement to him.   So what with her own and Deborah's cherishing and attention, he was soon laid in his bed, after suitable refreshment, and almost instantly sank into that deep repose which the angel of assimilation asks to carry on his marvellous work of refection throughout the frame.   His mother watched and prayed to a late hour by his bedside that night.   Perhaps her instincts were right. Heaven's protection was especially needed here. Woe betide you, Oberon Spell, should you ever fall under the claws of the future legal hyena of Edelstone !

CHAPTER V.

THE morning brought much and very serious reflection at Myrtle Cottage. Oberon Spell may have played the part of a hero in more ways than one, but he now looked very like a ruffian. He had an ugly black eye, his lips were swollen, his face, neck, and chest vulgarly scratched, and his right ear strapped up with sticking-plaster. The plain, unmitigating light of day presented all this hideously enough. His mother, whatever were her deeper and inner feelings, could not but express herself both pained and offended. Her son was evidently the aggressor. He went out prepared for the fight, determined to provoke it, if an apology were not tendered. The result was a savage and brutal conflict, of which no one could feel proud, accompanied, as it was, by horrible and dangerous gashes and wounds, shouts, struggles, and the necessary interference of the surgeon and police. What could appear more blackguard, not alone in a gentleman, but a youth of intellect, attainments, and presumable morality? Cubborn's hurts were reported to be of a malignant character. His mother was a virago, and compelled her husband to acts of persecution and tyranny. He might prove a troublesome antagonist—his son a life-long enemy. The accident was most untoward for Oberon. That very morning he was to be at the Priory, availing himself promptly of an invitation given by Sir Roger Wheatley. Of course, he could not go now. But how to excuse himself! Moreover, Mr. Ajax Lever, his uncle, or rather his aunt's husband, was expected that day. The object of his visit was to see Oberon and confer on his future profession. Mr. Lever was an eminent engineer much occupied in foreign railways. As he had no sons of his own, it struck him that his nephew, Oberon, of whose literary productions and letters he thought very highly, might find suitable and emolumentary employment on his own staff, while at the same time the youth would be mastering a foremost and thriving profession. Besides, there was a kind of arrangement subsisting between Mrs. Lever and Oberon's mother, that if matters should cohere, both the cousins, the engineer's only child, the heiress to a large fortune, and the son of the widow, should one day become husband and wife, and thus keep the wealth within the Spell family, to which both ladies were tenderly bound. Mr. Lever knew of this arrangement, and approving of Oberon, it met his hearty sanction. Mrs. Spell had all this present before her, and it grieved her deeply that the expected visit of this gentleman to her son must take place under circumstances which would most likely, for the present at least, put an end to such favourable prospects.

While she was calmly ruminating on so signal a misfortune, Deborah announced an early visit from Dr. Trensham. He called uninvited to see his young patient. He was a new settler in Edelstone, was a single man, a great contriver, and had some remote idea of the widow. He certainly did not know Mrs. Spell, or understand her character. But he had made up his mind to have Oberon, if possible, as his pupil and assistant in carrying out a grand scheme he had *in petto* to make a rapid fortune. Dr. Trensham was a very bad surgeon. The use of the knife, and sore flesh and broken bones troubled him. But he was a subtle thinker and clever theorist, and treating internal diseases only, might pass for a prodigy. He therefore became a physician.

"And how is my young patient this morning?" said he, bowing to Mrs. Spell, and taking the outstretched hand of Oberon.

"I feel well enough. Only I wish I could get rid of these ugly scratches and bruises."

"The badges of your valour. No, my young friend, they must remain till nature wipes them out. My system is never to interfere with nature. A sad accident this, madam. But from all I hear the fault was not Mr. Spell's."

"No, but the peril of entering into such broils!"

"I believe it is impossible," said Oberon, deprecatingly, "to pass through life with independence, manliness, and honour, without sometimes coming into rude collision, it may be personal, with others."

"But these others, my child, may be ruffians not worth the soiling of a gentleman's fingers."

"One's schoolfellow, however bad, is an equal."

"Ah! we must forget it all, my lad, forget it all. Get well, and have done with mischievous bookmates. How should you like to be a doctor, eh, and have them all under your thumb one day?"

"It would be rather hard to get one's living by the maladies of others. Never to be called to the side of intellect, valour, or beauty but when these were in abeyance. It is hard to become familiar with the sick-room and the charnel, unless, indeed, with a strong sense of duty."

"There it is. To remedy disease, to set all these charming beings on their feet again! This is our triumph—this our profession—one worthy of the most refined and benevolent mind!"

"But, then, you have to succeed."

"There, I grant, you have me, or long ago I should have made a fortune. The science of therapeutics, though as old as Adam, is still, sir, in its infancy. There must be a new science—the science of health—HYGIENE. We must cease to be jobbers and begin to be builders—not called in to mend and patch a broken body, but to keep it whole. Our conversation then will be with strength, health, valour, intellect, beauty, and wisdom, not with disease and decrepitude. Look you, sir—look you, madam, what to eat, drink, and avoid is the great principle—the panacea. The amount of carbon, oxygen, hydrogen, nitrogen, required by each constitution, whether sound or diseased. This is my system. I reduce everything to its elements. I regard the human frame as a laboratory, and with-

draw or supply the fundamental sustenance just as
its presence, or the contrary, is necessary for health.
The doctors do not know what disease means. They
confound effects with causes—symptoms and mani-
festations with the real source; while these are
only the efforts of impaired nature to break out and
cure herself—to cast away her impurities—efforts
which physicians foolishly arrest. What, then, is
disease, madam?   Ah! a profound question that.
It is—mark me—it is the congenital appetency of
the constitution to produce an abnormal secretion,
or it is this tendency—this injury to vital force,
caused by accident, whereby the tissues are over-
stimulated or under-stimulated, as the case may be,
through the organism of the nerves. This appetency,
tendency, proneness, inclination, lesion, or whatever
else you like to call it, madam, is the real defect—
the genuine disease—the *causa causarum*, dear
madam.   Now, the physician is good for nothing,
if he cannot check or destroy this irregular motion
in organic life—if he cannot wholly eradicate what
are called the seeds of disease, or more properly
defecate and purify the unhealthy ovarium in which
these wandering seeds are lodged.   I can do so,
madam.   Herein is my secret—my arcanum—my
mystery.   How to master and modify vital power—
how to order the tissues—how to regulate the secre-
tions—what to put into the stomach—the way to
make pure and vigorous nerve matter—healthy
blood, sound bone and muscle—and normal excre-
tions.   That is my cure.   I prevent disease, or I
extirpate it."

" But how ?"

" Observe, dear sir—observe, madam—do but note me. A certain amount of vitality or vital energy is given to everyone when born. This is his dowry of life. As long as this lasts, no matter what the pain and suffering, he will last, if not cut off by accident. It is the wick of the candle, madam, which will burn to the end, if not snuffed out before; and, as you know, madam, there are many ways of snuffing out a candle, so there are various modes of destroying vital force. There may be congenital disease to waste it, or induced disease—the winding-sheet and thief on the candle, madam; hereditary taint, inborn proneness, or acquired malady, will shorten our days and fill them with pain, or defect, or suffering of some kind, and cause an uncertain dim and flickering or brief light for a strong and lasting one. You may, as I said, madam, put out the flame altogether by a power sufficient to destroy it. I could kill you with a hatchet, madam, or a dose of poison. Premature death, no matter from what cause, is homicide—it may be murder; murder by the doctor, murder by neglect in various ways, the total destruction of vital energy somehow. Now, sir, in my system, what I steadily regard is this original principle of vitality, this life of our life, this normal measure of our being—the wick of the candle. I cannot increase it, for it is a predetermined quantity. It is out of the power of medicine to add a moment to existence; but it can prevent its waste, or improvident destruction, by removing from it all impediments to its free and regular motion. I can make my candle burn bright and bravely on to the end, madam. I let my patients live as God intended they should live. I do not slay them, sir, or allow them to commit self-murder by contracting disease, which many do involuntarily, labouring under ignorance which is fatuity, sir."

"But how do you save your patients, doctor?"

"On the drenching system, sir. I wash the frame with medicated drinks; I prop the frame with medicated viands; I supply good oil to the cotton of my lamp, good grease to the wick of my candle. I turn the body into what it should be, madam,—a doctor's shop. I banish disease through the stomach —that is, through wholesome assimilation."

"Then you do not hold with our neighbour, Dr. Atomcraft's new theory of the globules?"

"Ah! the infinitesimal doses, Homœopathy, the *similia similibus curantur*, and all that. Preposterous quackery! No, thank God! mine is the very opposite system. I would not, 'tis true, make the stomach a physic jar; for there must be no excess even of a good thing. But I would constitute every morsel of food taken into it a medicine. Instead of having a farthing candle—a puny thing—out of my wick, I would give it sustenance enough of the right kind for a full strong light, sufficient to illumine and cheer all around."

"Good; if one only knew the proper oily matter —the true substance to feed the vital force. Where to find this is the question!"

"Nonsense! Where? Everywhere. The elements; carbon, nitrogen, oxygen, hydrogen, are above, below, around, about, within, without, beside, beyond us. We are in the midst of genial nutriment. The flesh, fish, vegetable, fruit, and liquids we partake of are all medicinal; and for direct remedies, the pharmacopœia is full of them; 'tis only to swallow enough to get well—small doses do more harm than good. You must saturate the system with your curative when found; saturate, I say, but not drown. I want people to eat and drink their physic. This will not protract life beyond its natural term; not lengthen the wick, but it will prevent guttering and premature extinguishment. So we must make our meal of drugs."

"But people wont. It would be too repulsive."

"Not more so than beer, vinegar, spirits, mustard, and a hundred other things we take into the stomach at our ordinary meals. Why need medicines be rendered disagreeable? Is there no means of blending them?—of making them palatable? I know there is, and in my new system of cookery I intend to propound the art of serving-up physic as an agreeable luxury. But before I have done, I would impress one thing on you, madam."

"What is that, sir?"

"To keep the sewers of the body all free and open, in particular the main-drain, madam. Only imagine, for instance, what your neat house would be with a cesspool stopped up in the middle of it; that is what our poor human frame would be, madam, with its numerous and intricate natural sluices and gully-holes clogged-up or out of repair. Now, Master Oberon, you have heard the mystery

of the system; you are initiated.   Will you become
a votary and make fame and fortune?"

"These matters are all rather premature at present," said Mrs. Spell, rising.

"And I wish you could cure the scratches and
bruises on my face, doctor," added Oberon, with a
quiet smile.

"To tell you the truth, young sir, I am above
small cures; they do not suit me; I leave them to
the great doctor—Nature—or to my inferiors.   I
attend the grand maladies—typhus, phthisis, gan-
grene, hydrophobia, and cholera.   But you are
standing, madam, and my patients are waiting for
me.   I will call again to-morrow morning."

"If Dr. Trensham thinks it necessary," and presenting him with a guinea fee, which she had prepared while he was lecturing, she added, with a
smile, "the time of a medical man ought to be of
value."

"And so it ought, dear madam," said Dr.
Trensham, pocketing the *honorarium.*   "I wish you
both a very good morning;" and the professor of the
drenching system bowing very low, took his departure.

"An original that, mamma, one of our natural
quacks with diplomas."

"With all his eccentricity there is something in
Dr. Trensham I admire.   I like his taking to you,
and his idea of making you a doctor is not altogether
so preposterous.   There is something in the man
not disagreeable to me.   But I must hasten to
Deborah, as I expect your uncle Lever now every
moment."

CHAPTER VI.

BOUT a quarter of an hour after the proceedings with which we closed the last chapter, a cab drove up to the door of Myrtle Cottage, and the burly, portentous form of Mr. Ajax Lever, C.E., F.R.S., F.S.A., made its comprehensive appearance. Oberon, the moment he caught sight of the giant, was rapidly escaping to his own room.

"There is no occasion to avoid me, sir; I have it all here, black and white, in the columns of the *Morning Herald*. I am sorry for it too;" and saying this, Mr. Lever handed the journal to the youth, who immediately returned to the place he had previously occupied. Mr. Lever was a remarkable man. He was as big as any three men put together, and breathed so hard and moved so unwieldily and unceremoniously, that he quite disconcerted and agitated the small room into which he was ushered, as well as its two inmates. The arm-chair, though thoroughly well made, groaned in every joint, as the ponderous body of Ajax settled into it. Then the very pictures and paper-hangings seemed to suffer from the large spectacled blue eyes, which searched through and through them at every corner.

4—2

UNIVERSITY OF
ILLINOIS LIBRARY

Mr. Lever had surveyed the room, and could lay down a plan of everything in it, to the flowers of the hearthrug, which by some unaccountable accident were that day turned the wrong way. Of course he absorbed the fair widow and her disfigured son at a glance.

"That is an ugly tag at the end, is it not?" said he, addressing Oberon.

"But it is not true."

"What is it, my dear?" said his mother.

"The *Morning Herald,* which uncle has just handed to me, contains a very glowing account of our yesterday's exhibition. But the report winds up with this passage :—' It is to be regretted that the day closed with a very vulgar and very unfair fracas between the leading prizeholder and captain of the school, Mr. Oberon Spell, and the son of Mr. Cubborn, a highly respectable local solicitor. Young Mr. Cubborn is a very serious sufferer from a violent and, we must add, un-English attack by his adversary, who, it appears, was the first aggressor. The wounds are of so malignant a character, that we have no doubt ulterior proceedings will be taken to punish this unprovoked and outrageous assault.' "

"But nothing can be more false than that statement," said Mrs. Spell.

"That will scarcely alter its effect," replied Mr. Lever.   " How did it get into the papers?"

"One of Cubborn's clerks does penny-a-line business," said Oberon.   " That is the source of the report.   Dr. Flowers paid him for the first part, and

his master for the second part; and he gets a penny
a line from the newspaper for what is inserted."

"You seem to know it all by heart, Master
Oberon. But were you really the aggressor?"

"He grossly insulted my mother and me. He
wanted to make me out a literary impostor—the
pirate of others' writings, and I own I went out in
the evening and challenged him to fight, offering
the alternative of an apology. His only reply was
an additional insult, and an attempt to kick me.
Then, I admit, I gave him a blow on the nose, and
thus prevented his outrage."

"There it is, you see, you struck the first blow."

"I did; I could not well do otherwise. But
after that a regular ring was formed in a paddock
hard by, and we began a fair stand-up fight. I
aimed at his face, and the original wound was increased. He got badly punished; his seconds
wished him to give in, but he would not, and instead
of this he rushed at me, flung me, overlaid me,
began clawing my face and gnawing my ear, and
would have eaten me had he not been dragged off.
The doctor and police will tell the rest if called
upon."

"I have no doubt you played fair in this bout,
and that you had received ample provocation; but
the fight itself was wrong, the challenge was wrong
and silly, and the first blow was a downright
blunder. Only blackguards indulge in fisticuffs
now."

"Then is every school in the kingdom full of
blackguards? 'Tis the way we settle our differences."

"You settle nothing, but make ruffians of yourselves. You must write to the editor of this paper, and get to see the others. No doubt 'tis in all of them, so you must answer them all if required. They are bound to insert your letter, or stand the consequences."

"I am sure Oberon is to be excused in this instance," said his mother, "though I disapprove of pugilistic encounters altogether. But let us change the subject;—how are Frederica and Caroline?"

"I hope they are well. I have not seen either of them this fortnight. Pleasure after business. I wind-up for the present by my visit here. Then for home and respite a few days from labour."

"It was indeed very kind of you to give your attention to this affair of the placing of Oberon. He is now sixteen years of age. But here comes Deborah with some refreshment. First recruit yourself, and we will enter on the other matter at your leisure."

"Thank you," said Mr. Lever, "there is something practical in that. Cold ham and turkey, pastry and fruit, sherry and pale ale, my favourite cognac, French roll and butter, cheese and salad. It can't be better, Martha. I'll discuss this first, then to business. I'm off from here in two hours. I see you are a minute slow," pulling out a huge chronometer. "I am longing to get home."

"I shall trouble you with a small parcel for Frederica and another for Caroline. They will both go into your pocket."

"Ah! she is a charming girl. You do not fatten

your own turkeys, of course, Martha? This is very fine flavoured."

And no doubt Mr. Ajax Lever thought so, for without any evidence of gluttony, on the contrary, with many signs of good breeding, fairly tested in our manner of taking our meals, he managed to make a very hearty collation.

During luncheon Oberon, who had withdrawn, was busily occupied in writing a letter to the editor of the *Morning Herald*, which, when finished, he submitted to his uncle. Mr. Lever carefully read the document, and approved of it.

" Of course you will not send it off till you have made a copy? Should anything be said in the other papers, you must act in the same way. These matters are very troublesome; but one must be always careful in vindicating character. This is never done I can tell you, Oberon, by fighting, I think you ought to know that. The best way, however, is, if possible, to avoid offence; and in particular such awkward collisions as are sure to get into the newspapers."

" A good plan that, uncle, to grow-up a sneak and a milksop."

" A good plan, young master, to grow-up a man —a successful, respectable man. Look at me. I am now among the foremost of my profession; yet, I began life as a call-boy on board a Thames steamer. I hope I have augmented every way. I believe I am universally respected,—I could get into parliament any day I liked. Now, hear me, Oberon Spell, and as you listen note what I say. I owe my success as much to negative qualities as to positive—as much to forbearance as exertion—to tact as to talent. I never made an enemy; I could not afford to do so. No man can. I have made a thousand friends; I am rich in men's good-will and amity. If this is growing-up a milksop, I trust I am a fair specimen."

" You look as if you would not bear an insult, Uncle Lever."

" Of course I would not; people would pause before insulting me. But there is a way of treating these petty annoyances, when they do occur, as if they were beneath one's notice; and there's a better way still—never to provoke them, and not to be too sharp in spying them out. And now, Martha, what is to be done with this boy, that is if he will allow anyone to do anything with him ?"

" But Oberon is very docile, — I have always found him so. Dr. Flowers likewise; and indeed every one with whom he has had dealings. You must not be misled by this untoward affair; more-over, he must not be regarded as a mere child. He is forward for his age."

" All the better for that, only he must not be too forward with his fists. The highest object of life, next to seeking the hereafter, is to live longest of use to ourselves and fellow creatures. One cannot begin that too soon."

Deborah entered, and whispered her mistress.

" Tell Master Graff to come in. Hugh Graff, my dear, come to see you. One of Oberon's schoolfellows and youthful companions. Master Hugh Graff, Mr. Lever, Oberon's uncle, my dear."

"Hugh bowed and smiled a recognition, passing on to Oberon, whom he shook warmly by the hand.

"I was so sorry, very, very sorry indeed, you took any notice of Cubborn. Why, they set about chaffing me in the same manner at the tea-meeting. They said that sketch of Iris could never be mine."

"And what did you say, my little man?" asked Mr. Lever.

"Nothing, sir."

"What! nothing, and bear that?"

"Well, I felt within myself that I did do it. I knew that everybody I cared for believed that I did, and I thought that I should live to do better and convince people in time. It struck me, too, that there must be some fault in myself, or no one would doubt me. I am only a beginner, and persons require to know me."

"Well said. The burden rests with you, then, to live down this small scandal. You will do it, mark me."

"I hope so, sir. I am going to Sir Roger Wheatley's, Oberon, and I am so grieved that you cannot come with me. But I see you cannot."

"The member, of course, he means?"

"The same," said Mrs. Spell. "Oberon had intended being at the Priory this morning. However, I believe, my love, the invitation was general."

"Oh, quite so, ma. No time was specified; 'any morning,' were the exact words."

"Otherwise, you should write an apology; but now there is no occasion."

"The invitation to me was just the same. I will not go till Oberon goes," said Graff, putting down his portfolio.

"There's a dear boy," said Mrs. Spell; "but your parents wished you to go, and you have come out prepared; so I advise you not to disappoint them. You may mention, if you have an opportunity, that your friend here has met with an unpleasant accident."

"I will be sure to do that. The policeman told my father all about it. He said Cubborn was to blame; and his conduct, when Oberon was down, was not right."

"These are very clever drawings, my little man. I have been looking at them. I like them, and I approve of what you have said and done. My name is Ajax Lever. There is my card. If ever you want a friend, and I can serve you, do not fail to call upon me. I will remember you."

"Thank you, sir."

"I am sorry, Martha, our friend here is not in a fit condition to go to the Priory. I wanted to cultivate Sir Roger Wheatley for reasons of my own. It is confoundedly awkward."

"I fear it must be borne," said Mrs. Spell, with some dignity. "Good morning, Hugh, I wish you a pleasant day."

Hugh whispered his companion that he would slip in on his return, and tell him all that had occurred; then taking him warmly by the hand, with a low bow to Mrs. Spell and Mr. Lever, he left the room.

"That little creature said all that is necessary, or right to do or think, about petty malice and slander. It is a challenge to good behaviour. Contradict it if you must, but try and live it down would you avoid a life of turmoil. I had some idea, Martha, of asking you to let me have Oberon in my office, to act as a kind of private secretary to me, at the same time that he obtained every opportunity of learning my profession thoroughly. But he must put self-will at the door."

"Do you think, uncle, that the hard, matter-of-fact engineer is a calling which would suit me. I fear I might not like it."

"But you must live, my dear," said the anxious mother, "and uncle Lever's position is a very high one; he could, aided by your own abilities and labours, push you forward into the formost ranks of the profession."

"But, mamma, the engineer's is a very rough blacksmith-like trade, for there is the mechanical art to learn as well as the intellectual profession. What, if I should not like it?"

"Do not try it, Oberon. I have been looking at my hands and yours; there is some difference. But what will you do?"

"Well, I should like to continue at my studies for another couple of years at least, to master Greek and Latin composition, and then go to College."

"Greek and Latin what?"

"Composition, sir."

"Composition—trash!—what you must forget, and never practise in life except as a teacher. No, a smattering of these things may be necessary, since we must all pretend to a great deal in this world. It will answer every purpose."

"Is Mr. O'Kane a proficient in Greek and Latin composition?" inquired Mrs. Spell of her son.

"He is accounted a profound classical scholar, mamma, and eminent for his knowledge of this very subject. I need not tell you how much of genuine intellectual supremacy such high attainments imply."

"How comes it then, my dear, he is only an usher under Dr. Flowers, who, you know, is no scholar at all?"

"I am sure I don't know, mamma. I believe there is some kind of engagement between him and one of the Miss Flowers. I suppose he best understands and pursues his own happiness, as I wish to do mine."

"Well, my dear, but you must be able to get your bread, to keep house respectably, to marry and maintain a position in the world."

"I am not ambitious of grandeur. What I aim at is felicity."

"Felicity—fudge! Oberon Spell," said Mr. Lever. "You were never made for an engineer, so let us drop the subject, it only provokes me. I had my plans, as your mother well knows. But no matter, Oberon, you can command me in whatever profession you may choose, only let it not be that of a civil engineer."

Saying this, Mr. Ajax Lever rose and stood up

like a tower in the room. One could well be proud
of such a friend, certainly of such a relation ; for
Ajax Lever was a creator among men. He had
spread more beauty and usefulness over the earth
than the whole race of poets put together. Notwithstanding Oberon regarded him only as a kind
of behemoth, an uncouth form out of the great ocean
of the world, a Titan, if you will, but with the ima-
ginative eye out. There he was wrong ; for the
engineer was brimful of invention. However,
Oberon was glad when he saw the huge Cyclops'
back receding from the small precincts of Myrtle
Cottage and Edelstone, glad as we all are when we
have got rid of a weighty and puzzling contradiction.

He was scarcely gone when Iris Dove was
ushered into the reception-room.

" Oh, Oberon, what a figure you are ! I wish
I had been near when that fellow, Cubborn, insulted
you !"

" Why, what would you have done ?" said Mrs.
Spell, struck with the girl's air of vigorous demon-
stration.

" I would have smacked his face well, that is all ;
but I am glad you paid him home. He had no
right to annoy you. I can see his impudent looks
at me ; but I know how to keep such animals in
their place. You are a great fright, Oberon. Is it
anything serious ?"

" No, only these scratches."

" And the ear he had bitten. I hope he was not
mad. But I am so glad you will not lose your good
looks. I only ran in just to see you. I must

hurry back, for papa has company this evening."
And bidding the invalid a hearty good-bye, she
curtsied to his mother and departed.

"A bold girl that, and an acquaintance I do not
approve."

"Dear mamma, pray leave me something I do
like. Iris is my friend, and I will not forsake her."
With this Oberon ascended to his own room to
glance over all the daily papers, which had just been
supplied, and if necessary to dispatch letters to the
editors.

CHAPTER VII.

MRS. CUBBORN had strong ideas on the subject of pugilistic encounters. She on occasions did something privately in this way herself, and her only notion of fair play was to go in and win. Of the art, or science, or law of combat she knew nothing and cared nothing. Her sole aim was conquest; and whether this was obtained by blows of the fist, scratches with the nails, tugging the hair, biting, or kicking was all one to her, provided there was victory. This was her rule of right, and made everything square. She could not conceive that any one would voluntarily stop short in the grand rage to follow some absurd regulation of the prize ring. She certainly was not going to stand the nonsense that her son's nose had been broken without a stone in the hands of the enemy.

"That's it; I see it all. The villain had a stone in his hand."

"There was a mound of flints hard by," said Jonathan, with a groan, and anxious to catch at anything to bring Oberon Spell within the clutches of the law.

"A mound of flints, eh, darling! I knew it. I saw it all. I am never wrong."

"If that were really the case, and he had a stone

in his hand, I think I should know how to tackle
this brave youth," said Cubborn, senior.

"You would know how to tackle him—you!
Why, you had not a word to say until I thought
of the stone; now, of course, when I speak you see
your way clear enough."

"Ah! but legal proof is different from conjecture.
You were not there, and cannot speak to the fact."

"I was not there! But who wanted to be there?
Must everybody be there who proves an event?
You saw the stone in his hand, did you not, Natty?"

"I did, mother."

"My own son : brief and to the purpose."

"Of course you cried out that he had a stone,"
edged in the lawyer, cautiously.

"No, I did not."

"Why will you puzzle the child? Do you think
in his present state he can answer your cross-
questions? 'Tis plain, the whole case will require
careful consideration. I shall weigh all the particulars and deliver my judgment to-morrow morning."

The next morning the lady was all activity.
Attired in a rich brocade wrapper of crimson, a
thick nightcap on her head, spotlessly white, with
its border and long pendant strings deeply fringed
with Mechlin lace, and wearing a profusion of rings
on her fingers, Mrs. Cubborn took her seat at the
desk in her inner office, the centre of a circle. The
whole arrangement of the business chambers attached
to Mr. Cubborn's mansion was the design of his
managerial wife. A small compartment was assigned
to each clerk, but they could be conveniently ob-

served from Mrs. Cubborn's room without the lookers on being seen. In the lady's apartment was a series of bells worked on to the large writing table before her. These she touched when she desired either her husband, her son, or any one of the clerks to enter. They were strictly forbidden to appear through the double door of the principal room until the small tinkling bell had announced the permission. In this way everything was conducted with privacy, and confidential business was not bruited among a body of clerks to be circulated through the whole village. Mrs. Cubborn was a great and original woman, and had peculiar ideas of the capabilities of her profession; for though not as yet formally admitted on the roll of attorneys, she had her notions that at no distant day the sex would enjoy that privilege. For the present she was the moving power of the firm, and ordered and controlled all its business. She thought that business capable of wide extension, but despairing of her husband, she steadily fixed her hopes on her son, who, compound of malice as he was, was yet entirely her slave and of her special moulding.

She now rang the bell of her managing clerk, and in a moment Mr. Edward Trapper appeared.

"You were late this morning, Trapper. I expect all my clerks to be at their desk punctually at nine. I did not see you as I passed through. Do not repeat it."

"I had a call to make, ma'am."

"I suppose so, at the Merry Thought. Have you brought the papers with you?"

"Here they are, ma'am. The *Times* left it out."

"The *Times* is a monopoly. I hope to live to see the day when its back will be broken. Read the passage for me."

Mr. Trapper took up a journal, and hemming three times, began to read the full report.

"Not that tomfoolery. What do I want to know about Cramton Hall? I suppose Flowers and the newspapers have paid you—that is enough. Let me know what you wrote about the savage attack on Mr. Jonathan."

Corrected and subdued, or apparently so, Trapper read with due emphasis the extract from the *Morning Herald* which we have given in the last chapter.

"I saw all that yesterday. What can you be about? I want the chief fact which it omits—the stone."

"The stone !"

"Yes, the stone !"

"Is he—a—affected, ma'am ?"

"Yes, very bad—his nose."

"The stone—his nose." Trapper stared. There was something wrong.

"The stone—his nose ! Did I not tell you yesterday morning that the young blackguard had a great flint in his hand when he struck that atrocious blow on my boy's nose ?"

"The first I heard of it, I protest to you, ma'am. I am sure it was not mentioned at the station, and I think not by you."

“You are a fool, Trapper. Be sure of nothing. I tell you for the second and last time, that the villain had a sharp stone in his hand when the blow was struck. We have indisputable evidence of the fact; and I do not want you to conceal the truth from the people of the Merry Thought, or elsewhere. I suppose you could do nothing by way of correction with the papers now?”

“I might try the evening journals. But to do this I must lose no time.”

“Then set about it *instanter*. A shilling a line for what is inserted to the purpose—and, mind, the stone is a fact to everyone you meet. There is a large mound of flints near the paddock—and you know it to be a fact that Oberon Spell had one of those flints in his hand. Do you see?”

“Clearly, ma’am.” And Mr. Trapper, with a look of profound admiration for that great woman’s inventive faculties, quitted the room.

Left alone, Mrs. Cubborn rang her husband’s bell. He quickly appeared.

“I have rung for you, Cubborn, to know what you have done in Natty’s matter?”

“Done—nothing! I have other serious business to attend to. He got himself into a mess, and he must get out of it as best he can.”

“Inhuman brute! and this to a mother!”

“But, my dear, what would you have me do? The tale of the stone is all nonsense. The police will blow upon it, the men and boys present, and Trensham, the doctor.”

“Contemptible being!—just as if there was not

such a thing as palm-oil and counter-evidence. I tell you what, Andy, or Bandy, Cubborn—vile name!—if you do not stand by your son and see him righted, and that young scamp at the treadmill, you shall have nothing further to do with this business. I will have Trapper placed on the Rolls and you shall sheer off—off, I tell you. Oh! I only wish my boy were old enough. I would then let you know who is master!"

It may be asked why Mr. Cubborn submitted to this outrageous tyranny. He ought to be a highly-respectable solicitor. He inherited a professional practice of a hundred years' standing. His father and his grandfather had occupied that very house and carried on the business there. But Andrew had been forced to marry the daughter of his mother's cook, under threat of a felonious charge which at the time would have hanged him; and hence the source of his submission. He knew she was thoroughly and utterly wicked—that in religion she was an atheist—and in principle a thief—and in temper a demon. He was literally compelled to succumb to his wife's domination, or throw up his profession altogether and quit the country, if, indeed, that would be any protection. She would pursue him everywhere, and he scarcely could imagine the spot of earth in which her determination and energy would not find him. She was a woman of great ability and a sound lawyer to boot. Thus far, she was an acquisition, and in some measure compensated for her unbounded despotism. In her practice she made it a rule never to show mercy, and to avoid everything like concession, apology, or scruple of conscience.   Hard law—the *summum jus*—was her sole guide.   In this way, Cubborn—that was the generic term of the house, meaning mistress, master, and clerks, male attorney or female attorney—got to be accounted a capital lawyer—the best to win a cause—the best to squeeze a debtor—the best to grind the bones and blood of an enemy.   Truly, they were fearful people !

As she was launching out her thunders against her husband in the manner described, the stroke of a dumb-bell in the room announced a visitor.   She immediately rang for Snodgepole, her waiting clerk, and having ascertained that Dr. Atomcraft desired to see her, ordered that he should be admitted.

" Good morning, doctor.   I suppose you have seen your patient ?"

" I have just been with him."

" And you say my boy will be maimed for life ?"

" I do, indeed ; seriously disfigured."

" Oh dear—oh dear !   Well, do you think I should stand shilly-shally about the ruffian who caused it ?"

" Certainly not.   I would sue him immediately."

" Sue whom ?"

" Trensham, of course."

" Trensham ?   I am not thinking of him just now. I have him down in my books—all in good time. What I want is your opinion about the stone."

" The stone ?"

" Yes ; did not my poor boy tell you ?"

“Well, he did mention something about a stone this morning. But nothing was said to that effect on my first visit, and I have not read a word of it in the papers.”

“Oh, the papers are never correct. They are no authority. I thought I told you all about it. But I was so confused. Besides, I could hardly believe it till the full facts came out. But ’tis only too true, my dear sir, too true. The villain had a horrible pointed flint in his doubled fist, and with it cut open and broke my boy’s nose. I want your professional support in this matter, as a friend, Dr. Atomcraft. Why, how you sit there, Mr. Cubborn, without a word to say. One would have thought you would be glad to see our friend, Mr. Atom-craft.”

“The doctor knows, my dear, I am delighted to see him.”

“Well, there is that case of Skinner’s wants looking to. It requires careful consideration, and what, I fear, you have not got in you,—sturdy action, my dear. There, you may go. The doctor and I can manage our business.” The obedient husband left the room. “I am obliged to keep my people up to the mark, I assure you, doctor, or this large practice would go to the wall. I shall have a warrant out for that scoundrel Spell, or a summons, and I want you to state your opinion of the effect of the stone.”

“I should like to hear what Sir Astley Cooper has to say on the subject, my dear madam.”

“I am surprised at you, doctor. You cannot suppose I am going to drag my suffering lamb to

London, to pay Sir Astley Cooper ten guineas for telling me what I know already, and hundreds besides me know. All you are asked is to give your opinion, that only some hard substance, it might be a flint—of course we know it was—produced the wound. Will you do this ?"

" I can see no objection to this, for a knuckle is a hard substance — but the great offender was Trensham."

" Not a word about the knuckle—there is no occasion—as much as you like about the hard substance. Leave Trensham to me. I will extinguish him—only do you act the part of a friend here, and say nothing unnecessary. He is about to get up a company, and wants Cubborn to be the solicitor."

" Of course he declined."

" Well, I have not decided as yet. But do you do your part, doctor, and stand by your friends. I must tell you I like your new nostrum of small doses. I have been thinking about it."

" You have ! There is a great deal in it, I assure you."

" Well, when before the bench of magistrates just remember the hard substance and your friends, and you may put down Trensham as a ruined man, and your fortune made. Good-bye, doctor.—Show them their interest, and how obliging they all can be. He will see a flint in a hard knuckle. Well, so far so good. The villain! I will tar him, if I cannot brand him. Blood for blood, wound for wound—one that will stick—stick to his character —his vitals—his very soul, if he has one—or I am not Jonathan Cubborn's mother !"

CHAPTER VIII.

THE BROOCH.

HILARY DOVE returned joyously from his club, to which he had immediately adjourned on the close of the tea-meeting in the school-room at Cramton Hall. He had had his fill of exciting incidents for one day at least, and was brimming over with glee after the eloquent speeches he himself had delivered. His reserved, unsympathetic wife was, as usual with her at the hour, in bed and fast asleep, little recking the happiness she missed in not sitting up to share the recital of her husband's triumphs and pleasures.

The morning brought its duties and cares, and consequent exertion and bustle, in a house where there was no regular servant. Mr. Dove, in his eagerness to hurry to town, had barely time to mention that the brooch which he had confided to his wife's charge, or rather acceded to her wish to keep it till owned, belonged to Miss Wheatley, and was to be delivered to her maid when she called. Mrs. Dove took full five minutes to consider before she replied, then said calmly and slowly—

" They sent for it last night."

" Did you get a receipt ?"

" No."

" Well, I suppose it is all right; but in future

ask for an acknowledgment. We always do in business."

Mrs. Dove did not answer; nor was she surprised at her partner's pomp in giving directions. It was his way, and this just in proportion to his utter carelessness and disregard of every safe and cautious rule of trade. He left by the train, as usual, for London, and filled the whole compartment of the carriage with his loud and sonorous account of Sir Roger Wheatley and the magnificent display on the day before at Cramton Hall.

In the course of the morning a tall, respectable-looking woman, who presented herself in her proper character as Miss Wheatley's maid, called at Proscenium Villa for the brooch. Mrs. Dove heard her minute description to the end, and then said in her ordinary placid manner—

"I gave it up last night."

"To whom, pray?"

"A woman."

"What woman?"

"Jane Anderson."

"Who was she?"

"Miss Wheatley's maid."

"My name is Martin, and, as I said, I am Miss Wheatley's maid. There must be some mistake."

"There must."

"It may be a robbery!"

"It may."

"Have you any more information to give?"

"No."

"Then my best course is to hurry back."

"It is."

And Mrs. Dove proceeded to the hall-door, opened it wide, and let the disappointed messenger pass through the long walk into the road.

When Sir Roger Wheatley had heard this story, his first business was to send for Cubborn, whose skill in criminal cases, as a magistrate, he well knew. His instructions to the lawyer were concise.

"I place the whole," said he, "unreservedly in your hands, Mr. Cubborn; and I rely on your prudence and judgment not to entangle me in any ulterior proceedings. I wish you to use all proper means to recover the brooch. It is a family relic; its intrinsic value alone is more than a hundred pounds; though, of course, this is not the chief consideration to me."

The attorney promised to pursue the matter with all due diligence and caution, and making a very humble bow, took his departure.

His first professional step in the business was to consult his wife, who was on tiptoe to learn the news. Mrs. Cubborn was a hearty woman-hater—quiet, unobtrusive Mrs. Dove among the rest. Dove himself she disliked for three reasons — he was Oberon Spell's friend, he was a noisy declaimer, he had given the firm much trouble, and had brought some disgrace on it by awkward cross-actions wherein the house did not appear to advantage. Besides, was not Hilary Dove, the man who paid nobody, a proper subject for the virtuous indignation of an honest lawyer's wife?"

"And where do you think it is?" was the first

word she addressed to her husband when she had heard the story. "Where do you think it is?"

"That is exactly what we have to find out."

"Fool! the receiver is the thief. The brooch is safe in the possession of gentle Keziah Dove. She who hoards everything has hoarded this too. We must call in Gimlet into the business. Send Snodgepole express for him. Trapper will doctor a paragraph for the papers, mentioning Dove's name as often as possible, his wife's, and his daughter's. I have my reasons: Proscenium Villa is an odd appellation, and it will strike. Spell's name can be dragged in. What we first have to do is to show up the robbery—the robbery—the robbery, mind you. I will have no shirking the matter. Get that confounded old fool of a beadle, Tollard, to work with his bell and 'Oh, yes!' He will blow the matter far enough. We must spread this into a good stroke of business for the firm."

"Remember, my dear, Mrs. Dove's tale may be true. We do not know the full particulars, and must proceed with infinite caution."

"Infinite fiddlesticks. We must put on the screw. What lawyer does anything without the screw? Oh! I know how to squeeze the truth out of born liars, and the money from actual beggars. Press and bleed, press and bleed—there's your way to right. Meek Keziah Dove must go to 'Little Ease' and enjoy the pleasures of the lancet. To business; Cubborn, for once I confide this matter to you, and see you do it well. Leave me; I have

that affair of Blogg's to look into. It comes on
before the Vice-Chancellor on the 13th."

Mr. Cubborn left the room, prepared to carry
out his wife's instructions. After arranging everything for the loudest possible explosion, Trapper
and he proceeded to the railway-station to interrogate Hilary Dove, in order to recover the lost
property by voluntary concession if at all practi-
cable. The commission-agent, as usual, was bidding good-bye to a nest of friends left behind in
the carriage, when he encountered the unwelcome
presence of Cubborn and Trapper. Visions of
writs or arrest immediately presented themselves
to him; but he bore himself bravely. However, on
being made acquainted with the object of the interview, he appeared much more confused and guilty
than was compatible with perfect innocence. Was
he sure of all at home? Guiltless himself, could he
say in his heart that his household was pure? He
was guarded in his admissions, and rather pooh-
poohed the suspicions than scouted them. He took
care to warn Cubborn that he would make Sir
Roger Wheatley pay heavy damages, if through
that gentleman his character, or that of his family,
should be aspersed or injured. And saying this, he
turned from the lawyers and proceeded home. He
immediately addressed his wife—

"Keziah, I wish to speak to you alone. Iris,
love, leave the room. And now, my dear, I expect
you to be thoroughly candid with me in this very
serious business of the brooch. You must tell me
all—conceal nothing, otherwise I shall not know

how to deal.   Do you understand the true force of what I say?"

"Well!"

"Have you anything to add to what you said to Mrs. Martin this morning?"

"Nothing."

"You would not be a thief, Keziah?"

"No."

"If my wife—the mother of my child—became a robber, I would shoot her dead on the spot."

Hilary Dove was very pale and nervous as he spoke. His wife was as tranquil and collected as usual.

"Well, I believe you, Keziah.   I would, in fact, swear to your innocence."   He kissed her, and the affair dropped.   The commission agent took his tea from his wife's thrifty hands.   His dinner he had enjoyed in company with some choice spirits in regular course in the city.   He talked some light agreeable nonsense with his daughter, he petted his dogs, stroked his cat as she sat on his knee; he had quite a conversation with his parrot; he chirped to his canaries and fed them from his mouth; after a stroll in his garden he adjourned for the evening to the Merry Thought, as easy and unconcerned as if three writs and two summonses were not then in his pocket and a charge of robbery hanging over his house.   Who will deny after this that happiness is the pleasant fruit of natural disposition, which can charm circumstance, however untoward or burdened with evil and misfortune this may be?   Notorious malefactors have been merry in going to their final doom.

CHAPTER IX.

THE next morning all Edelstone was full of the lost brooch. To proclaim the intelligence there were the newspapers, there were the placards, there were the handbills, and there was old Tollard, the beadle, with his clamorous bell and quaint "Oh, yes!" Every name but the Wheatleys was given in full, and every particular included. The mysterious Jane Anderson had her portrait worked out of the most shadowy materials. Town and country were alike advised of her visit to the house of Hilary Dove; but around the description there was cast a cunning kind of veil, which left a doubt whether that clever impostor depicted by Mrs. Dove was not altogether a creature of the imagination.

Messrs. Gimlet and Picker, detective officers, now appeared on the scene. Although they regarded this and all similar duties as a matter of money and private interest, they had, nevertheless, their professional rules to go by. These they found to be sadly at fault on their visit to Edelstone. The whole matter, according to their mind, should have been kept in abeyance and concealed until they themselves had arranged their plans. As it was, everything was spoilt.

" You see," said Gimlet, on learning the full particulars at the Cubborns' office, " there is no probable case against the Doves.   The man finds it and proclaims it, and the woman gives it up to a likely messenger."

" That is exactly my opinion," said the lawyer.

" Hold your tongue! That is not my opinion," said Mrs. Cubborn, magisterially.   " Why was the brooch taken to Dove's house at all?   There is nothing in the story we have just heard, gentlemen, but the statement of the railway officials that a woman similar to the person described as Jane Anderson, went to London by the eight o'clock train ; there is nothing but this, which does not, to my mind, prove the guilt of Mrs. Dove, and doubtless also of her husband and daughter. Mr. Cubborn, unfortunately, has his feelings concerned in this matter.   Keziah Dove, they say, is a very pretty woman,"—(here the lady attempted a laugh)—" he, he! But for my part, I never allow feeling to enter into the profession.   I do not see what it has to do with the law."

" Certainly not, ma'am.   That is a principle I always inculcate myself.   We officers of the law have no business whatever with feeling."

" Well now, gentlemen, we have talked long enough, I think, in all conscience. I wish the search to be begun forthwith.   I have already procured the search-warrant.   I do not allow the grass to grow under my feet in such matters."

" Of course, ma'am, of course, since 'tis your

desire; but is it not straining a point to go at the Doves?"

"The magistrate's warrant is your authority, Mr. Gimlet; we must execute that. You and your friend were not summoned from London for nothing. We have our own constables; but we thought you would do the work better."

"Thank you, ma'am; but we must proceed in the regular way of business. I see nothing of a reward mentioned, which is not in the usual course. We officers are accustomed to do our duty, but we like to understand the ground we are going upon."

"I have been considering, Gimlet. I comprehend you. I see no objection to proposing a fifty-pound reward."

"Fifty pounds, Mrs. Cubborn!—fifty pounds!" said the astonished husband. "'Tis all very well for these gentlemen, but will Sir Roger Wheatley pay it?"

"We are his solicitors, and he must."

"But will Luxmore and Square allow it?"

"Luxmore and Square, mere attorneys! Really, gentlemen, I am ashamed of Mr. Cubborn, thoroughly ashamed of him. A respectable practitioner like him to put himself on a par with mere pettifoggers. It is plain Sir Roger Wheatley, who employs them about his estates, has no confidence in them, or he would have placed this matter in their hands. Thirty, however, will do, as fifty might tempt the Doves to be honest. I see, gentlemen, you must have some motive to work."

" Exactly so, ma'am.   Things now begin to look like business."

" Do you only convict Hilary Dove and his wife, and if possible, his daughter, and you shall both be well paid.   They are a bad lot, a shocking bad lot. I want to get rid of them out of the neighbourhood. They encourage that scoundrel, Oberon Spell. You have heard of that sad affair of my boy's nose.   Of course you saw it in the papers?"

" No, indeed, ma'am ; we never read nothing in the papers but the police, the assizes, the sessions, and the Old Bailey. You see, they concern us, ma'am."

" To business now, gentlemen ; that does concern you.   Call at the police-office, and they will lend you a woman to assist you.   I want to be alone with Mr. Cubborn ; I have a case of importance to settle with him."

Messrs. Gimlet and Picker for once did indulge in a feeling,—" Poor Cubborn !" but they quitted the room without adding another word.

On the door of Proscenium Villa being opened to the ordinary knock, Messrs. Gimlet and Picker, accompanied by a female, Mrs. Grub, wife of a local policeman, slipped at once into the hall, and thence into the reception-room, without stay or invitation.

" Take a seat, ma'am. My name is Gimlet ; perhaps you have heard of me. This is Mr. Picker, my friend. We have come about that brooch. You will be perfectly candid with us,—you can be quite confidential ; nothing passes from us. What do you know about it ?"

" Nothing."

" But you had it ?"

" I had."

" Just tell us what you did with it."

" I gave it to the messenger."

" Well, go on ?"

" I had rather answer you."

By this time the officers had begun to entertain doubts of Mrs. Dove's honesty. She was too guarded, they thought, for innocence. Unable to draw her into the usual voluble woman's conversation, they proceeded to question her most minutely as to every particular of time, place, and circumstance connected with her account of the brooch. The answers were invariably dry and curt, trim and bare, not a superfluous breath or syllable. The witness was cool and unmoved. Mrs. Dove was a puzzle to the two experienced police-officers.

" And you got no receipt ?"

" No."

" That is odd."

No reply.

" Well, ma'am, you perhaps have no objection to our searching the house ? We have a warrant for the purpose. Of course, it would save you much trouble, and exposure too, if you were to be candid with us. All that is required is the property—the brooch—we must have that. We have sure information that it is here. Have you nothing to say before we begin ?"

" I protest against the search. I am alone in the house."

"Oh, as to that, we are quite delicate, I assure you, ma'am, and have brought one of the feminine sex with us. If you will step with Mrs. Grub into the next room, she will examine you in the regular way of business."

When the officers were left alone, Picker said to Gimlet—"If she did it, she knows how to fence it. I never knew a woman say so little and give so small a handle."

"It may be her natural manner. She is wonderfully cool."

"As a stone at the bottom of a river. A barish place this, Gimlet."

"It has seen many ups and downs, like a tavern waiter. Here they come."

"Well, did it turn up?"

"Not about the lady's person. So far, all is just as it was before."

"Very well; now, Mrs. Dove, please show us over the house. Mrs. Grub will examine where you object to our search."

"Under protest," said the accused, in the same quiet manner, and the work of rummaging and prying began. It was indeed looking for a needle in a bundle of straw. The article was but small, and the house and grounds were ample and crammed with hiding-places. There were many things in that house which a sensitive mind would suffer keenly to see revealed. Several pawnbrokers' duplicates among the rest, and writs, summonses, and other disagreeable and degrading legal documents beyond number. But Mrs. Dove was quite passive, and seemed to regard the whole matter as *pro formâ*. She was not even moved by the disclosure of her own special stores. There was quite a profusion of worn-out goods. Old scraps, waifs and strays of all kinds, which should have gone in due housewife course long ago to the rag and boneman, were here stowed away and in trim order; repaired, where capable, at double their value, and packed with as much precision as if they were the property and gems of the wardrobe. The number of pins, needles, and nails was incalculable; and bits of linen, woollen, and cotton were arranged with the nicety and order of a draper's shop where the female assistant has not too many customers.

As these curiosities turned up, Messrs. Gimlet and Picker the more and more thought that they were in the track of the thief, if not of the brooch. There was so much hiding away and evidence of covetousness. Still they were not successful. Once they thought they had made a point. They turned out from a heap of shreds a silk glove curiously embroidered. Mrs. Dove, with a sudden start and exclamation, caught it up.

"Ah! I thought I had lost that. Give it to me."

"Not till we examine it, and all about it. Come, be a little plain; tell us the mystery of this old-fashioned glove."

"It does not concern your search—proceed;" and Keziah Dove, taking the glove from their hand, smoothened it carefully out, placed it among a heap of neat scraps, and resumed her passive demeanour.

The detectives were now all but at the end of their search. Gimlet and the woman Grub had left the last room. Mrs. Dove lingered behind, and Picker had his hand on the knob of the lock, giving a final searching eye around before quitting the apartment. One part of the work of detectives is to watch the countenance of the suspected person where the opportunity offers. Frequent were the examinations of Mrs. Dove's placid features by Gimlet and Picker. But nothing could be divined from a surface so tranquil and calm. The most exciting revelations continued to be made; the policemen themselves were more than once startled, and the woman who accompanied them was made alive to the scene. Keziah Dove alone exhibited neither surprise nor emotion. Certainly she betrayed no blush or sign of shame.

Picker, as we have observed, was about to leave the room, when his glance in its circuit struck upon the gaze of the suspected woman riveted on the very lock he held under his hand. Her eye was fastened there. Her feet appeared glued to the spot. She was fascinated; and though she felt the officer's observation direct upon her, she could not for worlds alter her fixed stare. She stood spellbound. The detective in a moment discovered this; he had the clue.

" Gimlet, give me your driver. I should like to unscrew this lock."

" Eh !" said the brother officer, and a look of meaning passed between the two. The gaze of Keziah Dove was like the sun's rays in a dark room. It poured a light on the hidden nook.

"Have you the key of this lock, ma'am?"

"No."

The respondent this time was deadly pale. It was the first change that had come over her countenance that day, if we except the slight transition connected with the glove. Her tone was calm but altered, and she made an addition to her wonted monosyllable. "The lock is not used."

"Here, give me the driver, Gimlet. There can be no harm in taking off an old lock, if only to dust out the cobwebs."

One by one the screws were drawn, and the whole lock turned down flat on the broad palm of Picker.

"These look pretty, don't they?" said the detective, advancing to a table, and displaying the lock with the wards entirely absent, and in their places rolls of uncovered gold piled closely together.

"And pray whose are these?" said Gimlet, drawing near with a chair.

"Mine," was Mrs. Dove's firm reply.

"Does Mr. Dove know you have so much money?"

"Inquire."

"How many guineas do they count?"

"Not one."

"I see they are sovereigns, yes. How many?"

"If you reckon, I will tell you."

"Count them, Picker."

"How many are there?" said the detective, after reckoning up each heap.

“Now that you know, I will certify that I know too ; five rolls of fifty in a roll.”

“Exactly, ma’am. We officers are honest men, and count straight. But this is not the brooch.”

“Every lock in the house must now come off, unless you will save us the trouble. We have the key to your hiding-place,” said Gimlet.

“Give me my money,” said Mrs. Dove—“my money ; it is mine.”

“Be calm, my good lady. If the gold is yours, why it is yours. Trouble or bother will not get it for you sooner. We are ministers of the law, and the money is now in the law’s custody.”

At that moment a knock came to the door.

“It is my husband.”

“Stop, ma’am, I will let him in.”

“What is all this about ?” said Hilary Dove.

“Only a search-warrant. We are getting through the business quite comfortably.”

“Is, then, an Englishman’s house no longer his castle ? Is Proscenium Villa an open common ? A search for a brooch which I was the first to find and to publish my discovery to everybody. Wheatley shall suffer for this, and Cubborn and the rest of them. I am a long leaseholder here, an old and much respected inhabitant, president of the Planet Club, and I carried the last election for Wheatley. By-the-bye, whose is all this money ?”

“It is the law’s,” said Gimlet.

“It is mine,” said Mrs. Dove.

“Yours !” said the astonished and alarmed husband.

"Be calm, my dear sir," said Mr. Picker. "Two hundred and fifty golden sovereigns in safe legal keeping;" and he swept the whole into a bag he produced from his pocket.

"But the search must go on, Picker," said Gimlet. "Off with the locks as fast as you can, and then for the grounds."

The spirit of Hilary Dove for the moment was crushed. How could his wife have come by so much money? If honestly, her heart must be black and indurated. He had suffered, his child had suffered, and she herself had suffered bitterly for want of means. If the gold was stolen, or the produce of a theft, what a depth of misery yawned upon them all! How if she were really guilty of the theft of the brooch! Should they discover it, as most likely they would in one of those old locks, what would be her fate?

But the officers did not find it; though stimulated by their singular discovery in the lock, they pursued their inquiry with renewed sharpness and vigour. Meantime, Dove had an opportunity of questioning his wife. Her cut and dried answer was, "The money is mine." She did not further satisfy his curiosity. He had large faith in her, he loved her, she was his wife, and he believed her.

The officers, with somewhat of an apologetic tone, bore off the bag of money. The whole matter next day was brought before the magistrates, and after a lengthened investigation the gold was restored to Hilary Dove. The case of the brooch was dismissed on the very probable supposition that it was delivered to the pretended messenger. Mr. Cubborn was severely reprimanded for having used many exaggerated statements, in order to induce one of the magistrates assembled to grant the search-warrant and summons. The whole ended in the triumph of Hilary Dove. He had his bag full of gold; his wife was discharged without a stain on her character; and a brilliant action for damages against Sir Roger Wheatley was rising now in gay prospective. The Merry Thought and Proscenium Villa were jovial that night. Good had flowed in from a sea of troubles.

CHAPTER X.

A FOUNDATION IS LAID FOR FUTURE TROUBLES.

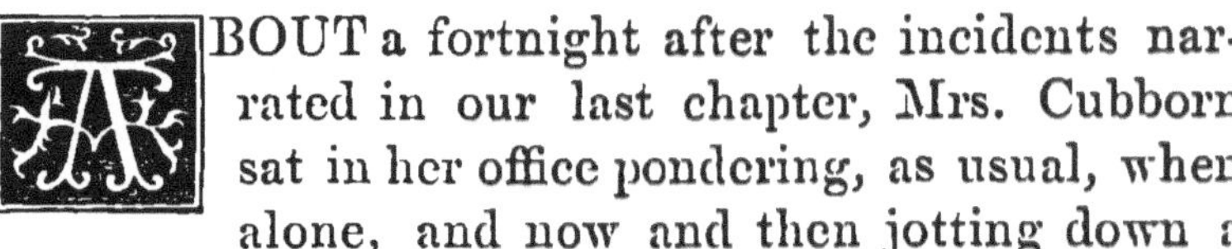

ABOUT a fortnight after the incidents narrated in our last chapter, Mrs. Cubborn sat in her office pondering, as usual, when alone, and now and then jotting down a note or two in a character only intelligible to herself. She seldom committed her more recondite thoughts to paper in the ordinary chirography, for reasons she approved, except when she allowed others to transcribe them and work them out in action. After about half an hour's deliberation, she rang her husband's bell, and he obediently attended the imperial summons.

"Well, Cubborn, I have been looking up matters a little, and I think you are conducting this business very badly."

"What business, my dear?"

"What business? Why, our business—the office business—the profession."

"I only do what you tell me. I have no voice of my own, as you well know. If things go wrong, I am not to blame."

"They do go wrong, and you are to blame, and you shall be to blame, or what are you good for as a husband and the head of the family? You ruined that affair of Dove's."

"How, may I ask you?"

"How?—why will you stare like an idiot? Listen to me, and I will tell you. That money, which you know in your heart was stolen, should never have left your hands."

"It never was in them, my dear. The police held it fast, till ordered to deliver it up by the magistrates to the lawful owner."

"The lawful thieves, you mean. The rolls were in gold. You should have pleaded some pretext for delay. I had intended to find an owner."

"Then you should have said so. Besides, I do not approve of those crooked ways."

"You shall approve of my ways, fellow, or quit the house, as I have often warned you. And so this is all the apology you have to offer me for losing the firm at least some two hundred pounds. I know one who would have been glad to claim it for the odd fifty."

"I dare say you do. And for your pains fall into the cunning clutches of Gimlet and Picker."

"Well, that is done with now, and cannot be mended. But what excuse have you to make for allowing that scamp Dove to swindle Sir Roger Wheatley out of three hundred pounds as a compromise for an action for damages?"

"If you will know, my dear, I had nothing to do with the matter. Sir Roger was thoroughly disgusted with our whole proceedings, and gave himself entirely over to his regular solicitors, Luxmore and Square. They were resolved not to let him off lightly for taking the original business out of their hands, and fell in easily with Dove's exorbitant demand."

" That's the way you suffer every trumpery fellow to over-ride you.   Had you not a tongue in your head?   Could you not expose their motive ?"

" I thought I had gone far enough in the matter, unless I wished to get kicked completely overboard. As it was, I was glad to have seventy pounds for the job and to cover all our expenses.   Gimlet and Picker had a consideration."

" Thanks to me for publishing the reward hot foot.   Though they didn't succeed, they deserved something.   But seventy pounds from such a chance! I believe you would be glad of sixpence.   Don't you know there is the printer to pay, and a thousand other small expenses ?"

" I should not like to be called on for the bill, my dear.   I was delighted to receive the cheque, and to get rid of the matter without explanation."

" But don't you know that Wheatley hates us, and would have kicked us overboard long ago if he dared?   He can't do without us at the election. There you knew you had him, and should have skinned him while in your power.   A pretty firm this is likely to become under Andy Cubborn's management.   But is it true that Dove has turned Radical ?"

" Quite so.   He says only the innate tyranny and absolute training of the Tory system could ever have made Wheatley persecute him on the baseless suspicion, that he or his wife had kept that brooch ; and so he ratted."

"A good job too; his absence will make our services of the more account. He stood in our way and claimed this election. He made you look only a poor sheep in his presence."

"I don't know that. But he is an enthusiast, a capital talker, and a renegade now. He may help to fling Wheatley from his seat at the next contest. Nutmeg, the grocer, promises he will stand."

"That is likely to be a long way off. However, you must go to Wheatley, warn him of his danger, and tell him boldly we can stem it. I want to continue that connexion for a time. It is necessary to my plans. But it was not for this, or anything about that fellow Dove, that I wanted to see you. Do you think, Andy Cubborn—as your old grandmother used to call you—do you think that I can look upon you as a husband and a father, while you let my poor boy be outraged in this most scandalous manner without redress or damages?"

"I did my best, and so did Trapper."

"Never mind Trapper. You are always leaning on somebody, and every one is in fault but yourself. Don't you know if you had not been entirely devoid of sense and spirit the bench of magistrates would never have made our charge against Spell appear malicious and groundless?"

"But I tell you the case broke down utterly at every step."

"And whose fault was that? Are you so gentle a sucking-dove that you could not have those present who would have propped it up, and sworn they saw the stone in Spell's hand, or saw him pick up one, or throw one down, or something else likely? A precious attorney not to know how to back up his own cause! I should like to know what we go into a court for but to win?"

"But the very witnesses you subpœnaed were our ruin, and proved the direct contrary to what you wished them to say. As to Atomcraft with his hard substance, Scriven gave him a rap on the knuckles he will not easily forget. And those seconds of Natty's, Wildbore and Blunt, they turned tail and called him a savage cur."

"Did I not tell you how their evidence would turn out? But was it not easy to get witnesses to contradict them and make them out young perjurers and liars, as they ought to be? I do not know what the law is to come to, if an attorney is to let his cause slip through for want of evidence when it is always to be had for a little liberality and management. I wish from my heart you were dead, Andrew Cubborn; I might then find a suitable helpmate. As it is you are my utter curse and ruin."

"If I am, all I say is that you are my prompter in the work of destruction. And as to Jonathan, your pet, his character, as well as his nose, is damaged for life."

"'Tis a lie—'tis a lie, fellow. The triumph is mine, in every way mine. I was listening to you, and trying if I could get any wit out of that thick skull of yours. I tell you the Doves are tarred for life. Everybody can point the finger at them henceforth, and say they were charged with robbery; and that brooch may yet turn up against them. Oh, I

would go all the way to Spinsterton Towers to see
that cunning piece of silence and her impudent
daughter treading the wheel! Then, do you think
people will believe that heap of sovereigns her own?
No, no; I say, black is my mark, and my mark is
on the Doves. And for Master Oberon Spell, I
have branded him as a young assassin. He is
pitched—defiled—the charge will cling to him.
Masters Blunt and Wildbore did not get clean off
either. The impression must be that they prevari-
cated. Atomcraft is a half-knave, a demi-perjurer,
the worst witness a case was ever curst with; he
will never recover his character. Besides, he is
poisoning my boy with his globules, and I know
how to let the world know it. As to his baronet-
ship of the Priory, I am delighted to know that he
has been tortured and cheated. His haughty slut
of a wife, and creature of a daughter who would not
play with Natty long ago, but used to hug Oberon
Spell and call him her husband,—well, she and they
all have been pulled down a bit with their fine county
airs and family exclusiveness. They have lost their
brooch, Hilary Dove their trumpeter, and three hundred and seventy hard pounds in the bargain. I
suppose you think I am like you, a fool, and conduct this business without hedging. I have an eye
to two issues; the one may fail, but the other is
sure to bring in a measure of favour. I will plant
the venom in the wound, if the blow does not reach
home."

"Sarah Cubborn, you are a fearful woman."

"I am, and I am your wife to boot. You shall

know more of me and this profession by-and-bye. We are both in our infancy—the principal and the business. Now, look to that action against Trensham. See that it holds water."

"It is desperately leaky at present."

"I am glad you perceive it. You must stop the gaps, and go into court with a sound case. I have my eye on Spell. I shall not forget the Doves. Blunt and Wildbore, and the rest of them, are all my enemies."

"They are legion."

"So much the better. We are legion for them. Are we not feared, dreaded, abhorred? And who is respected that is not so? A hated lawyer is sure to have plenty of angry business. Ours is a giant power, and I will use it like a giant. I shall be on the Rolls yet—then you will see. What is Dove going to do with that money? Five hundred and fifty pounds is no small sum to touch at one lump."

"It will be soon swallowed. Hilary Dove is one of those persons who do not know the use of money. He is going to repair and improve. He is going to furnish. He is going to start a new company."

"A company!"

"Yes; Trensham's Hygienic Food Company, with Scriven for the lawyer."

"Scriven again! That fellow is ever in my path. Only for you, we should have had this picking. Our old clerk will be sure to make a good thing of it."

"A pity you drove him away, Mrs. Cubborn. He is taking up all our respectable business."

" And whose fault is that, idiot ? If you had kept the whip hand over Trensham and Dove, as I planned, they dared not refuse you anything."

" You forget, my dear, that the extreme measures were yours."

" I forget nothing. How dare you tell me that I forget ? It is because they were not kept to the extreme and reined in with a tight hand, that Scriven steps in to snivel where we should rule. However, they have had their brand hot, hot ; all but Scriven, and his shall come. He is in my books. What is that French saying about excusing ?"

" *Qui s'excuse s'accuse*, my dear."

" Well, I'll take care that all our foes through the whole of their lives will have to be excusing themselves."

" From false accusations ?"

Ay, from false accusations. All the moredifficult to disprove. There will be one incessant round of defence—a constant indictment against them. Think you I do not know the force of calumny ? It never wipes out—there is always a stain."

" For this they call the great calumniator *diabolus* —devil."

" A capital name, though I don't believe in him ; but I like his power. Call me the great slanderer —the devil, if you will—anything but a meek woman. I hate amiable people. Half your beggars and gaolbirds are amiable. Go now, get to work ; see that a *ne exeat* be taken out for Major Conyers, another of the county worthies."

" But he is in actual service, my dear. The proof

will be impossible : unless, indeed, he is prepared to lose his commission."

"I want no argument, sir. I have said take out a *ne exeat*. Let the proper affidavits be made—manufactured, if you like the term. If you wont do the business, Trapper shall. Take out a *ca sa* for Sir George Trebaston—a county magnate too. Put a detainer on that fellow Talbot without loss of time. That bothering widow's goods must go. Serve writs on Lyddon, McGregor, and Trevelyan. There must be no compromise, every farthing, with costs, must be paid down, or off to Spinsterton Towers they go, the vagabonds."

The patient husband had nothing to do but to obey. A hundred times did he try remonstrance, attempt opposition; a hundred times did he signally fail. Mrs. Cubborn made light of a row. To maintain her supremacy she would have pulled the house to pieces and let the *débris* tumble upon all belonging to her; resistance was hopeless. She would go from door to door and proclaim him the greatest swindler living, and give her *pro* and *con* for her charges. There was only the one escape—to cut and run, or be satisfied to mount with her to wealth and power—the easier alternative, though the ultimate conclusion might be total collapse, explosion, and bankruptcy.

Immediately her husband left, Mrs. Cubborn rang Trapper's bell. The managing clerk appeared.

"Trapper, what about Trensham's new company?"

"It will be started."

"But it must not succeed."

"No fear of that. The thing is too absurd to last a twelvemonth."

"I do not know that. Trensham is a clever man, though a poor surgeon, and Dove could push anything into notoriety. You must be down on them from the beginning, in the way of paragraphs, *quasi* friendly, but keeping the connexion between the promoters and recent unpleasant circumstances alive. I want to stab Scriven here if I can; he is eating into the practice wofully, drawing off our best clients and business."

"Everybody speaks well of him. He pays his clerks liberally."

"Oh! he does?"

"And you will excuse me, ma'am, but there is that little matter of increase standing over."

"Trapper, you are covetous. Be satisfied. I make your newspaper business for you. Succeed in ruining this company, bringing in Scriven with a swinging loss, and sweating Trensham with heavy damages for my boy's nose, and it will not be my fault if you are not remembered. You must apply for an injunction in Scoppin's case, and I think we must boldly charge Edmonstone with fraud and forgery. You will see that it is well sustained. You may settle that affair of criminal assault against Sydney for a handsome consideration. I think we can't do better."

"Very good, ma'am, your instructions shall be attended to. Any further orders?"

"Not at present. You will duly report progress. Go."

Mrs. Cubborn next rang Cotching's bell.

The second clerk put in his head and wriggled his body into the room.

" Yes, ma'am ?"

" Do you patronise the Crowbar ?"

" I do call in there now and then, ma'am."

" I find no fault with you for that. The house is respectable enough in its way, and a man at your time of life must have his glass, though I can manage on water. Cotching, you might be useful to the firm. Mr. Trapper is really so much taken up with his newspaper hobby that he has no time for the serious matters of the profession."

" Yes, ma'am."

" I want you to get hold of the chairman of the Radical committee at the Crowbar and learn their moves. A sovereign a secret, if I consider it worth the money. We must not appear in the matter."

" It is a bargain, ma'am. I think I can manage Rumball. And as to secrecy, honour bright, ma'am, I am true to the backbone."

" Why, there's the door for those who are not, and I didn't care if the whole town knew our secrets here, only it would not be business. Keep your eye on Hilary Dove; he attends the Crowbar meetings."

" So he does now, ma'am. What a loss to the cause! Oh, he's a splendid speaker, a wonderfully clever man. I do feel surprised we ever lost him."

" Your master lost him, not I. But you must not call him clever now. He is on the wrong side. ' Stupid,' ' dolt,' ' ranter,' and ' fool ' are the words."

“ I understand you, ma’am.”

“ You may go now; remember, a guinea a secret.”

Mr. Cotching gathered himself together, and again thrusting his head forward, drew his limbs after him out of the room.

Mrs. Cubborn rang Snodgepole’s, her waiting clerk’s, bell. That personage appeared.

“ Snodgepole, I am not to be disturbed on any account for two hours. All clients and others are to be shown into Mr. Cubborn’s room. Go.”

Once more Mrs. Cubborn rang a bell. This time it was for her son.

Jonathan, as obedient as the rest, speedily appeared. His face was still strapped up, and he looked altogether a deplorable object; enough to arouse any mother’s indignation.

“ Sit down, my love, sit down. I am avenging you, Natty. I am making them suffer. But your fool of a father with his conscience and caution and scruples and honour spoils all my plans. I want you now, child, to study a little. It will divert your attention. Here are the pens, and here are what you are to imitate. There is tracing-paper, there is sand, and there is a blotter. Will you begin with the broad-nibbed quill pens, or the fine springy ones ?”

“ It doesn’t matter to me. Suppose I take the steel ones first. This will require one like a hair.” And Jonathan Cubborn began his studies under his mother’s instructive care. We merely indicate their nature. Their full development will appear in the extension of the Cubborns’ professional business.

CHAPTER XI.

PATRONAGE.

E have seen with what trim preparation and earnest intention and hope Hugh Graff wended his way to the Priory, in order to lay his portfolio of humble drawings before the county member and his family. He was but a rare visitor to the Park; for admission now was given only by special application to the steward; unless, indeed, as was the case with the upper class of families, among whom the Spells were included, the privilege was considered to be generally granted. The Graffs and Doves and persons of secondary grade, were not in this favoured list, but under the exclusive restriction. The young artist soon got to be interested in the noble scenery around him. It had every charm of richness, extent, variety, and beauty. But it cannot be said that he enjoyed either the sentiment or the poetry of the picture. He was rather occupied, so to speak, with the several objects and views as they rose before him. He was studying within himself how best to copy them, and for this purpose was fixing the images fast in his mind. Any enjoyment he felt was derived from the practical sense of storing up useful knowledge, rather than from a subtle association of idea or luxuriance of fancy. Perhaps Hugh Graff

had to be educated into the poetry of his profession,
if ever he should attain to that intellectual pre-
eminence. At present his pursuit was imitation,
and could he have sketched as he went on, he would
doubtless have presented some marvels of exact
delineation of scenes which could not be copied
ever so rudely without embodying forms of much
picturesqueness and beauty. He was learning, as
he walked, the strokes and pothooks of description.
At the same time he was insensibly imbuing his
mind with the spiritual life inherent in the artistic
examination of the various shapes of nature.

Perhaps the most satisfying landscape in the
world is a well laid-out old English park. Not,
indeed, the grandest or most beautiful, but the
easiest of approach, and the most varied in scenery,
and containing the greatest variety of pleasing
spots and associations. Hugh Graff enjoyed his
walk to the full. The sky over his head was, in
the language of his friend Spell,

> "One broad arch of sainted blue."

There had been a gentle rain in the early morning,
and the verdure and flowers were everywhere re-
freshed. The wind blew lazily from the south, and
lightly fanned his brow as he proceeded. There
were some very fine elms in the park, and three
long avenues of chestnuts full three hundred years
old, some being of great amplitude and beauty.
But it was the presence of a number of magnificent
oaks which constituted the glory of the place, many
of them growing in spots of much picturesqueness and

poetic and romantic suggestion. There were vast expanses of fern from which at times the antlers of a noble stag appeared, while at a short distance, in quiet seclusion, a whole herd of deer might be found browsing on the short herbage.

There was a large lake fed from a series of cascades, and pouring its redundant waters into a variety of brooklets which, here and there crossed by bridges, gave an infinite freshness and variety to hill and valley, and spoke their guttural language to the solitudes around. As the range was very extensive, a part of the lower ground was enclosed for rearing a few choice herds and flocks, and not far off from these was another large fenced space for the stud of horses attached to the Priory. Such a park would have been imperfect without a goodly stock of game ; this was there in profusion. The plantations were numerous, and you could not pass them without being made aware of the presence of pheasants, while hares and rabbits started forward and frequently crossed the path of the wanderer. There were foxes, stoats, polecats, weasels, and badgers in the grounds, but only rarely visible. What pleased Hugh most were the gambols of the squirrels, which he watched running up the stems of tall trees and leaping among the branches. The keen eye of a keeper, too, now and then met his gaze. But he passed on, merely inclining his head and smiling. In fact, the young artist was lost in the study of the varied scenes which continually arose before him.

In this way he got through the park, and was

now in the beautiful walks which led directly to the mansion. The shrubs and flowers here arrested his attention. Being quite uninterrupted, he had the opportunity of witnessing the effects of skilful horticulture in floral decoration, and he paused more than once in order to master thoroughly the absorbing volume of pictorial instruction set before him; for in this light only did he regard the choicest production and disposition of the garden.

The house was a comparatively modern structure, built on the ruins of an ancient priory. A goodly fortune had been laid out in its erection, and both architect and builder did ample justice to the very liberal terms and margin allowed them in the original contract. The ecclesiastical character of the foundation was sought to be preserved where this could be done without injury to the convenience, beauty, and grandeur of the edifice as a manorial dwelling. The attempt was highly successful, and the building was admitted to be one of our best specimens of the fitness of the Gothic style, judiciously used, for purposes of state and residence.

When the boy came directly in front of the pile, he was not struck with the mass so much as with the variety of parts and the difficulty of embodying so many ornaments, quaint figures, and proportions in a picture. As he continued to gaze, a sense of an indistinct whole and a certain solemn grandeur and feeling of the presence of antiquity grew upon his mind. The thought arose within him that he could best give an idea of the Priory

by expressing in pencil that vague picture without
much attention to detail or the filigree and orna-
mentation which at first had so much perplexed him.
Pondering thus, and adding to his stock of knowledge of practical art, he approached the great door.

"Well, youngster," said the porter, " what do
you want ?"

"At the request of Sir Roger and Lady Wheatley, I am come to pay them a morning visit, and to
show them my drawings."

" Oh, your drawings ; and your name ?"

" Hugh Graff is my name."

" Any relation to Graff, the carpenter ?"

" His son."

" Oh ! now I know you."

Poor Hugh came as an artist somewhat filled
with his own importance, but was sadly taken down
when he found he could only make himself known
as his father's son, the child of a carpenter.

"And you wish to see Sir Roger and her ladyship ?"

" If you please.　I came early, not to disappoint
them."

" I fear they cannot see you to-day.　They are
too busy."

" Perhaps, sir, you would like to have a peep.
Have you a taste this way ?"

" A taste—oh, a taste ?　I should rather think
I have.　I give the cut for my own livery ; and
Stultz says I am first-rate ; only I must keep within
bounds for the style of the family.　A purty one
that."

"It is. Will you be pleased to select one for yourself?"

"Thank you. I should like that. It so resembles my niece."

"No, not that. It is not mine to give. It belongs to a young lady. Will you accept of this one?"

"Well, I suppose I must;" and the artist placed a sketch of the room where he was born before the jauitor. "I suppose," continued he, iu his mildest and most winning tones, "if I waited a little, I should not have my journey for nothing?"

"Well, I will see what I can do for you. If you were the tailor or dressmaker or barber I might manage it; but I don't think they want pictures. The house is chock full on 'em. Ah! perhaps this gentleman"—and he addressed another portly personage, not in livery, but solemn black—the steward or butler—"will do something for you. This young lad, sir, says he came, invited by Sir Roger and my lady, to show his pictures."

"I have come by express invitation, otherwise I should not be here."

The major domo scanned him narrowly, and answered placidly—

"We are all very busy this morning. But step in here, my lad, and I will inquire her ladyship's wishes. You will find some of the choicest gems of art there to entertain you."

Hugh Graff was tired and quite subdued. He had come out with grand prospects, and thought his fortune was made. He even conceived he looked big and important to the tall trees and affrighted animals in the noble park through which he had passed. He now began to realize his utter insignificance. Had he been a tailor, a mantua-maker, or a hairdresser, he would be something—a tradesman; as a poor artist he was nothing. It was his first great lesson. He had been, moreover, hard at work mentally since his entrance into the park. At best he was not a strong boy, and the walk had exhausted him. He felt naturally disappointed at the cold character of his reception, but more at its utter common-placeness, where he had expected so much elevation, generosity, and kindness.

The chamber into which he was ushered was entirely devoted to engravings, and contained the very prizes of the art both from the schools of our own country and those of the Continent. But charming as they were, and suited to the taste of the visitor, they had now few attractions to arrest his weary attention. He took a turn or two about the room, glanced cursorily at the glorious scenes surrounding him, and then, dropping into a very easy chair, fell into a profound sleep.

The young art student was weary in mind and frame. His slumber was at first deep and refreshing, he was wholly lost in unconsciousness; but by degrees the active mind began to stir, the lobes of the brain ceased to press so heavily one against the other, the corpuscles of grey matter were in slow motion, the material ministers of the soul had commenced work. The sleeper sighed, stretched out his arms, turned on his side, and began to dream a dream. He thought Priory Park was enchanted ground, and that he was flitting about it on angels' wings. After enjoying the ecstatic luxury of floating over all things in a balmy summer air, he suddenly came upon the mansion. Against this he saw a huge ladder, and hundreds of people toiling up rung by rung with loads on their backs, in order to get an entrance. But as for himself he had his wings, and fled in at once through the window. He met the big porter, now translated into a golden-robed keeper of the gate, and by him he was ushered forthwith into the state chamber. There sat the genius of the place, Sir Roger Wheatley, his lady and daughter, all radiantly clad, and with piles of gold, diplomas of honour, ribbons of various orders, and admissions to high places all in heaps around them. Graff thought they welcomed him most graciously, and smiled ineffable things at his drawings, for they had the portfolio before them. The dream went on this way for some time, broken here and there by strange combinations and contradictions. Iris Dove was actively busy in his fate, and now it was the Levers, and now it was the beautiful young spirit Ernestine herself. But he suddenly thought in reverie fashion that he was not himself, but Oberon Spell, and that all his vision concerned his friend.

He might have been there a couple of hours when the steward pushed open the door, and found him in a perturbed slumber, his portfolio beside him.

"What! you still here, poor child? They have

forgotten you, my little man. Start up, it is getting late."

" Yes, yes, sir.—Oh, sir, yes. Oh, dear! oh, dear! where am I? What a pity,—such a change! I beg pardon, I don't know how it occurred. I suppose I was tired. Am I to go, sir?"

" Well, I thought they would have sent for you long ago. But stop, I will take up the portfolio myself and place it before her ladyship."

" Sir Roger particularly requested to see it."

" You must not always take those things for granted, my lad. He is rather too busy now to see you; but wait here, and I will try what I can do for you."

Mr. Glover, that was the steward's name, was not absent more than five minutes on his mission of kindness. He brought back the portfolio, from which some of the best and most promising drawings had been extracted, that of Iris Dove being formally left; and, with a cordial smile, presented the artist with a sovereign and a shilling.

" There, my little boy, I have succeeded in getting a guinea for you. Her ladyship is engaged, and had forgotten you. You must want some refreshment; come with me."

" First allow me to thank you, sir, and present my duty to Lady Wheatley and say I am much obliged. Will you, sir, accept this drawing from the few left ? I know there is not much in it, but one day, I hope, it will be of value."

" I understand you,—I accept it with pleasure. Come now with me," and taking the lad by the

hand he led him to a large room filled with cup-
boards in the panels, and ordered him a luncheon
of cold bread and meat and sweets, and a glass of
very mild ale.

"I have obtained a privilege for you from her
ladyship. On mentioning your name, you have
permission to enter any of the gates of the park,
and make what sketches you please in the
grounds."

"Oh, thanks, thanks; this is a favour. Now I
shall know where to spend my Wednesday and
Saturday afternoons and my holidays."

"Good-bye, my little boy." The steward rung
a bell. "Harper, show this young gentleman the
way to the western door."

Bowing very low to the great man of a greater
man, the youthful protégé left his patron's house
with a guinea in his pocket and his portfolio
lightened of the best of his drawings. Still he had
gold, and those were but pictures. He had sold
his wares and was satisfied, although the visit was
not what his youthful aspirations had anticipated.

He called in on his friend Oberon as he passed,
and somewhat amused him and Mrs. Spell by his
naïve account of his journey, his reception, his
sleep, and his dream, with the final result of a great
man's patronage.

"Ah, Hugh," said Oberon, smiling, "we must
both stand on our legs, and not depend on walking-
sticks. Your gold-headed canes never yet supported
anything better than footmen and foplings. It
was as well after all, mamma, that my illness pre-

vented my visit to the Priory. I should not have pocketed the affront so complacently."

"My dear, I do not think any slight was intended; great people are not always at leisure, and if we look on things rightly, there is always some compensation. You are satisfied, and our friend Hugh is satisfied."

"Oh, thoroughly so. It is my first guinea, and fairly earned."

"A good beginning for a tradesman, not for an artist, Hugh," said Oberon.

"Well, I don't know, but I suppose you are right. I said I would call, and I have called. But I must get home now;" and after an affectionate adieu, the friends parted.

CHAPTER XII.

FTER much and serious deliberation on Oberon Spell's future career of life, it was finally resolved by his mother, with his own hearty consent, that for a couple of years or so he should dedicate his time to his classical, mathematical, and general studies, under the occasional direction and guidance of Mr. O'Kane, who was really a very superior scholar; that, in fact, he should digest and assimilate his already-acquired knowledge, read extensively and discursively, preparing for a successful college course, and in a remote degree for the bar, his ultimate destination, should no intervening circumstance interrupt and alter this programme. But there was a deeper and more absorbing intention in Oberon's mind. He had long meditated the production of a poem which should illustrate the several departments of art, by a series of beautiful tales and allegories, in themselves classical models of the special themes they explained. To this his reading and the studies of his leisure were all, one way or other, directed. Artist-like, he drew out a regular plan, set diligently to work, and daily added to his choice stock of manuscripts.

Priory Park opened its scenes for his rambles and

contemplations. Here were delightful walks, soul-entrancing vistas, and arbours delicious for meditation or repose. Oberon was not always alone in his excursions. He frequently met the Wheatleys —father, mother, and daughter, and had brief conversations with them. He sometimes came upon Ernestine, accompanied solely by Martin, her maid, and without any familiar communication on either side, there was much to arrest the attention and interest both, and for after-reflection and remembrance, in the scenes and observations which presented themselves on these occasions; the one generally springing out of the other, and the inquirer, for the most part, being the young lady, who was fond of seeking information on every conceivable subject, and found in the student an inexhaustible mine of intelligence and knowledge.

But the poet had also at times other companions. Hugh Graff was frequently by his side, and more than once Iris Dove ventured to accompany him. She, like the Graffs, had never been included in the regular aristocratic admissions to the park, and might now be regarded as formally shut out by reason of the violent political opposition of her father to Sir Roger Wheatley. But quiet Hugh Graff in his inner nature was encroaching and presuming, and conceived there could be no harm in extending his own *carte-blanche* to his almost inseparable lady companion. As to Iris, she never gave a moment's thought to the matter, and Oberon somehow took it for granted that two were comprised in the permission accorded to the young artist. It was thus that the three young friends were often in the park together.   Many were the bright, sunny afternoons and glowing evenings they passed in each other's society among these delightful solitudes. As the range was very extensive, and included a circuit of some twelve miles, they were most times to themselves, as they desired, each pursuing the task he liked best.   Hugh sketched, Iris worked, and Oberon strung verses together, or was lost in contemplation ; at times even indulging in that sweeter employment than doing nothing—thinking nothing.

One evening the three were together in a bower which commanded the most magnificent landscape the park exhibited.   Hugh Graff was pausing in his sketch of one of the glorious old oaks which thronged the scene, and presented a hundred quaint images to the spectator.   As usual, he submitted his work to the judgment and criticism of his friend Oberon, and listened to his observations with profound attention and reverence: although Oberon was, in truth, but a poor draughtsman himself, the pictorial force of his mind and his descriptive powers in words were wonderful.   He saw objects not as matters of hard, dry outline, but through the imagination, embodying always some grand or beautiful sentiment.   Hugh Graff found his best and most genial instructor in the poet.   He could fill in all the rest himself, but he felt his capacity as an artist expand under Oberon.

After thanking Spell for his instructions, he fell back, as a break in their studies, on his old love of hearing Iris recite some of his friend's poems. There may have been a certain secret or insensible policy in this, but the wish sprang truly from the heart, and Hugh could scarcely feel a greater pleasure than in listening to the composition of Oberon recited by the lips he thought most capable of doing it justice, and which he knew gave most satisfaction to the author.

"Iris, dear, have you completed your study of 'Life?'"

"I did my best for it; but I don't like it. 'Tis in blank verse, without that spring which makes rhyme so glib to declaim."

"'Tis very grand, young lady, I tell you; and you must recite it for both of us now."

"Not, surely, if Iris dislikes it," said Oberon.

"No, I don't dislike it; but I cannot feel it."

"Oh, no matter for that; you must try and feel it. Your father is quite in love with it."

"Oh, I believe if Oberon only wrote nursery rhymes or doggrel, pa would be in raptures with them. But since you wish it, dear Hugh, and Oberon is serious, I will recite one of his poems which somehow is a favourite of mine. You know the story; it is about that Italian singer and her handsome lover. But I will begin.

I.

"Light of my soul, when I was born
The Sun-God ruled my destiny,
And filled me with a love of morn,
To make my life a dream of thee.
There is no night when thou art near,
But summer day for evermore,

Such singing of gay birds I hear,
  Such darling flowers their fragrance pour:
Apollo's brow I'll kiss, and kiss,
Dissolv'd and lost in love's abyss.

II.

" Thou heard'st me sing, my love, last night,
  Thou saw'st me move, a dream inspir'd,
Whilst bravos pour'd and bouquets bright,
  And thousand rapturous hearts admir'd.
O! pulse of mine, I saw but thee;
  I heard alone thy precious breath;
There's only one dear world for me—
  Within thy breast—without it, death.
My bower of love! my fame's fond strife,
My inspiration and my life!

III.

" 'Twere strange to tell th' eclipse of tone
  That dimm'd my feelings from a child;
How love-warm genius brooded lone,
  And grief-clouds marr'd affections mild;
Till glorious darkness wrapt my soul,
  And lurk'd soft lightnings in the gloom,
And heaven's great echoes o'er me stole,
  Like Chaos wailing Nature's doom—
But Phœbus shone with am'rous dart,
And summer-noontide charm'd my heart.

IV.

" No marvel I should love him well,
  For who can view that godlike brow,
Where might and light and beauty dwell,
  Nor feel entranc'd as I do now?
And once I gazed with eyes elate,
  But sudden paled with eyelid quiver,
And felt the flash of woman's fate,
  The fire within her heart for ever;
And from that consecrated hour,
I share my glorious Smintheus' power.

v.

" Why art thou beautiful, my love?
    Why young and chivalrous and kind?
Ah! who can deep affection prove,
    Where bright perfections charm the mind?
Would it were otherwise, if so
    Thou slept'st more calmly on my breast,
And felt in age, or pain, or woe,
    A vigil couch for thy unrest.
I reck not form, or grace, or art,
But love the love born in my heart.

VI.

" Play to me, dearest, I will sing
    With thine own soul of thrilling fire:
The ravish'd earth and skies shall ring,
    The very stones will join in choir.
O! beauteous tone! O! pulse of heaven!
    Th' electric trembling of the stars!
To that soft, dulcet touch is given
    More than the conq'ring power of Mars.
Leonora sings! Apollo plays!
They're come again!—th' Elysian days.

VII.

" I've had a dream—a summer dream,
    Of bosom fancies and sweet loves;
The cold North world did dimly gleam,
    The South sent forth her rosy doves;
Rich bloom and fruitage warm'd the ground,
    And forms of beauty graced the sun;
Whilst mirth and music bubbléd round,
    And genius golden guerdon won.
We dwelt apart in vine-clad bower,
And laughing Cupids whiled the hour.

VIII.

" And, as we slept in dewy trance,
    The dreaming of my dream reveal'd

Thy searching spirit's arrowy glance,
  Which life's prophetic book unseal'd.
I saw the truth, like burnish'd gold,
  The present, past, and future—one !
Man's sum of being briefly told—
  The daylight of a winter's sun,
A sun though wrapt in twilight cloud,
A sun when cold in midnight shroud.

IX.

" The vision of my vision changed !—
  We were together through long years,
Grown young in love ; for time estranged
  All selfish, unconfiding fears :
There was no age upon thy brow,
  Nor shriv'ling care to cramp my will ;
Thou wert as beautiful as now,
  And I thy fond reflection still.
The constancy of wedded truth
Embalm'd our hearts in roseate youth.

X.

" A life-long love !—oh ! kind self-death,
  Sweet suicide !—thns wholly thine !
Thine to the last, devoted breath !
  Thine absolute each pulse of mine !
To be all this even in a dream,
  Or a dream's echo, is such bliss
As seraphs rapturously stream
  Through heaven in their communion-kiss.
Then, dove-like, wake, and, nestling, sigh—
' O ! 'tis no dream !'—feel this and die !

XI.

" Come with me, sweetheart, leave this shore,
  Where darling love was never young ;
Where life is labour evermore,
  And faith and genius are earth-sprung.
Oh, come ! and breathe my sunny land !
  By Como's waters shall we dwell,

> Embower'd by Nature's fost'ring hand,
>   And charm'd by Art's divinest spell—
> Joy! joy! oh, heart!—dear Italy!
> With mine own love I welcome thee!"

"Thanks, dear Oberon," Hugh exclaimed; "thanks, dearest Iris. It was charming. Oh! you never looked so beautiful as when you described that 'Godlike brow.' I do not wonder at your choice of the subject. I will never rest till I paint that picture, with you as the singer and Oberon as her lover."

"And who is this bold lady who declaims so loudly in Edelstone Park?" said an excited voice, breaking in on the astonished trio.

"Oh, Miss Wheatley," said Oberon, rising, and at the same time deeply blushing while he took the hand outstretched to him alone, not with the usual friendliness, but with somewhat of offended dignity.

"Yes; my maid and I were on our strolls, and we heard voices. At first, not knowing from whence they came, we approached, but unwilling to interrupt so enthusiastic a declamation. I now perceive who your choice is. I have seen this young person before; I think, Hilary Dove's daughter."

"I am Hilary Dove's daughter," said Iris, stepping forward into the walk with the sweep of a tragedienne.

"Come, Martin, we are intruders here. I was not aware that Priory Park had become a common;" and inclining her head slightly to Oberon, the daughter and heiress of Sir Roger Wheatley passed on with her maid.

“ There is some mistake,” said Oberon. “ I must run forward and explain.”

“ Miss Wheatley, I beg pardon. I trust you will not think me an intruder here.”

Ernestine Wheatley was very pale and somewhat confused and annoyed; she, however, replied with tolerable composure :

“ No, Mr. Spell; with you it is altogether different. I have seen you in this park as long as I can remember; your young artist friend has had, I understand, permission; but there the privilege ought to stop—must stop; that young person shall henceforth be excluded. Her father, Hilary Dove, is one of Sir Roger Wheatley’s most active political enemies. He is a renegade, if not something worse.”

“ Hilary Dove is my friend, Miss Wheatley, and his daughter Iris my chosen companion. We shall however be sure not to obtrude again ;” and raising his hat to the young lady, Oberon Spell hastily returned to his friends.

Miss Wheatley stood a moment, puzzled, and then walked on in haughty silence beside her maid. Her feelings had been deeply wounded, but nevertheless she perceived that her conduct was unladylike and wrong.

“ Come, Hugh,” said Oberon, giving his arm to Iris. “ What can you be about ?”

“ About ? why, finishing my sketch, to be sure. I do not see why we should take up the quarrels of Iris or her father. We are not politicians. Besides, it would be very awkward; this is such a capital place for sketching. I will try and see Sir Roger myself and get you permission, Iris."

"Never for me. I know myself better. That young lady hates me, and I think I know the cause."

"Come, dear, we must go. If Hugh chooses to remain we cannot help that; we must leave."

"Well, walk slowly," said the artist, steadily going on with his work. "I shall be sure to catch you up in Blackberry-lane."

Oberon Spell and Iris Dove were speedily on their way, arm in arm, to the next gate, which opened directly into the road mentioned. As they passed, Ernestine Wheatley saw them from the distance, and felt her heart, young as she was, throb with conflicting emotions. However, she quickly mastered herself, and appeared only annoyed at the presence of the daughter of her father's political enemy to the simple, earnest woman who attended her.

"Hugh is of a peaceful disposition, as mamma says," said Iris, casting a regretful look behind. "I wish he were here."

"For his own sake I wish he were; but I am not sorry that we are alone. Iris, there are many things I wish to say to you which we cannot well mention before others."

Iris was silent and blushed a little, very little.

"I was thinking," said Oberon, "you ought to commence a course of studies. I shall be most happy——"

"To be my teacher. Oh, that was what you had to say. Pray don't think of it, if you would not be my torturer; and not a word of this to papa."

" But should you not like to improve yourself?"

" No, not in book-learning; I can't see its use, nor can mamma. There's the Skelmers; the eldest brother is a scholar—a very learned man, they say, and a poor scrub of a writer. The other, I believe, never read a book in his life, not even a novel; he can't spell, and his writing is a scrawl; but he was thrust into a warehouse when a boy by his elder brother. He picked up the trade of slops; he knows this, and he is one piece of pushingness and cunning, so mamma says. Well, he gets seven hundred a year, and an interest in the business as manager of a department, in the great city firm of Higginbotham & Co. He is cautiously and slowly undermining his employers in the house, and making a party for himself among the chiefs and men. His design is to succeed as principal one day. He lives in a villa, and keeps his wife, who knows nothing, in luxury; while his brother, with all his conduct and knowledge, has to shift from lodging to lodging, constantly struggling to maintain that poor, proud lady his wife and three ailing children."

" With all those drawbacks he may be happier than his elder brother. He is not a pretender, like him."

" A pretender, indeed. I should like to know what the reality is good for, if the base coin passes better? I tell you, mamma says that in this world appearance is everything. I shall stick to that.

I shall do very well with a little scraping of knowledge here and there. I can talk as well as you now, and perhaps think better. Oberon Spell says—

> "There is a soul of wisdom in the world,
>   Beyond our written knowledge; broad and clear,
>   Germane to ev'ry mind, which shines on all,
>   And makes men's genius equal."

Ha! ha! What do you think of that, Mr. Preacher?"

" And what do you think of all my labours to be a scholar ?"

" Why, that you are a fool for your pains; a make-believe, like me, will do much better. We know when it is wise to show off. I never bore people, as pedants do. Now, if you could paint like Hugh, you would have value for your labour, and could turn it to profit; so mamma says."

" Indeed."

" Indeed ! Why, I heard yourself say that the wisest of men—I do not mean Solomon, but Socrates—you see I know that—with all his knowledge only knew enough to know he knew nothing."

" True; human intelligence is very circumscribed."

" Oh ! give me the man who knows slops well, or chimney-sweeping, or anything that will bring grist to the mill; he is my master of arts—and hearts too," added she, laughing.

" Iris, I fear you are incorrigible."

" If I were I should not know so much of your poetry. But where is Hugh—my Hugh—little Hugh Graff ? I must run back to meet him."

"No, Iris, you must not condescend to that. He did wrong in lingering behind."

"I don't think so. Come, come along!"

And saying this, the arch, tantalizing girl caught Oberon by the hand and tried to drag him back. Just at the moment a rustle was heard in the hedge, and Jonathan Cubborn passed rapidly along the field it enclosed, coughing significantly as he hurried forward.

"An eavesdropper here," said Iris, checking her exuberant action.

"To warn you, Iris, that, as your mamma says, you should never forget appearances. But I see Hugh coming."

"Oh, I am glad you joined us," said Iris, quitting Oberon's side for the approaching artist. "We were getting prosy and should soon have quarrelled. Well, dear, have you finished your sketch?"

"All but a few touches which I can give it at home. You look dull, Oberon. I hope you are not offended with me."

"We must act in unison, Hugh, if we are to be friends." And saying this the student walked on by himself in silence. After a time Iris once more drew to his side.

"Oberon dear, I hope you are not meditating another battle."

"No, Iris; to contemplate is my mood."

"Oh, I had forgot—a bookworm. Save us from stale thoughts and musty tomes! I must rejoin Hugh. He is economizing time; not losing it on me, but finishing his sketch on the road. Come, cheer up. I know I am naughty at times; but take the light with the shadow, the good with the evil."

"But why should there be evil?" Pondering this question in other than its metaphysical and moral bearing, Oberon Spell did not reply, but took the turning which led to his home, leaving Iris to finish her walk with Hugh Graff, whom she had rejoined. She soon missed Oberon from the road, and said, while a tear started to her eye,—

"Dear Oberon! I am a sad girl, and annoy him often when I do not intend. It was all your fault for staying behind, sneak as you are! But who have we here?"

"Oh, Mr. Cubborn," said Hugh, blandly. "I did not know you were behind us."

"Hard for you while Oberon Spell was here," said Iris.

"It was fortunate for you, miss, that I was here when that fellow forgot himself."

"It is you, I think, who forget yourself now and forgot yourself then. But it was well to have a hedge to run behind for shelter; it prevented another ugly accident."

"Come, come; let there be no bitterness. We are all friends and neighbours here," said Hugh, interposing. "I hope Mr. Cubborn is too well bred to play the spy or annoy a lady; and, by-the-bye, as you are here, perhaps you would charge yourself with this sketch of a Royal Oak for your mamma. It will save me a journey. Do you like it? You know you were always clever at drawing, Mr. Jonathan."

" Well, I used to be ; but I attend to another department now. I wonder, Graff, a hearty good fellow like you, can chum with that cur, Spell."

" He is my friend."

" And mine," said Iris, in her most emphatic manner.

" Oh, two to one—one too many. Good night, Graff—good night, miss."

Hugh and Iris were alone together, but the sole conversation of Iris was about Oberon Spell and his noble bearing and conduct. In all these eulogies Hugh cordially joined ; though he somewhat regretted the tiresome monotony of the conversation, for in the bottom of his heart Hugh Graff was most covetous of admiration.

" We are at home, Hugh. Good night. Poor Oberon ! I did not say good night to him ! God bless you !"

" And you, dearest Iris. Good night."

And so they parted.

The very next day Oberon called to take a hasty adieu of his young friends, Iris and Hugh. The previous night he had had a very long and serious conversation with his mother, and the result was that both resolved to accept immediately the invitation of Mrs. Lever to join the family in London. An attempt was made by mother and son, each in a peculiar way, to sever the ties of early companionship and maturing affection.

CHAPTER XIII

NCE fairly launched on the great ocean of metropolitan life, Oberon Spell, ever sensitive to new impressions, stood in some danger of forgetting his boyish love. But that was inrooted in his being, and however concealed for a time by circumstances, it was sure to peer forth again at the genial season. Nor was his cousin Caroline exactly the person to wean him from an early and deep affection. She had not the recommendation of beauty essential to his notion of feminine excellence. In fact, the young lady was rather plain. She was not a bad diminutive of her gigantic father. Middle-sized, fair and burly, with large blue eyes, a ponderous forehead, a heavy cast of countenance; she resembled him, too, in the strength and breadth of her intellect. She evidently had been taught to place her forte in her mental attainments and accomplishments. But then she was so chiselled and finished in all her ways, so concise and weighty in her language and argument, so much the creature of a very superior education! She spoke well, and always with sound sense. She wrote well, and with the neatest angle of that peculiar penmanship of English ladies. She played well, drew and painted well, and even danced well, considering her *embonpoint*. She knew the

leading foreign languages, with a certain proficiency
in their conversation and literature.   She had
passed some years on different parts of the Continent,
and could discourse freely on their manners, usages,
places, and scenery.   She had a smattering of
Greek and Latin, and in mathematics she could
work and demonstrate the problems and theorems
in the first three books of Euclid's Elements, and an
equation of the second degree came easy to her
clear perception of the relations of numbers. Then,
she was fairly read in history and in other topics indispensable to a well-cultivated and full mind.

With all this, it could not be said that Caroline
Lever was a bluestocking.   She certainly was not
devoted to books.   Her disposition was rather playful than otherwise.   But she was just fresh from
tutors, travels abroad, and a round of professors
and learning, and her mind was filled with nothing
else.   She still breathed of the desk and the
governess and the pedagogue.   So that persons
could not say what she would turn out by and by.
For the present she had just those qualities and
attainments of which Oberon himself had had his
fill.   There is a freshness even in ignorance, many
are pleased to call it simplicity, and unquestionably
of this wild natural plant Caroline Lever had little
share.   Then she was Oberon's senior by nearly a
couple of years.   To him she appeared, and was, in
fact, a matured woman.   In the damsel of nineteen
he forcibly missed the untaught hoydenish girl who
commanded his love.

The young pair visited the great sights of London

in company with their mothers. Caroline was not a little gratified at being chaperoned from place to place by such a handsome beau, for though but a mere youth, Oberon was tall and commanding in his appearance. In their rambles they left nothing unexplored, and, like most visitors, the student saw more of the metropolis than thousands born and reared in the city itself. But although their tastes and judgments generally agreed, their sentiments and feelings were many times apart. Caroline often thought her companion too much of the teacher. She had been schooled to regard such beings as learned machines—persons to be listened to attentively and respected, but never anything more. To admire them would be positive crime. We could, therefore, easily understand the relations of these two young people, if the handsome features and elegance and the real superiority throughout of Oberon had not awakened something like love in the bosom of the lady. This was not lessened by the frequent dependence of this well-educated damsel on her youthful companion for accurate information. What she had merely learnt, he had digested, and she had continually to appeal to him to confirm or correct her knowledge. It may be, too, that she had been taught by her mother to regard Oberon as her future husband, and began thus early to discipline her mind to a certain feminine submission and obedience; or was it that she was secretly and unconsciously smitten? However it befell, there existed an essential difference in the kind of regard each bore the other. But certain it is, that their feelings were not those of brother and sister, rather of unassimilating acquaintances brought into close relation.

Their mothers failed to perceive the heart-distinction prevailing between them. Mrs. Spell was only too well pleased at the contrast of her niece to the forward girl they had left behind at Edelstone. She conceived it impossible that her son Oberon, so chaste and classical in all his ideas, should not regard his cousin as the purest reflex of his own mind, and therefore come to esteem and love her in time. The want of personal attractions did not forcibly strike her. They never do a woman as strongly as a man. Besides, Caroline, though rather stout and heavy looking, was on the whole a most accomplished and agreeable young lady. As to the affection of her niece for her perfection of a son, she conceived it to be impossible that any woman could behold and know him without owning within herself the sentiment of love.

Mrs. Lever was not a very deep or calculating woman; she desired the union of her daughter with her nephew; and, making sure of the event, she left circumstances, which must at present be immature, to the ripening issue of time. In this way a very pleasant season passed off in London.

But it did not close without a visit from Hugh Graff to the great metropolis. He came at the express invitation of Mr. Lever himself, who had taken a solid liking to him, and was desirous of thus testifying his regard in the most prominent and substantial manner.

The young artist was much improved in appearance. He had grown taller and was less rotund. He was still the same subdued, quiet, smiling youth as ever, with a soft, bland manner, a gentle voice, and an eye full of observation. He had been winning his way all around his native village. Everybody teemed with praise of the clever painter; and as his prices for sketches and portraits were very reduced, his pictures were to be found in houses of various degrees in Edelstone and the surrounding neighbourhood, one of them dangling as an attractive sign to the Merry Thought. His earnings were carefully stored up for him by his father, who began to have a fixed hope at last that the lad might make a comfortable livelihood in time by his work as an artist. This was a great step in faith for a man who had associated in his mind painters, poets, and all of that tribe, with the starvelings of society.

The master to whom Hugh had been apprenticed, and who took a great interest in the boy when he saw the real direction of his mind, of which he was a rather competent judge, had no hesitation in giving up the indentures and cancelling them, with the following proud endorsement:—" This document was given to insure that Hugh Graff of Edelstone should serve seven years of his life to learn the trade of a grainer from me. He has by talent and industry acquired all I can teach him in half as many months, and is now competent to teach me or my foreman. I, therefore, release him from his engagement, and send him forth to win a high reputation as an artist."

It was with no slight pleasure the young painter showed this honourable testimonial to the appreciative engineer, who read it aloud, and was not sparing in commenting on its real force and significance.

"Well, sir, you have succeeded, as I predicted. I understand that your late master is a man of crotchety disposition, very hard to deal with. You must have had many rebuffs and difficulties to please him; but to triumph as you have done, is a greater tribute to your temper and management than even to your genius. We must see what we can do for you. Should you like to become a pupil of the Royal Academy?"

"By all means, sir; that would be the height of my ambition."

"You shall draw upon my funds until able to sustain your own position."

"I thank you, I thank you, indeed, very sincerely; but I have sufficient money saved in my father's hands, or rather in the bank, where he placed it for me, to support me till I shall get a connexion here. I hope soon to add to my stock by adequate exertion. I only regret that my friend Oberon is not about to join me, we have been so very long together; but our careers are now to be different."

"So it appears; nothing will prevent my nephew from pursuing the flowery paths of poesie."

"Doubtless," said Oberon, with that cool, independent manner so characteristic of him, "I shall be as happy following the bent of my genius, as you in yours, uncle, or Graff in his."

"True, sir; only rhymes do not jingle so sweet as money."

"Literary pursuits, I presume, are not incompatible with the study, attainment, and practice of a paying profession."

"Assuredly not; but I have not heard to what profession or calling, if any, you wish to attach yourself."

"I believe we are to confer with Sir Roger Wheatley on that subject," said Mrs. Spell, with her usual quiet dignity. "I think Oberon's destiny is in safe hands."

Here the conversation dropped, and while it was going forward the artist was busily occupied in showing the collection of sketches in his portfolio to Caroline, who expressed herself delighted, as she really was, with her examination. Mrs. Lever joined them.

"I suppose, Mr. Graff, you will take up your residence permanently in London, when you enter the Royal Academy?"

"I presume it will be necessary, madam."

"If you do we shall be glad to see you occasionally. Mr. Lever I am sure will be pleased to learn of your continued success."

"It will be a hard struggle for me to quit Edelstone, where I have so many dear objects of affection—my parents, my relations, and I think I may say, numerous friends. Moreover, there are many houses in the village, and round about, where I shall leave some memorial of my hand. I feel, as it were, bound to the spot. But in this world, madam, we must progress and grow rich. I shall, however, feel myself amply recompensed by an occasional visit here, madam, if permitted, whenever I can snatch an hour from the course of arduous and severe study I am about to enter on."

Mr. Lever now moved his portentous body to the group, leaving Oberon and his mother seated at a side table.

" I have just been telling your young friend, my dear, that we shall feel pleased to see him now and then when he comes to settle in London."

" Certainly we shall. And so this is your port-folio now? How well stocked, and richly too. When you advance a little further, you shall try your hand on a portrait of Miss Lever."—(Caroline smiled, and the artist bowed very low.)—" Mean-while, you will allow me to make a few selections from these; they will be a valuable addition to your portfolio, Caroline."

" They will indeed, papa."

Mr. Lever and his daughter, assisted by the artist, made a very careful choice. There was some little difficulty about payment, but the engineer, in his rough and ready way, soon got over Hugh's scruples, and insisted on his receiving a ten-pound note, which, to say the truth, was not too large a sum for the drawings. At an aftertime they might fetch eight-fold that amount.

All this time Oberon and his mother remained where the engineer had left them seated. They spoke together in a low voice.

" I find no fault with your friend Graff, my

dear," said Mrs. Spell, " but I cannot conceal from myself and you, that somehow he very materially interferes with your popularity. Even at Edelstone you have ceased to be the prodigy of the village. It is all Hugh Graff, nothing but Hugh Graff, that clever youth, that astonishing genius."

"Well, dear mother, I rejoice at my friend's success. He can never be to me but a friend and a brother; his progress and praise are alike mine."

" God grant they were; but in him I perceive a marvellous alacrity in seizing occasions and circumstances, and in you their scornful neglect."

" Because I truly despise them, mother. I am full of one great idea; only wait, do wait, dear mother, till my poem is finished and published, and then judge of the wisdom of my present mode of action and conduct."

" It is so long to wait, dear child. I do not wish to dishearten you, but I fear years will intervene before the completion of that poem."

" Time must not be considered on such an exalted theme."

" But you have to go to college, and then there will be your foreign travel. Surely it will be time to look carefully to a profession after so much preparation."

" But, dear mamma, all this while at intervals I shall be pursuing my poem. But if I could ever feel offended with Hugh, I should take umbrage at the marked predilection of Iris for him; and yet I do not know that I do not like both all the better for their mutual attachment. It binds them more closely to me as friends."

"I wish from my heart they were old enough to be bound far otherwise; they sadly block the way. But pray, my dear, put Iris Dove and all such nonsense out of your head."

"And substitute for her such a lump of putty as I see before me. You do not know me, my mother. But come, let us join them. Why, Hugh, how wonderfully you have improved!—Oil-colours, too! You know I always said you would be an artist."

"Yes; and I answered I wished to be one, and you encouraged me even against hope. I verily believe that had I not known you, I should never have taken pencil or brush in hand, except as a carpenter or house-painter. You taught me, as you say, to look up and beyond."

"Tut, tut, man!" said Mr. Lever, rising; "you had it in you, just as I the engineer in me. The artist would come out under any disadvantage."

"But I owe so very much to Oberon. Like you now, dear sir, he was my encourager, my inspirer, and my guide."

"Well, it is all right to be grateful. But come below with me to the library; I will give you a letter of introduction to my friend, Sir Strutter Lomax Looney, the great picture and engraving dealer, late lord-mayor of London. If he takes to you, gad! sir, your fortune is made."

Patting Hugh on the back, as was his manner, they both descended to the library together. Caroline and Oberon prepared to take a walk in the park,

and Mrs. Spell and her sister-in-law were left alone
together.   Mrs. Spell, who had heard the proposed
introduction to the great Sir Strutter Lomax
Looney, was inly pained and grieved.   There was
just an inkling of soreness and envy in her heart at
Hugh Graff's marvellous good fortune.   Had she
consulted her son, who, from his various readings
and habit of observation had a correct notion of
many things, he would have enlightened her as to
Hugh's chance of making honour or fortune by any
connexion with the printseller and late lord-mayor,
Sir Strutter Lomax Looney, who was noted for
using young artists.

CHAPTER XIV.

HEN the young people had departed for their ramble, Mrs. Lever, addressing her sister-in-law, took occasion to observe that she was afraid that Oberon was but a careless lover.

" He is so very young, dear, it is almost a sin, and certainly somewhat of an absurdity, to talk of such matters in regard to two mere children."

" Children ! Well, it is the foible of parents always to regard their offspring as boys and girls, never as men and women : but I tell you what, Caroline will be nineteen next January, and she is just of the same age I was when I married Lever. Then she is such a truly superior girl, she has been so well trained, that she would be an ornament to any establishment."

" But Oberon, dear ; I am referring to him principally. He is only a mere youth ; seventeen the first of August last. I fear he is not of years to fix his affections."

" You see, my dear, it is really a matter of indifference to us. Caroline is a girl who has been sought, and is now sought, by a whole swarm of admirers. Independently of the large fortune she will receive, her accomplishments are amply sufficient to recommend her. It was only for dear Oberon's sake, whom we all love, that Ajax and I were desirous of establishing him well in life, at the same time duly caring for the interests and happiness of our child. We all know Oberon is a handsome youth and the promise of a very fine man. But I have to tell you one thing, dear."

"What is that?"

"I believe Mr. Lever is seriously offended with Oberon."

"I should indeed regret that, if his resentment were founded on any just cause."

"Oh, there is no resentment—there can be none; only that peculiar, independent way which Oberon has, I often think, somewhat displeases him."

"Independence is a fine quality in a man, Frederica."

"To contemplate, dear, to contemplate; in practice it is very bad—almost the road to ruin. But what on earth does the boy mean to do with himself? His poor father did not leave him a large fortune to idle and revel in; and although your management has been wonderful, it cannot be supposed he will have much to start with. He ought not to expect that we can give him Caroline without an adequate prospect of his being able to maintain an establishment."

"I do not believe he expects anything of the kind; I rather infer that he thinks nothing about it, or if he glances at it, his feelings at present—he is so young—are not much interested."

“That is, in other words, Martha, he does not really care for Caroline.”

“Do not be hasty, dear. The lad is barely in his teens—a mere schoolboy; he has to go to college and on his foreign travels, and to select and make a certain way in a profession, before he can even think of marriage. I find we are all rather too precipitate.”

“Mercy, Martha, what a career you have chalked out for my nephew! I know that Lever’s idea was to take him at once into his own office, and to make him an engineer; and, I need not tell you, the probable successor to a gigantic business.”

“Well, my dear, do not suppose I am insensible to the advantages of the offer.”

“But hear me out;—and then, when he became of age—that time will now come quickly round—to give him our daughter. Can we do more?”

“Trust me, Frederica; I, his mother, must feel the confidence and love this selection implies; but, as I said, he is but young yet.”

“Surely not too young for the engineering.”

“He has decided against that, and I cannot, indeed I will not, contravene his choice.”

“So that he not only rejects the profession designed him, that he might be able to marry our daughter, but he is foolish enough to manifest a marked indifference to her attractions.”

“It is very difficult, in truth I find it impossible, to control the affections of children, Frederica.”

“Oh, then he has affections! the boy, the immature youth entertains his own juvenile passion. We all know how headstrong he is. Be candid with me, dear. Since I must infer from your admission that, young as he is, he is already in love, pray, dear, who is the fair lady? Is it any one I know?"

"My general reply, Frederica, is in strict accord with my observations all along; that Oberon is at present of too youthful an age to hold him engaged to any one, or to regard his sentiments as fixed and decided. We must give him time. Let him come of age."

"And Caroline in the meantime is to reject a score of eligible matches, in the end perhaps to be thrown aside on the shelf by Mr. Oberon Spell. No, Martha; this will never do. The matter had better be ended this very day. I shall speak to Mr. Lever on the subject."

"Do not be rash, Frederica! Perhaps you do not consult Caroline's feelings sufficiently."

"Oh, as to that, I had not thought in that direction. I do believe the poor girl likes him; but she has been well disciplined, and, if needs be, she must learn to forget him. Better now than at a later period. It shall never be said that Caroline Lever, the sole child of the great engineer, was the rejected of Oberon Spell."

"Again I say, Frederica, do not be so prompt to decide; let the affair remain open, as it ought to be —neither party engaged, as they really are not. Should you find a more eligible match for Caroline, by all means let her accept it. She is quite marriageable. It is different with my boy. I presume, should he not be so lucky as to obtain Caroline, he might even be fortunate enough to find some other heiress not indifferent to his poor perfections."

"Oh, indeed!—another mystery! And pray, dear, who is this fair charmer for whom my child is to be rejected?"

"I am not at liberty to tell. All I can say, in the utmost candour and sisterly affection, to you, Frederica, is, repeating my former expression, the lad is too young yet for us to determine anything in regard to his future marriage. But one thing I have made up my mind to, and that is never to interfere between him and the true object of his matured affection."

"Which, of course, you know will not be Caroline. Well, dear, I suppose he will turn out like his father, marry the woman of his choice against the express wishes of his surviving parent. I trust his selection will be as fortunate."

"You stir painful memories, dear. Pray let us change the subject."

"Then I am to let that question of Caroline's marriage with Oberon continue in abeyance at present. Is not that it, Mistress Precision?"

"I think, my dear, that will be the better course."

"Well, I will consult Ajax on the subject."

Here the conversation dropped. There was to be a dancing party that evening, and each lady retired to perform some necessary act of duty in a large household, where one aided the other in the domestic administration. But the faithful wife did not fail to communicate to her husband the substance

of her colloquy with Martha Spell, deferring, as she
was always wont to do, to his opinion.

"Well, my dear, I have no objection to regard it
as you ladies have wisely left it—an open question.
But mind you, if we really meet a more eligible
offer, Oberon Spell shall never have my daughter.
He is impracticable, Frederica; like his father,
headstrong and self-willed. 'Tis to be hoped the
final result may be more fortunate. I loved that
lad; I was proud of him; but I have done with
him."

The evening came, and Mrs. Lever, as usual, was
equal to the task of receiving numerous guests and
making them perfectly at their ease and happy, so
far as she was concerned. Her husband was at
his post in the vicinity of the Houses of Parliament,
attending to private and public business, giving information here, directions there, but in all cases extending his own connexion, practice, and fortunes.
His ponderous proportions, little adapted to the
drawing-room or ball-room, were not in much request by the company. He was thoroughly well
represented at home.

Caroline had dressed her best, but it was un-
deniable that a ball costume did not become her.
It only brought out her *embonpoint* more prominently, and made her look unwieldy and even
awkward in the midst of a bevy of English beauties.
The young lady, too, had evidently had her lesson
from her mother. She was not to be too marked
in her attentions to Oberon. Her papa might
ultimately not approve of the alliance. Most pro-

bably it would never take place, and so on. Whatever was hinted or said, Caroline was unusually sad and gloomy. Scarcely a smile escaped her the whole evening; and her chagrin was sensibly increased by seeing Oberon quite unconcerned at her melancholy, and dancing away light-hearted and gay with the acknowledged beauty of the party, who seemed quite charmed with the handsome stripling's society. As a matter of politeness, he with his accustomed careless familiarity asked his cousin to dance, but, as she declined, he did not press the suit, but made another and more attractive selection. The ultimate consequence of an evident slight was that Caroline Lever had to withdraw from the ball-room ill.

"I feel rather unwell, dear mamma; allow me to retire."

"By all means, my dear child; go to your room and ring immediately for Watkins; she will attend to you. I will join you soon."

Nothing was said that night about Oberon's open neglect of his cousin; but the next morning the whole matter again formed the subject of another long conversation between the two mothers. This time there was more animation, more point, more satire, and some bitterness. The two sisters-in-law almost quarrelled. The result was to hasten Oberon's departure for college; and in a week from that day he started for Oxford.

CHAPTER XV.

T is not our intention here to enter on a narrative of Oberon Spell's university career. There was in it nothing remarkable; and the same course has been so often described before, that unless accompanied by some special features, little new can be said on the subject. We prefer giving an extract from one of his numerous letters to his mother, as embodying his views of a university education, and because it shows the state of his mind at the time.

" It was well for me, dear mother, that the plan of my education included a regular university course. Without this, I should have gone forth a literary upstart to the world—a mere sciolist, with half-formed notions and much empty vanity. Nature had, I believe, endowed me with a certain appetency for knowledge, and I have had the best instruction that Cramton Hall and O'Kane's zeal and learning could impart. But for all that I was not educated. I was almost in a worse state than an unsuccessful student; for my repeated scholastic triumphs had led me to believe that I was at the top of the tree —that the horizon of knowledge was clear before me, and that, as I had no compeers, my researches and labours could not go much further.

" How was I undeceived when I found myself a mere dwarf in the presence of the intellectual giants now around me. No single subject do I know accurately, completely, and well. I have, therefore, resolved to begin at the foot of the ladder, prepared to climb it step by step, sustained by the ablest instructors. Is it not much, very much, in life to know that I am drinking from the highest sources of human intelligence; that whatever in science or letters has been communicated, received, or discovered is understood and taught here; that here is the latest and final depository of existing but progressive intelligence and knowledge? What an amazing advantage to have for instructors and guides—often as companions—the very foremost scholars, thinkers, and geniuses of the age— the intellectual Titans of the modern world! Rightly appreciated, dear mother, a college life is the heaven of mortal existence—the empyrean of the mind, and one of the great spiritual contributories to the exhaustless fountains of the soul. To me it is an elysium—a sublime poem in itself—the realm of truth approximate and real—a scene of serene and lofty enjoyment, which I would not forego for all earth's pleasures beyond!

" I strive, my dear mother, for excellence in everything—not alone in the field of intellect, but in sports of various kinds; balancing carefully one against the other—the brain's exhaustion with the body's exercise and refection."

Such were the thoughts of Oberon Spell communicated to his mother, not as mere first impressions, but as his real appreciation of a college-life. We will not say they were not afterwards in some degree modified; but they must be admitted to be in the main elevated and just.

It cannot be said of the chiefs and leading men of our universities, that they are very active in the selection, encouragement, or recommendation of merit. So many clever youths appear, so many prodigies, that it requires their experienced eye to discriminate between ephemeral, self-exhausting precocity, and true and enduring mental power. But whenever this rare endowment is disclosed, and the possessor happens also to be gifted with an attractive person and manners, he is almost sure to become a marked favourite in the university. It was Oberon Spell's good fortune not only to be on the best terms with the master and tutors of his college, but to have conciliated the attention and regard of the Bishop of Boroughcliffe, one of the most eminent scholars of the age, and formerly Regius Professor of Divinity in the University. The distinguished prelate one day took the trouble to inquire into the successful student's prospects in life, and on receiving a candid explanation, he strongly advised Oberon to enter the Church, promising him his protection and patronage. This implied a condition of existence which our hero deemed humiliating and slavish, and to which he could not bring his mind to submit. He therefore very politely declined the proffered suggestion and kindness, and thus permanently displeased my Lord Bishop, who, it must be conceded, had put himself considerably out of the way to hold out a helping hand to the young scholar in his future career. The truth is, Oberon had notions of authorship ever floating across his mind; and if he at all thought seriously of a profession, it was to the Bar and not to the Church his attention was turned, the former career being most congenial to his public views and independence of character; though it must be stated that even this loomed only in the very far distance—his grand, his absorbing ambition was to be the poet of his epoch.

In this way some two years of the student's life had passed at Oxford, broken by the usual vacations, and also enlivened by occasional visits from his friends, among whom the Levers and Hugh Graff were the most prominent. It was just barely noticeable that the young painter appeared to have obtained a rather permanent footing at the engineer's mansion. He accompanied the mother and daughter once or twice to the college, and was on those occasions on terms of marked intimacy with both. The great man himself was far away in Canada, bridge-building and railway constructing. Caroline was still a spinster, though Oberon had more than once ascertained from his mother that her marriage with a certain Scotch baronet in search of a fortune was positively expected. This information produced no other effect on Oberon's mind than to wish that the alliance were speedily accomplished, as he should be then relieved from Miss Lever's rather too marked attentions. Though he could better judge of this young lady's feelings towards him from her letters than from her bearing and conversation when in his society. The epistles of the heiress were in truth very superior productions. She evidently laboured to make her best impression through them. They teemed with just thoughts, correct reasonings, accurate and comprehensive information, and pure and religious sentiments. But in them all was a manifest, though by no means prominent, desire and anxiety for Oberon's welfare. She took a genial and hearty interest in his successes, and tenderly sympathized with his crosses and failures, rare and exceptional, indeed, as the latter were. But all these amiable displays of intelligence and feeling produced no manner of effect on Oberon Spell's heart. In that direction he was unassailable, and this began to be thoroughly felt at the Levers'.

How different was it when his sympathies were really aroused! While in the midst of many learned speculations, some successes, and here and there a dream of ambition, his college career was one day suddenly invaded and stopped by a most unexpected visit. Occupied in the composition of a profound metaphysical essay, his attention was in a moment called away from the regions of abstraction by a very realistic note from no other than Iris Dove. It was brief, but to the purpose.

"The Caxton Hotel, Oxford.

"DEAR OBERON,—I am here—just staying for a day. Papa is with me. I thought you might like to see me. I know I should like to see you. I

shall stop in all day to meet you.   Pa will be out.
But that will be all the better.   .Be sure to come,
and soon.

"Yours affectionately,
"Iris Dove.

"Oberon Spell, Esq."

A sudden blush suffused the student's face
when he saw the handwriting in the address.   He
kissed the note gently, as if it were some reverent
thing, before he broke the seal, a delicate glow at
the same time overspreading his countenance.   He
was no longer a student.   He was the enthusiast
and lover again.   He threw his learned disquisition
aside, read the billet three times over, kissed it
tenderly again, and hastened to put himself in
visiting trim.   In about twenty minutes he was
beside Iris in a small room of the hotel.   It was
now more than two years since he had seen her.
She too had been away, going a round of visits with
her peripatetic father, assisting him in various ways
and adding to what he valued most—display and
observation.   Iris was greatly improved in appearance—quite a radiant beauty in face, size, form,
and figure—a being of such commanding and
elegant exterior as is rarely met with even in a
sphere to which she had no pretension—among the
acknowledged and reigning belles of the English
court and aristocracy.   Oberon was quite enraptured
at the sight of so much loveliness.   Ah! what a
rich and glorious contrast to the severe and disciplined forms, scenes and themes so long before his

eyes. Here was Iris, fair Iris Dove, the same merry, confident, unartificial and affectionate being as ever —but how much more fascinating and beautiful! It was impossible that Oberon should not love her. The meeting was on one side exquisitely happy, on the other teeming with sisterly affection and eager curiosity.

"Why, Oberon, how you have grown! You are a great man—I cannot say you are improved. I fear I shall not like you half so well as when you were a boy. Ah! my brown-haired boy, where is he gone? But I want to see where you are—and all about you—and all over all the places here. We have only to-day, so come, and let us be off and make the best of it. You see I am quite ready to start—it is only just to run on my bonnet. Here, take a biscuit and a glass of wine—I shall be with you in a moment. You dine with us at six—pa made me promise him."

How the bonnet was run on was one of those miracles which only scenic transformations can realize. True to her word, Iris did return in a moment, and as elegantly and precisely attired to the disposition of a ribbon or a single hair of her rich fair locks as if she had devoted hours to her toilette.

"There, you see, I have not kept you long waiting. But, you know, I was quite ready before, and this is such a love of a bonnet; pa bought it me yesterday to see you in, that it is just like putting on a smile, or something equally easy, to slip it over the head. Do you like it, Oberon?"

"Well, I think it becomes you, dear Iris."

"And is that all? Oh, this humdrum place has spoilt all your gallantry—why, pa says it makes me look— Well, no matter; let us go."

It may be safely said that two such remarkable and handsome personages were seldom seen in the ancient seat of learning. Every one believed that the pair were sister and brother, for there was a resemblance between them in the lofty and commanding carriage and in the open sunniness of countenance, only that Oberon's face was of the Greek mould, while that of Iris was decidedly of the fair-haired Norman—a cast of features far more charming and elegant. It cannot, however, be denied that in the few introductions Oberon was compelled to make, the young lady's general conversation with the bland and courteous individuals who addressed her, by no means justified the expectations raised by her intelligent countenance, her clear, ringing, cultivated voice and elocution, and her very imposing exterior. Iris herself was quite unconscious of any deficiency. If the truth were known, she thought she was very polite in entertaining here and there a staid young man—Oberon took good care to make his introductions select—or a learned old fogy, with a little agreeable chit-chat not exactly within the round of letters or polished society. However, there was evidently no pretension about her. She was at home on the subjects she broached, and was listened to, if for nothing else, for her *naïveté* and sound sense—a vein of solid understanding and clear and direct statement characterizing all her observations.

Their ramble through each spot was almost as

brief as this notice. They had much to see, and, in truth, Oberon was not too willing that Iris should extend her acquaintance in his college, or the university, until she had acquired a little more polish and superiority in tone and language, if indeed he should deem such friendship necessary to his and her future career. Six o'clock was drawing on, and both were not sorry to return to the hotel. Hilary Dove—the same joyous Hilary who made Edelstone ring with noise and pleasure—was present to meet them; and right glad and happy was that father to see his child in the company of the only man he desired to be her husband.

"It is a long time, Oberon, since I last saw you. I must congratulate you on your vastly improved appearance. Two years have made a man of you; I am really delighted once more to see you."

That was a happy evening in the life of Oberon Spell,—one of those soft, sunshiny hours of felicity which glide into the blood and warm the heart, leaving a perfect feeling and savour of summer delight and perpetual gladness. It was all conversation—most agreeable, racy conversation; each had to tell the other something new, something pleasing and interesting. Oberon had a thousand amusing incidents of college life to relate. Hilary had a whole budget of humorous news; and as to Iris, she was most pungent and animated, and always to the purpose in her witty criticisms of the various characters she had met with in her travels, "here and there, roundabout, and everywhere," with her father. Not a word of sentiment was spoken, and yet, for Oberon, those few hours teemed with love. He saw, or fancied he saw, in Iris not only a glorious form of beauty, but a mind capable of the largest thought and intelligence. He was really struck with the total absence of nonsense in all she said that evening. How different from the airy and flippant nothings which fell so glibly from her father's lips, and which he deemed the most winning turns of éloquence. At length the hour came when the three friends were to part. The separation just forced something like a tear from Iris; Hilary Dove was painfully moved. Whatever were Oberon's feelings, they were buried deep in his breast; but in his final gaze at her he loved, he appeared to drink in, and did drink in, the whole witchery of her countenance.

> " The soul is set with one bright image of
> The beautiful beloved."

And the picture which formed there on Oberon's heart was the one permanent likeness of Iris which alone through life he ever knew. It was inefface-able,—it could not be altered. Here was a contrast to the dull routine of the university; here was a treasure to be cherished with his palpitating life's-blood during that severe and stern course of literary discipline he had prescribed for himself till his college course should be run.

'Tis true that course was interrupted by this flying visit, but it renewed in Oberon's breast an affection which had for years lain dormant. It gave him new impulses, new motives, new hopes, and new pros-

pects. He would raise Iris to his own height—to
a height her intellect could command, and they
would both, hand in hand, stray through life
together.

The student went to work again as diligently as
ever, but with more zeal and ardour. There was a
renewed freshness, manliness, and vigour about him,
and he made himself more sensibly and powerfully
felt, not only at the examinations for honours, but
in those sports which add more popularity to the
winners than even the high scholastic distinctions
themselves. It would be almost superfluous to state
that Oberon Spell greatly signalized himself throughout the whole of his Oxford career. His college,
and even the university, were proud of him not
only for his proficiency in the walks of learning and
science, but for his skill and mastery in most of the
athletic games then coming into such general vogue
among the students. He carried off nearly all the
university prizes and filled the class lists, while
maintaining at the same time the highest character
for manliness and gentlemanly conduct. He took
a first, and was solicited to stand for a fellowship,
but this he declined, as his views extended far beyond a mere university career. So that after passing three years of happiness and triumph at Oxford,
and when he had taken his B.A. degree, Oberon,
with only a slight intermission, devoted to his mother
and his most intimate friends, among whom he still
ranked the Levers, prepared himself sedulously for
some two years' travel over the continent of Europe.
For this he carefully read most of the authoritative

books on the various subjects connected with the places and sights he intended to visit. Iris Dove and her father were still away on a business tour through the country, and he was denied the pleasure of a meeting with them in Edelstone. 'Tis true he could return the flying visit at Oxford, but Oberon had the tenderest regard for the feelings of his mother, and whatever may have been his heart affections, he forbore to make them prominent by any formal or special notice of the young beauty, when not immediately brought into his society. He was always looking forward to a future when he could, with his parent's sanction and approval, gratify the one joy and hope of his existence.

He saw Caroline Lever more than once, accompanied her to the theatre and the opera, and to other places of amusement; but with the same feelings on his part as ever. He was a friend—certainly not the least of a lover. That the engineer's daughter regarded him with a deeper affection than any she had felt before, she could not now conceal from herself, or from the discerning eyes of her mother. Ever since their last meeting at Oxford he had grown in her estimation far more handsome; but it was his supremacy as a scholar which entirely captivated and subdued her. She was brought up with the idea that Oberon, the brown-haired youth, would when a man be her husband. She had looked upon him as her own. Her parents also regarded him as more than their nephew—he was their son. With this predominating notion all that concerned him interested them, and it was not until his obstinate contradiction of Mr. Lever at the meeting in Edelstone that any thought of a divided house and, palpably, of a divided life, existed. Her mother had been too confidential, as mothers will, with her very clever daughter, who was led to believe that Oberon was her own, and though she was not in the least impulsive or demonstrative, nor remarkable for too lively feelings, she could not forget the fond and intimate relation with which she had formerly viewed him. She could not now conceal from herself that there was not the least reciprocity, and that her young love was sown in an ungenial soil, where, tend and cultivate it as she would, it could never take root or flourish.

On Oberon's side and on that of his mother, they were careful to note the various rumours spread abroad of the intended marriage of Caroline with the Scotch baronet. Mrs. Lever herself had taken no little pains, after her conversation with her sister-in-law in her own drawing-room, to let her friends know, always of course in the most delicate manner, that her daughter was in the matrimonial market, and no doubt by many the young lady was regarded as a prize with considerable attractions. Through some mismanagement or *contretemps*, as it was believed, the union with the baronet never came off. The real reason was Caroline's fixed aversion to him. He was much her senior in years, while her heart was brimful of a very young lover. Then, whether from her reluctance, or diffidence, or want of personal beauty, no formal proposal came from others; and the possibilities were many that if Caroline Lever could not have her cousin, Oberon Spell, she would remain all her life single.

Still there was a chance, a mere probability, that Hugh Graff, the rising young painter, might one day—it must be distant however—carry off the heiress. He was a great favourite, as we have seen, of Mr. Lever's, he made himself always agreeable to his lady, and was regarded with some little friendliness and kindness of feeling by Caroline herself. It was astonishing how this young man had made his way; but make his way he did, and that in every direction; at the Academy, among wealthy and noble patrons, at the Levers, with the chiefs of the press, and in fact in all places and among all persons, till he began to acquire a public name, and became decidedly popular. He was getting rich too —ay, rich is the word to apply to the once poor artist. Hugh had a trick of the miser, or rather of the severe economist, in his character; and whatever money he made was not wasted in superfluities, but carefully put out at interest, and nearly always under the suggestion and guidance of the worldly-minded and experienced engineer. He kept eligible acquaintance, mingled in good society, and bade fair to be made an Associate at the very first vacancy. He frequently met the leading Academicians and the President himself at the Levers' and other parties, and by his quiet and gliding disposition and un-assuming manners managed to render himself very agreeable and friendly with his superiors. Hugh Graff was on the high road to fame and fortune.

All this time Oberon Spell was wandering in the land of dreams. He was preparing for some speculation, some shadowy, indistinct course of life, which had not come, and which doubtless would never come, over all which his unalterable love for Iris Dove dominated. With this kind of feeling and aspiration uppermost, and a desire to attain to universality and perfection in his knowledge, our hero set out on his travels.

CHAPTER XVI.

AN is the lord of the globe—why should he not see the whole of his estate, or some goodly part of it at least? Why pass his life cooped up in one corner? The world is wide—it is diversified. Not a country but has its special scenery, its special climate, often its special language, usages, and manners. The human family are in a great degree strangers to one another—foreigners—why should they not become acquainted and have the same united interest? The strong could protect the weak, the civilized instruct the barbarous, the energetic and rich diffuse their industry and commerce among the idle and poor; in this way the light of Christianity might be universally spread, and the one Lord and one Faith of the Gospel preached and received everywhere till true catholicity became the stamp and the character of religion.

Thoughts like these were passing through the mind of the poet and scholar as his foot for the first time touched that vast Continent which certainly was the cradle of all modern civilization, and which ages ago had made vast strides in the lore and intelligence of the world. The two years which he had given himself is a long time, when devoted to regular sight-seeing. Oberon visited all the leading capitals of Europe, and saw everything worth seeing—churches, museums, art galleries, prisons, hospitals, public buildings, and institutions; places of amusement, of interest and note, sublime and beautiful scenery, and more than all, the people of each country, the various classes of the common family—rich and poor, small and great, industrious, lazy and criminal, pious and profane, believing and infidel; ascertaining, as far as possible, the actual condition and habits of the numerous social divisions into which the inhabitants were distributed. Of all this he made ample notes, designing one day to publish the whole as a comprehensive tour of Europe. Alas! how many such masses of thought and labour lie stored among the MSS. of literary travellers, destined never to see the light; or if published at the cost of the author, doubtless all too late for correct and useful present information. The world is moving on, and the description of this year will be stale, flat, and profitless the next. The newspapers and literary journals have almost superseded books of travel.

Oberon did not much care for companionship. He had set out alone, and brought with him only a very few letters of introduction. He enjoyed himself most in self-communion, and when actively employed in some kind of authorship. A latent love of solitariness and uninterrupted thought had begun to develope itself in his character. But we are never masters of ourselves. An unexpected incident recalled the wanderer to scenes of home and heart affections again.

One day, weary from exploring Alpine scenery, he sat himself down by the side of a crumbling rock up which vines were crowding now in wild luxuriance. It was the middle of July, and the sun shone fervidly down the hill, on one of whose banks he had found shelter from its rays. Around was an utter solitude; and satisfied with his retired position, Oberon, placing his knapsack under his head, soon addressed himself to sleep. He may have been enjoying this refreshing slumber some two hours or more, when a solitary female passed the road, and on seeing the reclining form suddenly started. She had left her companions behind, and wandered on alone as had been her wont for some time. But she had strayed too far to make herself heard. Nor was she desirous of doing so, for a single glance at the countenance of the reposing figure reassured her. It was Oberon Spell, and he would never harm Ernestine Wheatley. She was riveted to the spot. She could now fairly behold him. She had never seen that noble expression before, or realized the brown-haired man, boy-husband of her childhood. Their meetings had always of late years been in the presence of others, and the lady was naturally timid and shrinking, or rather perhaps too proud to have it thought she had taken any special notice of the handsome scholar whose praises had at one time filled the whole of her own delightful village of Edelstone. He was now asleep; profoundly so; and she could gaze on him at her will.

But even this had its fears. She hesitated. The
situation was awkward. They had ceased to be
friends. He might awake. Her companions might
come upon her or some stranger might pass. All
this time, while pondering on what had best be done,
her eyes and, it may be well said, her heart, were
rootedly fixed on the slumbering poet. How stately
he had grown! how magnificent that face and brow,
and that thick, flowing beard and commanding
moustache. Here was a living picture of one of
those grand Middle-age heroes over whose history
she had so many times passed whole days, instructed, animated, and delighted.

There he lay on the mountain's side, with God alone
to watch him ; and she—might she be permitted ?
Yes! she would feed her eyes on her love. They might
never be gladdened with that sight again—nearer—
still nearer. What graceful tapering fingers and
small high-arched, compact, springing feet ! Surely
here was one of nature's true nobility. Oh ! how
different from that creature—that libertine—Earl
Summers ! Ah ! that fly creeping about under his
lashes ! It will wake him, and for worlds upon
worlds she must not be found there. He awakes—
he starts—he brushes the insect from his brow—
and he beholds Ernestine Wheatley stooping over
him. Both utter an exclamation of surprise—
Ernestine is transfixed—caught—undone ! In a
moment the traveller was on his feet, and apologized
for being found in such a rude trim and situation
before a lady. But that lady was very nervous
and pale, and tottered near to fall. Oberon had all
his senses and energies about him.

"Permit me, Miss Wheatley—you are evidently not well—there, lean on my arm. Ah! had I been aware that you or any one were so near, I should not have thrown myself thus carelessly on that hillock; but the shelter the foliage afforded tempted me. Will you be seated? There, make a seat of my knapsack, and rest a little till your friends come. I suppose they are in the vicinity."

All this time Ernestine did not utter a single word. She was helpless, and mechanically did what he told her. Oberon hung over her silent, and, it must be owned, he was deeply affected. At length a warm flood of tears came to the lady's relief, and she indulged in them for some moments, then drying her eyes, she said in a choked whisper, "I thank you." She began to recover rapidly. She arose and approached Oberon, who had retired a pace or two from motives of delicacy.

"Mr. Spell, this meeting is indeed most wonderful—most unexpected. Surprised at beholding a stranger, you found me at the moment when your well-known features arrested my attention. I am very glad, believe me, to see you. And have you been well—quite well—and your mamma?"

"Perfectly well, thank God, and thank you. I trust you have enjoyed your long tour on the Continent."

"I have not been all along here, we visit England occasionally; but for some time I have not been to Edelstone. I think I am somewhat better, but still they say I am not quite well. My party are not far off, just above at the bend of the hill; may I ask you to walk with me a little of the way. I am but such

a feeble mortal; and the sudden sight of you!"—
(Oberon gave her his arm, and she proceeded.)—"I
am very delighted we have met. There may be a
Providence in it. Oh, those social distinctions, how
I have lived to despise them. I have, through the
public journals, followed you to a certain extent in
your college career. What a series of triumphs
and victories! And you are not—— Well, never
mind; I was going to say something,—but never
mind."

Oberon well knew what was uppermost at her
heart and lips, but he forbore to prompt her; he
rather turned her attention to her father and to
other subjects, which he knew would interest her
and wean her from the oppression of present
thoughts.

"We stop here; sad to say, we part here. I
own I should like you to join our little group. I
can hear their voices; they are now only a few yards
beyond. But circumstances are against me, Mr.
Spell, and perhaps you would not desire the meeting?"

"I shall consult your judgment entirely, Miss
Wheatley."

"Well, I think this wonderful interview must be
to ourselves, a secret—for the present at least. Can
I in any way serve you, or papa, or any one I know?
I am so anxious to do you some good. We are
fellow villagers, Mr. Spell; I too was born at
Edelstone."

"And I have that honour. But, at present my
course is somewhat fixed."

" Fixed ?" and Ernestine paused. Recovering herself by an effort, she continued, " and your poem ?"

" It is in abeyance for a time. When this tour is over I shall once more begin, not to leave off, I hope, till I finish."

"I have many of your fugitive pieces in my scrap-book. I wish you would collect them; they would make a very delightful volume."

" You think so ?"

" I must think so. They are truly witching and beautiful."

" I wish everybody thought so," and Oberon laughed. His thoughts glanced at the wilful girl on whom he had set his heart.

" Do you know," said Ernestine—" come, we will go back a little, not to keep you waiting here —I was going to tell you that a General Count Spell is one of our party. He belongs to the Austrian army."

" My family originally came from Vienna."

" The same. They are of much consideration, I assure you, in the Austrian capital. I wish I could introduce you. But it is so embarrassing; mamma is with us. Where are you staying? Give me your address, I will write to you."

" For the next three days my quarters will be at the humble auberge indicated there," and he wrote the direction on a card; " but at present, dear Miss Wheatley, I need no introduction. Should I ever desire to trace back my family, I believe I know where to find them; and I also believe that neither they nor I will have occasion to be ashamed of one another."

"I think not," said Ernestine, fervently. She had turned back again towards her party. "Perhaps 'tis better as it is. Well, Mr. Spell, thank you; once more the voices of friends bid us part. Good-bye; this meeting is a secret, remember. Adieu! May God watch over you."

Oberon pressed the hand so fondly—we will say—given to him; and, repeating his farewell with a deep emotion, caused by the lady's agitation, he led her a few paces up to the brow of the hill. They then separated without another word, and Ernestine, taking the first turning to her right, was soon in the midst of a very joyous party,—a lonely and desolate heart in a scene of festivity and gaiety. Oberon went his way and pursued his wanderings, ruminating much on the strange destiny which appeared ever to follow him. Could Iris Dove be compared with the glorious being who had now left his side, where no doubt she would wish to cling for ever? But no; he would banish contrasts. No good came of them. He would be true to his heart's love, and stand the hazard of the die, no matter what the consequences.

Time wore on. The tourist had now been away a year and nine months on his travels. Almost his sole correspondent was his mother. To her he gave from week to week a full account of all his adventures. But he felt restricted as regards that strange interview with Ernestine Wheatley at the foot of the Alpine hill; on this he was wholly silent. He

had in the beginning of his journey received a few
letters from Hugh Graff and the Levers, but these
gradually dropped off as the distance increased between him and them, and he was not sorry when
the correspondence had entirely ceased. Letter
writing where the heart is not set, becomes, if to
be often repeated, a nuisance and a burden. Iris
Dove and he had never but once communicated
by letter; he would have given worlds to be her
guide and instructor, and to press her dear original
missive occasionally to his lips; but here, as elsewhere, he was restrained in his affection. There
was no manner of engagement subsisting between
them. He was not by any means sure that he
was or ever would be the object of that strange
girl's love. His mother, and indeed his circumstances, were opposed to the match; so a thousand
prudential reasons prompted him to silence.

It was a part of Oberon's design to return through
the north of France to England, taking Brittany,
which he wished to explore, on his way. He ar-
rived in that picturesque country about the commencement of the autumn season, and was much
struck with the several sights presented to his
researches. The people were in a manner new to
him; the scenery was beautiful and grand, and the
historical recollections connected with this remote
colony made it a special point of interest to the
traveller.

One night he took up his abode at a neat lodging
in one of the primitive hamlets of the interior.
The owner of the mansion was a middle-aged lady,

whose reduced circumstances caused her to open her doors to eligible inmates. Her brother, somewhat her junior, was the curé of the village, and generally passed his evenings within the walls of his home. Oberon was rather surprised to find in Père de Foix a gentleman and a scholar in a very humble clerical guise. They spent many a pleasant evening together, discussing some of the higher subjects of science and learning, in which the Oxonian often found that he was not always the superior. But what puzzled him most was to discover that such acute logic, such amazing stores of knowledge, and such a mass of common sense withal, should submit to be the minister of an enslaving superstition.

" My child," said the priest, in answer to some rather direct inquiries, " I never discuss points of religion. Where faith begins reason ends ; who thinks otherwise is on the downward road to atheism. The child and the moribund believe ; they do not argue. I have been the one, and owe it to my creed that I was not brought up an infidel. I shall soon be the other, mayhap am so now, and I have no time to quibble or even to reason. ' I believe, O Lord, help my unbelief !' Here commence and cease my polemics. We have a wedding to-morrow ; that is a sacrament, and the pair are taught by due religious preparation not to profane it, but to enter it holy. We shall have a christening, please God, by-and-bye ; the infant will be admitted within the sacred circle of the Church which embodies the purest morality and sublimest knowledge in the world. When capable of knowing right from wrong the child will approach the sacrament of penance, be taught the nature of sin and guilt and to form a conscience; and on his hearty sorrow he will be granted forgiveness by God through his minister. At a maturer age the boy will have to prepare his soul—his whole interior—to receive his Lord and Saviour, and to walk as one incorporated with the Incarnate Word. His powers now strengthened, he is supposed to be able to undertake the entire responsibility of his religious profession. He is confirmed as a soldier of Christ, and receives the seven gifts of the Holy Ghost, if he partakes of the sacrament worthily. Should he wish to enter Holy Orders, here is another sacrament to bind him to God and his altar, to his Spouse and his Home; and when about to undergo the perilous journey of death, there is the last sacrament—the extreme unction—to comfort, to sanctify, and to embalm his spirit. He is dead—passed from earth; but the communion of saints—the sacred correspondence between all the good on earth and in heaven—makes him no stranger in our prayers and intercessions. All this may be, in your estimation, dear sir, superstition, but I think it must be conceded that it leads to a pure life and a happy death, two great purposes of religion. Take from me or my poor people our faith, and what hollow carcases we should remain!"

"I own," said Oberon, in reciting this conversation to his mother, "that I was powerfully affected by what the good father said, and I never will in my life strive to shake the Christian faith of any man, unless I am indeed prepared to say he will

accept my better substitute; without this assurance
I only stir up doubts and turn a Christian into an
infidel.   On the whole, dear mother, this spot is
charming to me—so filled with pleasing associations, that I shall revisit it should I ever be in
Brittany again, and I will counsel my best friends
on their foreign travels to take the little hamlet of
Beauregard and the mansion of Madame de Foix,
as a most interesting point in their rambles."

Not many weeks after, Oberon having completed
his two years' excursion, placed his gladsome foot
once more on the soil of England.   He was a
larger-minded, more liberal man for his travel, and
had vastly lessened in himself the distance between
the Englishman and the various races of foreigners,
all brethren of the same large human family.   "And
now," he would say in after life, "as these are days
of international competition in works of art and
industry, why not the great chiefs of learning and
science contend for the mastery?   University against
university; always the very best men; principals and
fellows, with scholars of the like pretension and
position abroad, till the highest reach of mental
excellence which the world could evoke were attained?   This only would appear to be wanting to
make our modern system of promoting peace and
civilization complete."

CHAPTER XVII

THE GRAND POEM.

HE real business of life commenced! To sit down to learn a profession whereby a man may be enabled to marry and support a wife and family, rear, educate, and portion off the latter, and then die; this was the grand problem which Oberon Spell had now to consider.

"There is a shorter way than all this, dear Oberon," said his mother, as they both sat beside a cosy fire at Edelstone; "there is a shorter and, to my mind, a better way."

"Will you name it, dear mother?"

"Suppose we begin to build the house at the chimney-top; marry first, and think of a profession after!"

"A strange proposition, mamma."

"No, not so strange. There is Caroline Lever with a fortune at command and a useful, intellectual calling too; and if you reject your cousin, it may not be too late for another and a nobler alliance."

"I understand you, dear mamma. But once for all, I reject both proposals, even if attainable, of which I am not quite so certain. Many things besides the affections of young people would have to be considered. I really cannot see why all this fuss should be made about my marrying. I can get on very well in my own way. Perhaps, mother, I shall never marry."

"That would be to disturb one of God's ordinances, Oberon. The divine government is that men should perpetuate their race legitimately on earth. Here is the noblest worldly immortality."

"I had rather be immortal as a poet, mother, than be the great father of mankind himself. And so I shall remain single, if——"

"I know what you would say, dear child. But that shall never be with my consent. And now to decide upon a profession."

"Well, dear mother, this is the more sensible part of our conversation. I have weighed the matter, and I think I shall take to the Bar. I shall enter on my terms at Lincoln's Inn ; that will not interfere with the progress of my poem."

"Be it so. I earnestly trust, my dear, that this troublesome work will not in the end disappoint you."

"Do not call it troublesome. It is a labour of love. If I produce the right article, trust me it will be appreciated. I shall win fame, fortune, and honour."

"God grant it, my dearest child !"

Here the conversation dropped. In the course of a few days Oberon consulted a legal friend who had become distinguished at the Chancery Bar, and was soon entered as a regular student of Lincoln's Inn, not with the intention of qualifying immediately for a career as a lawyer, but to enable him to acquire the name of a profession which he might follow or abandon at his pleasure.

Iris Dove occasionally visited Edelstone, but at this particular time she happened to be away on a lengthened visit to one of those numerous friends whom her father had made in his tour of inspection as manager of the Hygienic Food Company, and as peripatetic trumpeter of the great Liberal cause. Oberon was therefore left alone to advance his poem to completion.

Meantime he contributed some valuable papers to the reviews and magazines, for which he got well paid, and this, with the fame he began to acquire, though writing anonymously, became a matter of intense satisfaction to his mother, who thought that after all, her son might be right, and that his best course perhaps was to commence as an author.

He had resumed his favourite rambles in the Park during the absence of the Wheatley family. The place had grown familiar to him. His mother frequently joined him in his walks and enjoyed with him the delicious scenery. On one of these occasions they were joined by Sir Roger Wheatley, who was paying a flying visit to the Priory. The baronet came upon mother and son suddenly as they were admiring the grand effects of one of the artificial cascades which formed the most interesting and imposing feature of the lovely landscape around them. After an interchange of salutations and those general remarks which introduce more formal and regular conversation, Sir Roger said—

"And so I find, Mr. Spell, that you have at

length made up your mind to follow the Bar as a profession. Well, you are young enough yet to win your way betimes to eminence. I must say you bring high recommendations from college, and no doubt your late tour has vastly extended your knowledge of the world. A man of your calibre, Mr. Spell, generally makes a thriving lawyer. If at any time I can aid you in your professional career, I shall be most happy to do so."

Oberon bowed and looked at his mother, who was beaming with smiles and gratitude. He answered for himself.

"I am deeply sensible, Sir Roger, of your kindness. At present, though ostensibly going to the Bar, I am solely engaged in literature, and in particular on a poem now near completion, and of which possibly you may have heard—a work on which depends my future movements, and, I may say, my fame and fortune."

The baronet eyed the young man keenly, and with a smile.

"A poem, Mr. Spell; a great undertaking in these degenerate days. But "—(turning the subject as he perceived his quiet satire was felt, he continued)—" we have all been much gratified here by the absence of that troublesome mortal, Hilary Dove, from the country. For the last six years he has been endeavouring to plague me with his opposition. The general election, you know, is coming round, and we poor members are made to tremble for our seats. I trust the fellow will not oust me."

"That I think would be a crime, Sir Roger. I

ought to have some influence with Hilary Dove. I believe I have. With your permission I should feel great pleasure in exerting it in your favour."

"I shall feel honoured in becoming your dependent for this act of kindness, my young friend; and if I dare mention a return to you, I promise not to prove ungrateful. Dove, I assure you, is most mischievous, for ever speechifying about subjects he does not understand—Reform, the Ballot, Church-rates, Direct taxation, and other favourite Radical topics—he has succeeded, to a wide extent, in making people believe that I am little better than a legislative and social tyrant—an old Tory, grinding and robbing the poor, and checking the advance of liberty. But I fear I have interrupted your walk, madam."

"You have enhanced its pleasure a hundredfold by this fortuitous meeting, Sir Roger; and the admirable but delicate lesson you have conveyed to my son, who just now is lost in high speculations, too elevated, I fear, for busy, wayfaring life, but nevertheless, not to be ignored or neglected."

"Ah, madam, it would be a rude, coarse world without our poets. But a dull balance-sheet of my steward's awaits my rapid examination and signature, so I must needs hurry back to my library. Good-bye, and pray remember, not to make yourselves strangers either here or at the house."

There was something unpleasant in this meeting—it grated harshly on the sensitive nerves of both son and mother. Sir Roger Wheatley, the member of Parliament and ex-Minister, did not regard the spirit of independence exhibited by our hero as a quality to be praised in young men. On the contrary, he had set his own opposite conduct as an example and exponent of his genuine opinion. For this Oberon did not care; his principle was a high and noble one, and ought to have been better received. Why should obtrusive patronage persist in interfering with his occupations and plans of life? His true concern was for the displeasure, or rather the disapproval and disappointment, of his mother. She continued to walk by his side calm and silent. This lasted while they advanced some three hundred paces. At length Oberon broke the stillness.

"Mother," he said, "I perceive that my refusal of Sir Roger Wheatley's somewhat abrupt offer, though undoubtedly well meant by him, displeases you."

"I only regret, my dearest child, that you are so blind to your own interest. It is necessary to live in this world. Here is a great function and duty of our existence. You know my means. They have gone to their utmost tether, and your own, the result of our common retrenchment and saving, are but scant and limited. We cannot live without money; and that man defeats the designs of Providence who not only does not use the best means to promote his interest, but actually rejects great opportunities when offered. I would not for worlds discourage you, my dear; but however unwilling I am to believe it, from all I hear it is clear that in these 'degenerate days'—you remember the words

—no sure fortune can be made by following the profession of a poet."

" I could point to some instances to the contrary, mother. It all depends on the marketable character of the work."

" You see how you are obliged to use commercial terms.   I fear, dear, it is all—so far as success is concerned—an affair of trade, nothing more.   But I wanted to cultivate the baronet's friendship."

" Why ?"

" For reasons of my own—for you, Oberon."

" Ah, I understand you, mother; but let me beg of you to abandon all such delusions. To be candid with you — though I should be aware of Miss Wheatley's regard for me, and had even her parents' consent—she should never be my wife.   No—no— never !"

" Rash boy! you know not what you say, or what bright fortunes you are casting from you. Remember Caroline Lever! I fear she is lost to you."

" Oh, absurd, mother, to be hatching marriage plots for me. They never answer. Herein, mother, I believe in destiny.   Marriage is too grand an event ; too much of present and future depends on it to have it arranged and decided by our petty mundane plans.   I am pre-engaged, mother, by the will and wisdom of God.   Let us change the sub- ject.   There must be no difference between you and me."

" No, my love, I will gladly turn to a brighter theme."   And gradually and skilfully did the fond and judicious mother draw away the thoughts of her child from the object whom she knew was then uppermost in his heart. She spoke of a thousand things interesting to him; asked question after question, and required explanation of this, instruction on that, and guidance in some other matters, all suggested by their route as they passed along towards home. Oberon's attention was entirely absorbed in satisfying his mother's inquiries, and in admiration of some new beauty of the scene, well as he recognised each spot.

In passing from out the gate into Blackberry-lane, and when a little way on the road, they came face to face with Jonathan Cubborn. He was now grown a man, short and strong in frame, his disfigurement still prominent, he looked repulsive and forbidding. With a malicious smile and a muttered chuckle he pursued his course up the green lane, at the same hurried pace which had marked his approach. Was he fleeing from mischief?

He had passed.

"What a hideous sight, Oberon. I always regret meeting that man. I wish he had not crossed my path to-day. It bodes no good."

"It cannot bode evil. There is no use in a vain sorrow for what occurred long ago—the thing cannot be undone. I did not court the fray. Mine was not the first insult, not the first threat of a blow. If I struck, I struck fair, and on sufficient provocation. 'Tis past, mother; it was inevitable."

"It may have been so, but since it happened, Edelstone has not been pleasant to me. The evening draws in; let us quicken our pace." And mother and son, as if urged by an uncontrollable force, hurried forward.

"Ha! Oberon, what is that?" exclaimed Mrs. Spell, as she got into the open road leading direct to her house. "A fire-engine! and see, what a crowd! Look! look! there's a fire!"

"There is, but we ourselves are safe, dear mother, Deborah is at home."

"We have enemies, Oberon, my child, wicked enemies. Another engine! another again! Ah! God have pity on us. It is Myrtle Cottage!"

"No, mother, no; do not alarm yourself. Walk slowly on, and I will be back in a moment."

In a moment Oberon returned, agitated and pale. "Dear mother, fortitude. It is our home. Step in here while I run forward. I must be on the spot."

"And I too. I go with you. Oh, God! have mercy on us! My poor Deborah! My child's poem!" Saying this the anxious mother pressed eagerly forward, leaning nervously on Oberon's arm. It was in vain he essayed to console her; she continued to breathe in a half-whisper, "My poor Deborah! My boy's poem!"

"We must not anticipate the worst. It is yet daylight, and Deborah could escape. As for my MSS. they will defy the fire—they cannot perish. Let us hurry on, dear mother; ages are now in a moment."

They were at last fairly in front of the fire, in the midst of the crowd. A lane was cleared for them. Every one deplored their loss and murmured sympathy. The superintendent of police soon assured them that Deborah was safe, and that the fire had begun among Mr. Spell's papers.

"My son's papers! Merciful Heaven! His work —his noble work—all destroyed! Oh, Oberon!"

"Run, run," cried Oberon, "fetch me a ladder. Oh! this will do," seizing a chair and table. "I will mount to the room! They must not go! I will save them!"

"Madness, sir," said the chief fireman. "Come down, I say, there. Pull him down. Do you want to destroy yourself? I tell you, there it began. 'Tis all over in that room. Here, bear a hand. For God's sake, sir, do not add to the confusion. Now, boys, now, to it, my hearties!"

Excited by the scene, Oberon was among the foremost in labour; now pumping the engine with might and main, now dragging out the furniture vigorously. The cottage was but a small detached structure, with some few outhouses. No other building was in danger. The neighbours crowded to the rescue, in the midst of whom were Zadok Graff and his stalwart sons, exposing their lives to save whatever could be extricated from the flames. Oberon was everywhere; now rushing through the door, which had been left open by Deborah, as at the last moment she escaped; now huddling the moveables together in the road; and again at the engines, exciting all others to the charge.

"What trunk is that my son is dragging out now?" exclaimed Mrs. Spell to Dr. Trensham, on whose arm she leant as she stood on an elevation prepared for her on the opposite side of the road. "Can it be his precious MSS.? No, no! I see, it is only an old box of waste papers, belonging, I believe, to his grandfather. Why should he risk his life for refuse like this, lying buried in the cellar? Will no one check him? He will destroy himself! I shall lose all!"

"My dear madam, be comforted. The firemen have stopped him. The engines are playing beautifully now. But, oh! how awful! Had you not better retire, dear madam?"

"No, Dr. Trensham; I am in my place. My God!—my Father! what a terrible scene! And this is a fire!"

At that moment a pillar of flame started up like a giant through the clouds. But there was a full supply of water to dash it down again. The conquering jets of flame were met by still more victorious jets from the hose. They steamed and foamed and hissed together, till at last a black mass of carbon was the result. The roof fell in with a hideous crash. All was over. The fire gradually subsided into ashes, charred wood, and cracked and broken walls. Myrtle Cottage, the neat, the unique, was a mass of ruins. Oberon Spell's grand poem was lost for ever.

There was some mitigation and solace in the active presence of Sir Roger Wheatley in the midst of the disaster. The moment he perceived the direction of the flames he hurried to the scene, and rendered by his countenance and exertions no small amount of aid and encouragement. He had postponed an urgent call to the Carlton Club, in order to assist at this fire, and he was the first to offer the hospitality of his mansion to the sufferers.

"Your mother and yourself, Mr. Spell, will take up your abode at the Priory. I myself, and the family will, unfortunately, be away; but then you will have none to interfere with you. Rest is needed for your mother till the effects of all this dreadful calamity shall have passed away. You must indeed, both come. I have sent for the carriage."

"I must be on the spot, Sir Roger, and where I am, my mother will remain. Eternal thanks for your kind and hospitable offer, but my position is amidst these ruins."

"Well, sir, as you will;" and after a short time the baronet retired.

Oberon could not have well quitted the situation; and perhaps he reflected that, had it not been for his unfortunate delay with the owner of Priory Park, his mother and he would have returned earlier, and Myrtle Cottage might still have been standing; the work of the incendiary—for such he felt persuaded that sudden and rapid conflagration was, so long after he had left home—would, perhaps, have been wholly averted or defeated. As it was, his loss was irreparable, utterly and thoroughly irretrievable. He had no copy left of his poem, and the labour and triumph of a life was thus gone for ever.

But when in the midst of her great and overwhelming calamity, Oberon's mother heard Sir Roger Wheatley's generous and courteous invitation, and its curt rejection by her son, she exclaimed, "It is—it is destiny! the hand of fate is upon us!"

CHAPTER XVIII.

THE fire which swept Oberon Spell from the home of his birth made him a changed being. All his treasures of intellect were utterly annihilated. Not a vestige of a MS. or a book was left, the conflagration was so quick and furious throughout, but in particular in his own room, where by all accounts it commenced. He could never renew those works again. His previous career had been distinguished by a remarkable precocity, and by the rapid production of literary essays of various kinds. All the freshness, and it may be said, the fulness, of his genius were stored in those pages. The child, boy, youth, and man had each been a severe student, and had early acquired the habit of committing thought to paper. He was now twenty-three years of age, and it is questionable whether under the most favourable circumstances he could ever produce again works equal or superior to those irretrievably destroyed. Certainly he had lost the true heart for successful authorship. His great achievement —his poem—was buried; unlike the dead, it left no epitaph or monument. Reflection, memory, or reconstruction could never restore its creative pages. Differing from many a plaguy rhymester, Oberon

Spell had not the art of learning his verses by rote, and reciting them to willing, or far more likely, unwilling, listeners. This feat he reserved for the standard poems of his own and other countries. He was accustomed to write with a running pen, and was always satisfied when his ideas were hived, as he termed it, in MS. These MSS. consumed, his past intellectual life became a blank, and left no record behind. This to the young author was a terrible bereavement. And he felt and resented the shock through every fibre of his being. He was never the same person after. A blight had passed over his mind and heart. He thought, and spoke, and estimated himself not according to any existing merits he displayed, but by the standard of productions of undoubted value—productions which had never seen the public light, and of which he cherished only the bare reminiscences. Not that we would by any means indicate that the genius of the poet was extinguished or at all sensibly impaired. This would be doing his subsequent works great injustice; but he never wrote with the same power, verve, and originality again.

His mother, in her way, felt her special misfortune. We have described the furniture and arrangements of Myrtle Cottage, internal and external, as something unique. They were truly so; models of solidity, convenience, and taste. These could not be replaced; for they were the result of years of planning, contrivance, and collection. Even the fashion of making good and lasting furniture had passed away from the country. In none but rare and exceptional cases, and at an enormous cost, were houses garnished then, or are they now in a manner to combine the elegancies of art with perfect accommodation and durableness of make and material. Besides, there were gems in that house which only taste and long and careful selection could bring together ; and there were other treasures, as portraits and various souvenirs and memorials, which no skill of the mechanic or artist could ever replace.

House and furniture were both well insured, and the money was punctually and ungrudgingly paid by one of our principal fire offices. But though the bank-notes could rebuild the house, they could not restore Oberon Spell's precious MSS., or the Myrtle Cottage of the incomparable widow—the Myrtle Cottage of Edelstone, known as the bijou of the village for miles around. The calamity effected a change in everything ; but it likewise brought its consolations.

The universal sympathy expressed for the sufferers was in itself consolatory. From every quarter came letters of regret and condolence. The moment Hugh Graff read an account of the disaster, all his old feelings came back again. His grief for Oberon's irreparable loss was heartfelt and genuine. The misfortune was his own—it was a dear part of himself which suffered. He earnestly entreated Oberon to join him in the metropolis, pursue his legal studies, and thus endeavour to dissipate his troubles. Mr. Lever was away, but his wife invited her sister-in-law and her nephew to spend a few months with the family at the seaside during the rebuilding of the Cottage and until things should again get into their regular position. As to Zadok Graff, his great sorrow was for the handsome furniture. The books and writings of the young gentleman, and all that sort of stuff, could be easily replaced by a little money and exertion; but there was that marvel of a sideboard—never!—that was irreplaceable. He had done his best to repair and restore, and he had had the assistance of a first-rate working cabinetmaker. But their neatest efforts were mere bungles—the genuine finish and beauty could never be given back again to those choice bits. Then the total destruction by the fire, how could that be remedied? Many of these views were those of Deborah, too, who was inconsolable for her pots and pans, and the graceful and cleanly fittings of her unexceptionable kitchen.

Dr. Flowers, his wife and daughters, and especially Catherine, were even tender in their solicitude. They proffered the magnificence of Crampton Hall as a suitable mansion until matters should take a correct and normal turn. Dr. Trensham, too, was assiduous and kind, perhaps rather too much so, considering the almost stern solemnity of the occasion. But in the warmth and goodness of his heart, he offered his house as a quiet retreat till a calm and restorative system of things should reappear. This was most liberal; for the doctor was now in the flush of the great Hygienic Food Company's success, and his prospects were truly of the most dazzling description—nothing short of a for-

tune of millions—some great public testimonial—
and a baronetcy or peerage to crown and reward his
brilliant discovery.

As to Hilary Dove, he was on his travels for the
company all over the United Kingdom, and engaged,
too, in vast electioneering schemes; smashing
Toryism, as he described his career, wherever he set
his foot. But no sooner did the disaster to the
Spells reach him through the public journals, than
he came by express to town, and was down in Edelstone one hour after his arrival in London. Nothing
could be more cordial than his proffer of friendship. The only thing was that he promised a
hundred-fold more than he could possibly perform,
or than could with any sense of independence
be accepted.

The widow, her son, and servant were for the
present lodged in a quiet house in the outskirts of
the village. This indeed was a temporary abode;
but it answered every purpose of proximity and
management. As to the profuse offers of Proscenium Villa, the amiable companionship of Mrs.
Dove, and the near prospect of a visit from Iris,
with the speedy return of the promoter himself,
these temptations were all heroically resisted. Mrs.
Spell said, in her quietest manner, that Sir Roger
Wheatley had courteously placed the Priory at their
disposal for a few months, but that she had felt it
to be only consistent with the sense of independence
of both to decline the friendly and hospitable offer.
This was paying Mr. Dove in his own shining coin,
only the currency happened to be genuine not

spurious metal. Joyous Hilary, after despatching a very hearty luncheon, and expatiating in glorious flights of oratory on the wonders he had performed for the Hygienic Food Company and the political cause which he had only a few years espoused, and which the next general election would show, ended his visit by placing a letter from his daughter in the private hands of Oberon, not choosing to trouble his mother with these little matters of gossip and youthful recollection.

When Oberon was alone—and he soon took an opportunity to be so—he drew forth the precious missive. It was neither inviting in chirography, envelope, nor seal, for Iris was somewhat slovenly and careless in the style of turning out her letters; nevertheless, the poet and scholar, as he gazed on the well-known handwriting, felt a glow and visible light break over his countenance, and for the first time he owned a heart-smile since the evening of the fire. He kissed the impression reverently, shall we say more reverently than the text it concealed deserved? But yet it came from a pure and earnest friend, and one with whom the whole of his childhood and a good part of his youth were associated. The epistle ran as follows :—

"Grindthebones Mill, Shoddyshire.

"My dear Oberon,—The account I have just read of that horrible fire (I fear some horrible creature had to do with it) has made me miserable. I feel I ought to be near you; had I been, this hideous thing never would have occurred. But do bear up, my dear brother, bear up and comfort your mamma. She must be terribly cut up by the destruction of her nice house and furniture. Poor Deborah, too, she must take on about her kitchen. There was nothing like it in the universal world—nothing certainly here. These are all such queer people; oh, I do not like them at all—so stuck up and consequential. One had need be somebody to be acknowledged here. Their visitors are just as starched as themselves—country doctors, lawyers, and manufacturers, or buyers from the warehouses in London. Pa says they are all good Liberals; but they are as grand as bashaws. True mushrooms, don't they hold up their heads! What are kings, emperors, lords, and ladies to them! The people here can afford to despise sour grapes. I must tell you I have had no end of beaux since I began my travels; but the nabobs of fathers will not have it that I am good enough. I am not one of them-selves. Just as if I would look at their pieces of fustian. They are not such frights either; some of them are decidedly handsome; but 'tis plain they don't know the knack of making love: some are shy, some are rude, some are pompous; all are re-pulsive. Every scrap of their knowledge is picked up from the newspapers, and if you should chance not to be up in them, you are set down as decidedly ignorant. But, Oberon, there was one such nice creature, so like Hugh and you, both of you. They said he was crazy for me. Think of that, young gentleman! He proposed to pa, and then popped the question—you know to whom, and of course got his congé. I had the dear originals at home; I didn't want the copy. Besides, to tell you the truth, his father would not let him. I had not the needful. You have no idea of the aristocracy here. The porter wont speak to the errand-boy out of business, the clerk holds the porter at arm's length, the shop-walker looks down on the clerk, and the buyer thinks himself an emperor. They are all sneaky enough to the governor, as the principal is called. Oh! how they do toady and crawl to him. He on his side is truly royal and exclusive. He never invites his young men, he only uses them; they serve his turn, and when he has squeezed all the blood he can out of them, he sends them adrift and lets them go to the dogs. I wonder how they think of getting to heaven here; unless they can mount up on yarns, I don't see by what means they can ascend. Pa says the workpeople are either fanatics or infidels; and as to their superiors, they think of nothing from morning till night but making money. The disregard of truth is shocking; to fib cleverly in trade is the one great recommendation. Then to do the short-measure trick and the covers for bad articles, and the other frauds and adulterations, are, I can assure you, quite necessary to get on in business. Without this you could not meet the competition. Then they do so harry the poor workpeople—men and women, but the women the worst.

> 'Grind her fine and grind her sleek,
> She is but a woman weak.'

"But I must tell you a little bit of gossip. I was

last week at a party here, a Mr. Gusset's, and he
carried matters very high and mighty the whole
evening; not a word could be said, that he did not
pretend to be more learned and intelligent in than
persons evidently well-informed on the subject. The
good people—wife, husband, sons and daughters—
were all gracious enough to patronize me, and
among other things I was asked to recite for the
amusement of the company. 'With much pleasure,'
said I, promptly; and away I rattled with 'The song
of a shirt.' I don't know, Oberon, whether you
have seen it, but it is capital, and just out; 'tis by
Tom Hood, that witty writer in the magazines.
Believe me, I never declaimed better in my life. I
sent a shudder through the room. Poor Gusset,
every time I said 'stitch,' I put a stitch in his side.

"How I do run on, to be sure. I had almost
forgotten the fire! Do you know, dear Oberon, I
never began to think so much of the utility—I know
you dislike that word—well, the advantage, of poetry
as since I came down here. To see them all grub-
bing for money, and thinking and living for money
and nothing else, has made me see the necessity for
something to keep mankind from sinking into animals—something to give the soul, as well as the
body, of things. And just at this moment of my
new birth, as one may call it, this horrid fire comes
to destroy all your dear verses. I would have risked
my life to have dragged them out. I am sure there
must have been a want of management somewhere.
But Oberon, my brother and friend, I have heard
you say that nothing striking occurs without its

symbol and warning designed by Providence. What
mamma says may be all true: 'Poetry was intended
to amuse the mad or idle.' It demands money and
leisure, and was never made to meet the rough,
sturdy business of life. Do you know that the crazy
people in an asylum in Scotland write very good
rhymes? but I can understand this, for only imbe-
ciles are wholly mad; the language of frenzy may
speak out from a bursting heart.

"By the by, I should tell you that Hugh's—our
Hugh's—pictures are thought a great deal of here.
You often meet them in the houses about. Pa says
they are at a premium, and will one day sell for the
double of what they fetch now in the market.   I
am sure of this, or the shrewd folks here never
would buy them; but they are great patrons of the
arts.   The chief drawback to poetry is that it cannot be sold like a picture.   Do you know I would
propose, as a part of the divine art, that the author
should make a very neat original draft, and sell the
manuscript, bound, to the highest bidder, and that
the general copies, like engravings, should go at the
ordinary price, only letting the buyer of the manuscript propose his own terms.   I know the poets
usually write a desperate scrawl (you do not, dear
Oberon), but they might be taught to set a value
on a neat and characteristic penmanship, and thus
make their works just as they come from their
hands, of rare and special value.

"They tell me I am getting still taller, which if
true is wonderful at my age; I am up to pa now;
shall I ever be up to you? What a gander! Talking
of that, do you know I have always found that geese,

instead of being stupid, are the cleverest of animals. I do wish there was a kind of study of the intellects of the lower creatures. They never go to school, they are never taught. What little barbarians children would be if they had not regular instruction !

"I need not ask how you look after your two years' foreign travel. I only hope you are not handsome. Do you know I think your handsome men out of position ; they are admired and take our places. I should like to know, young 'Apollo,' what chance a poor wife would have with you ? You have no end of admirers ; there are four of them to my knowledge, but I leave you to guess their names. Oh, would it not be rare fun to set the dear fools by the ears. I wish from my heart we were all children again, and near our brown-haired boy to comfort him. Oberon, do you remember the long, long sunny evenings on the door-step at Edelstone? Oh, my heart ! They are shining and dancing pit-a-pat there now, like sunbeams on Easter morning. I shall be back soon, and we will try and make the best of the fire. It is a dire calamity, one that overthrows and overwhelms us all. But I will be near you, dear brother Oberon, to comfort and cheer you. My kindest regards and love to your mamma.

"Dear Oberon, brother,

"Your very affectionate sister,

"Iris Dove.

"Oberon Spell, Esq."

"P.S. What became of your darling cat ? The papers said never a word of poor Nelly. Do, dear, let me know.—Such a beauty !"

We will not say that the man of refinement and intellect was proud of this letter; but for him it had undoubtedly a certain charm; its very *naïveté* gave him an agreeable sensation which no polish of diction or elevation of sentiment could communicate. Nor was he seriously piqued at the marked preference shown in the context for his friend, Hugh Graff. Oberon had grown up with the idea that no comparison could ever be instituted between him and the young artist. In person, in intellect, in education, in position, aye, and in work actually done, though not at a monied profit, and in the world's estimation, he was entirely his superior. For the student had ever been a stern labourer, and his college career had given him a stamp to which Hugh Graff might in vain aspire. Oberon could never dream of him as a rival. This was his way of thinking, and the source and explanation of many of his actions in reference to the artist and the young lady on whom he had set his heart for a wife. Her artless composition and sentiments left him an enviable ground, as he thought, for the improvement of both. Her education, her true elevation, would be his genial work. And then, how beautiful she was; and with all her deficiencies in accomplishments and knowledge, how commanding and capable of extorting respect and homage from others, from others who did not know her intimately, and even from those whose acquaintance extended much further. Here was a block of beautiful marble left to him to cut, to shape, and to polish into intellectual life and grace.

He had been accustomed to show his mother all his letters, to make her a partner in his every sentiment and resolution. But here was matter now becoming exclusive and sacred, so esoteric and precious, so much within his being and heart, that he even dreaded the air around him, lest it should bear abroad those hushed, whispering words,—words of gold to him though imbedded in quartz,—words of ridicule and babble to all besides, and of stumbling and offence to his mother. That anxious parent should not behold it. He would spare her this contradiction and sorrow.

As to the cutting remarks of Iris on his writings, he had become inured to them; but he confidently looked forward to the time when his glory would be her glory, when what he loved she must love too, when both their hearts and their fortunes should be one. This was another victory which he had to achieve, another heart-rapture in store for him! 'Tis true, since the fire his thoughts on a career of literature had grown rather dim and confused. He stood like a man who had suddenly lost every vestige of his property, who cared not, who knew not how to begin the world again. Stupor, apathy, and inaction were upon him. For this he was the more inclined to mope along with the grand sentiment, to become the silent and secret victim of an absorbing passion.

He was in this mood, resting his forehead on his hand, whilst seated in the small room now assigned him as a study, when his mother entered with a smile on her face, a smile unwonted of late; for

Mrs. Spell had taken her son's loss and her own very deeply to heart.

"Here, Oberon," she said, "here is a letter which ought to please you, or awaken a deeper sentiment, if only out of common gallantry and to gratify me."

"From whom, dear mother?" and Oberon raised his head and stretched forth his hand for the letter.

"Read, and see, my dear child. Read it aloud. It will bear re-perusal. It is, as you perceive, addressed to me."

Oberon, leaning back in his chair, drew forth the sheet from its very neat envelope, and read as follows, first satisfying himself as to the person from whom it came.

"Oh, from Miss Wheatley! Well, what can that interesting young lady have to say?"

"The Ravines, Northumberland.
"25th August, 18—.

"My dear Madam,—The dreadful disaster which befel Myrtle Cottage reached me through the public journals this morning. I sensibly felt the shock just as if the blow had been dealt to myself, the Priory, or any other object dear to me. I lose not a moment in conveying to you my most sincere condolence and regret.

"Ah! this, indeed, is a great misfortune! What cunning hand can ever restore that neat edifice— that unique furniture—those rare and exquisite gems? But the books and the MSS. destroyed! Here is a great public calamity, a loss to me and to every one in the community; not, therefore, a private grief, but one to be universally deplored. Oh that it were in my power to restore one page of those precious poems, the publication of which I had so long and so eagerly expected. I would indeed give all my prospects in life to be of any real assistance; but lamentations and regrets are idle and unavailing. Accept my deepest sympathy, dear madam, and tell Mr. Spell to bear up under his heavy affliction. He must take heart. His Troy laid in ashes, an eternal Rome will arise from the dust transported elsewhere. I anxiously look forward to the hour that is to crown the public fame of Oberon Spell, the poet of Edelstone—that most charming of all spots for me, and the place of my birth.

" Alas ! dear madam, what can secure us happiness on this earth ? Not youth and genius, or the works of Oberon Spell would be extant, and your once delightful hearth and home standing now ; not riches, kind parents, hosts of friends, or the heirship to vast estates, or I should never know a sorrow ; but we must look to the merciful hand of Heaven and to the oblivion of time to cure our griefs—if, indeed, such a thing as forgetfulness be possible. Mr. Spell, however, and you, dear madam, must try to obtain consolation from whatever source is open to you. Surely the sympathy of kind friends is much. I can conceive a lonely sorrow which can never share this blessing, for which there can be no healing, no sympathy, no condolence, no oblivion ; and this may fall on very young hearts and be their

life's canker. But I fear, dear madam, that instead
of comforting you, I am indulging in a vein of un-
pardonable moodiness and melancholy. 'Tis my way
sometimes, especially so of late ; so pray in your
charity excuse me.

"One thing delights me. We shall be back to
Edelstone soon, and I hope to have the privilege of
personally comforting and soothing you. If un-
feigned regret for your irretrievable loss can be a
consolation, you have mine from the depths of my
heart.

" With my compliments to Mr. Spell, and every
expression of condolence and sorrow,

       " My dear Madam,

          " I beg to remain,

             " Your very sincere friend,

                " ERNESTINE WHEATLEY.

" Mrs. Spell."

" Well, what do you think of it, Oberon ? A
very charming letter, is it not ?"

" It is indeed. You must feel exceedingly obliged
to Miss Wheatley."

" And you ?"

" Oh !—I too, of course."

" But do you see nothing further in it ? Has it
no meaning beyond ?"

" No doubt there is a concealed meaning, an
irrepressible sentiment and allusion, a feeling scarcely
controlled even when writing to you. But I can
have no part in this. I do not, never have, never
shall share in the affection."

" Do you mean to tell me, Oberon, that if Miss

Wheatley—the young, the accomplished, the beautiful heiress of estates worth 60,000*l.* a year—were to indicate a regard for you, that you would be the dolt not to perceive it and rejoice at it?"

"Mother, why will you persist in totally misapprehending my nature and feelings? Once for all, to be very plain with you, if Miss Wheatley were not alone what she is, but ten times more accomplished, more learned, more lovely, and with double her prospective fortune, were she a royal princess, and if she came with her parents' consent, and I saw and understood her passion, I would not marry her: for this good reason, my dear mother, that I have no heart to give her, and I could never be happy where I had not settled and fixed my heart."

"Oh, yes you would, with Ernestine Wheatley. She would inspire you. Love begets love. We grow fond of what is attached to us. New ties would arise. You would altogether cease to be what you are now. You would be a father—a great proprietor—a statesman—a poet. Ah! my dear boy, do, for my sake, if not for your own, reflect on surrounding circumstances. Think that this shadow of a great substance at such an hour is a signal blessing from heaven. Do not, let me entreat you, reject and despise it!"

" Reject and despise what, mother? Nothing is proposed—nothing known—nothing offered. 'Tis all our own conjecture—probable indeed, but still conjecture. And then, have you never heard of a girlish fancy? Every young maiden in her lifetime has many of them. Some wear their hearts

on their sleeves, and are for ever, as they think, in
love.   Suppose this should be such an affection!
But even grant that it is true, real, genuine,
vigorous, and permanent, is it right, is it fair and
honourable, to encourage such a treachery against
this young lady's parents and friends ?   Is it grateful to the man who has been so graciously kind to
us ?   Is it just, moral, or honest to sacrifice his
daughter's name and fame, high position, grand
prospects—the prospects of one day becoming a
duchess and doubling her rent-roll,—all to raise up
your poor son—the broken-hearted poet—to a station
of riches and eminence ? As if rank and wealth could
confer happiness, while I believe they only increase
care.   No, my dear mother, this is one of those
temptations in life often set before very humble
people, which we must resist, or we should be as
mean and villanous as the abigail who perverts the
love of her young mistress to her own snob of a
brother, or the thief who finding the sole treasure
of a fond couple in his way, seizes it, and beggars
and ruins the owners.   We must not contravene
the laws of God—of honour—of gratitude—and of
true affection ; we must tell Satan to get behind us,
mother !"

"I stand rebuked and corrected, my dear son.
I was very wrong—and yet—but no, you are right.
I will say no more about it—at least for the present.   I must write a nice, adroit note, returning
the young lady our most sincere thanks."

"It is doubly incumbent on you to be cautious
and prudent, as I have no doubt that this letter was

written without the consent or knowledge of her parents—is, in fact, a clandestine communication."

" My dear child, you alarm me. But you are quite right, and take a just view of the whole case. I am so thankful to Heaven that you were here to lead me out of the snare. My fondest blessings on you, Oberon."

The subdued and corrected mother retired to her room, and there penned a very kind and careful letter, skilfully interweaving the most sentimental and impassioned allusions of Miss Wheatley in the body of her own text, and referring them all to the loss herself and her son had sustained, so as not in the remotest degree to appear to interpret or understand what were the young lady's real feelings. This done, she went to rest and calmly slept, with the consciousness of having avoided a great temptation.

Oberon too withdrew, and soon sank into a delicious slumber. He had placed the letter of Iris under his pillow, after fervently kissing it and begging God to bless her. He passed the night in a dream. He thought he was a sculptor. He was busy in moulding a piece of pure white clay to the shape of a Minerva, and was pausing at every manipulation to drink in the pleasure of the plastic artist. At length the statue breathed, and became Iris, but Iris beatified and exalted—and—and—but as he gazed, his idol fell down from its pedestal with the vulgar crash of broken crockery. He started and half awoke; but composing himself again, spent the rest of the night in gathering up

and replacing the pieces. These now appeared to
multiply and grow into other new and still more
pleasing forms and images. The sequel he could
not recollect or describe. It was lost in one of
those vague hiatuses which break and dissever our
dreams. At last he awoke. It was morning, and
he felt as if he had gone through a life's experience
in his vision. He sprang up, aroused by a strange
noise. The magic letter had fallen on the ground,
and a kitten was playing with it on the floor. Puss
had slipped in and claimed her own property.

CHAPTER XIX.

HE burning down of Myrtle Cottage did not take place without ample comment on its cause. As we have seen, the Spells, mother and son, had a host of friends in the village. The destruction of that neat abode was regarded by almost everyone as a personal loss. The total annihilation of the student's MSS. was universally deplored, and people the least capable of understanding them, were loud in their exclamations of sorrow. That the fire was the work of an incendiary most of the inhabitants believed. In the room where Oberon wrote, and which faced a lane and an extensive range of meadow and woodland, were two windows, both usually left open during close weather. It would be easy to cast a ball of combustible matter through one or the pair of inlets. That such was the operation no doubt was entertained. But who was the assassin?—what hand flung the villanous shell? Gimlet and Picker, who had been summoned, took counsel with the police and firemen. But after a very careful investigation, and with their conclusion unanimous as to the diabolical cause, they could not bring the act home to any special delinquent. Everybody pointed at the Cubborns. But

everybody pointing is not legal proof, and the breath of the suspecting was muffled. It was only here and there a nod, a wink, or a shrug, the dumb language; not a word was uttered, not a whisper escaped the lips of the nearest friends even in their closest confidence. They dreaded the tremendous power of the law in the hands of rascally attornies. Mrs. Cubborn had been seen flitting about on the night of the fire. This was more noticeable as she seldom quitted her house. Trapper, Cotching, Snodgepole and Co. were among the crowd. Jonathan, with his usual legal bag, was in the village before the conflagration, and the next authentic account of him we get is that he was in Blackberry-lane when it commenced. Much of what was advanced proved to be mere conjecture, and no one was willing to say what he knew. In fact, there was not a shadow of tangible evidence against any individual. Still the suspicion lurked about the village, and the Cubborns were made to feel that they were moving in a thick, suffocating atmosphere, where they could not breathe freely. The smouldering embers seemed to choke them, so oppressive had become the general condemnation.

It was the morning working-hour—nine o'clock. Mrs. Cubborn was at her desk in the inner room of the vicious circle. Her son sat before her. They both looked troubled.

"'Tis done, Natty, well and cleanly done too; but though I planned it, I wish it were undone!"

"And so do I too. They have the profit: they pocket the insurance money; and as to friends, swarms of them have sprung up. The whole village is mad after them and dead set against us."

"Let them go mad, let them dead set. Think you I cannot transform all this, and turn their heaven into a hell? Boy, we have had our revenge, that is sweet. Not all their smiles, and tears, and condolences, and that trash, will give them back the lost poem. No; while I behold your maimed face, dear child, I am ripe for any deed of vengeance. The whole world has become our enemy, and I hate it. I only want you to be true to yourself."

"Well, I am true, am I not?"

"You are. Leave all this fine froth of friendship to me; I will cool it down, I tell you—turn it into bubbling gall."

"But can you undo the suspicion? 'Tis that which strangles me, mother. I often feel the rope tightening about my neck, and the blood rushing like flames to my brain. I fear I shall go mad. I cannot sleep, I cannot work as I used to do. I am all fever and restlessness."

"Nonsense; you should take courage and be calm."

"Calm, indeed! It is well for you here, smugged up in your room, with no eye to look on you, to be cool and calm. What can you suffer? The world does not glare on you, dog you, spit at you! I tell you, the weight and oppression I feel of people's hate are crushing me. I am not the same since that night. The fire is not out yet; it is here, here, mother, raging within! I cannot walk, or talk, or sit, or ride, but everybody suspects me, and has his eyes fixed on me. They, the Spells, suspect me; the village suspects me; the police suspect me; Trapper suspects me; so does Snodgepole; so do they all. Father suspects me and abhors me—he drives me from him—he shuns me like contagion; the whole world suspects and hates me. Mother! mother! can you undo this hideous hell-glaring suspicion? Can you?—can you?"

"Of course I can—nothing so easy. Be quiet, lad, only be still, and you shall see it all pouring back like molten lead, to sink him, your enemy. There, boy, cheer up, be comforted."

"But the inquiry, that ugly inquiry, may go further. I was seen with the bag in the village."

"Bah! Did any one peep into it? You were seen with the same bag more than a thousand times before and since. As to the investigation, I have had a word with Gimlet here. He is all right; a twenty pound note has made him careful not to push his prying eyes too far. There is such a thing as the law of libel. He does not fear it, but he can make others do so."

"But he knows nothing of the fact, does he?"

"No, sure! That is where it is—entombed between my brain and right hand, which you are, Natty. Only, you understand me, he is not to encourage vague and libellous suspicions. The inquiry is already blown upon; as to that, set your mind at rest. 'Tis because you are new to it. I tell you the world is our enemy; we are both at war with the world. And see what they do in war—those brave and glorious soldiers! Don't they burn, and ravage, and plunder, and murder? Tut, boy, their great generals have more blood, arson, and robbery on their individual souls, than all the highwaymen hanged at Tyburn, Newgate, or all the gallowses put together. So take it easy, my raw recruit; you will get used to it by-and-by. And, mark me, not a single week shall pass away before the tables are turned, and this ugly suspicion shall point at him and at her, and make their lives the hell you now find it."

"Oh! if only I could feel that, see it, know it!"

"You shall, boy, I tell you. Now, listen to me, Natty, listen to your mother, and drink in her words, as you did the milk of her breasts. I am growing weary of your father; he is good for nothing. If it were not for that bit of election business he does for Sir Roger Wheatley, I would get rid of him and conduct the profession with you. I hope to live to see the day when women shall have their rights and be admitted on the Rolls. I am working for it quietly but deeply, and I think I shall succeed. Why not female attorneys and barristers, as well as doctors and what not? Why should there be any restriction? People ought to get their bread as they best can without let or hindrance, and especially poor, weak women, as they call us. We shall not have free-trade in food, and cowardly protection and prevention in the means of procuring it. No, no; none of that absurdity. But this is not what I am coming to. What I want to call your attention to now is most serious."

"Yes, mother?"

"Well, I have not had you taught penmanship for nothing, my son. 'Tis a great art is that of the pen; if well used, the highest art known or conceivable in a commercial community. With this talent alone, well applied, one might make thousands. I need not remind you that it has long been my opinion, that a great deal more might be made of our profession. We have everything in our hands. We have it really all our own way, so long as the power to issue writs is with us. But the profession requires development. Some do get the knack by instinct. We see attorneys sprouting from the dung everywhere. Why not? Our opportunities, our authority, are enormous. This, Natty, is an old, a respectable firm; let us see if we cannot turn the humdrum title to wealth and honour. You are a genius, child, a born genius at the quill and the faculty of exact imitation. Thanks to your mother, boy, for discovering and developing your extraordinary gift. I alone know its right use, and you know that you have the instrument. We have kept the secret well between us. This is the way to success; no boasting, no blabbing. Well, I want this Priory estate!"

" The Priory !"

" Do not interrupt me, but listen. Not the Priory alone, but the Ravines, Blackmines, and Erlam Court—the Staffordshire and Shropshire estates of young Summers. There, don't sit gaping, but hear me. All this will require time and work; time and work, boy, will do wonders. I see great prospects for my child, my Natty; riches, honours, high station, ample estates, perhaps a peerage; or, I tell you, if this be unattainable, and it is just possible that under our curst restrictive system it might be, I will try and upset everything, and strike for the presidentship of a British republic. Ay, boy, you shall be that, or it might be myself—a woman; and why not a woman? Queen Victoria is a woman. We will sweep away this rubbish of Church and State, Kings, Lords, and Ladies, if they stand in the way. I know no obstacle; I will not recognise one. But all in good time! There is nothing which an attorney cannot reach, if only he have the courage and ambition. We shall begin by throwing all this musty old Toryism overboard; yet, at its proper season. We must be prudent as well as brave. Oh! I have a vast plan in my head to develope the profession, enlarge its sphere, and avenge the scorn men heap on us attorneys, by showing that we are their masters. What think you, boy?"

" I think, mother, I would let well alone. You might be taking things too far. Your ambition gives you the fancies of a madman. All that peerage and president talk is sheer insanity."

" There spoke your poltroon of a father."

" I am no poltroon. But I bear my father's name; he has always given me good advice, and set me a fair example. This is an old, an honoured business. My father, my grandfather, and great-grandfather, all stood by it and built it up. Why should it not go on as other firms, in a legitimate, safe way, making money and fame? I don't want to be a lord or a president. I am satisfied to be a plodding, practical attorney."

" I know you are, for you are your coward father's son. But listen to me. You should have spoken sooner—said all this before; 'tis now too late. You must get power to save yourself; you must cut the knot, or it will tighten about your throat. Ha! do you begin to feel me? I tell you what, retreat would now be ruin! But why is all this nonsense of doubt and fear? Kings, emperors, and statesmen —the great rulers of the world—are hourly planning worse crimes—wholesale murders, widespread devastation, every conceivable horror daily, and they eat and drink like other people, and are as calm and good and pious. They are not called mad. Why? They have been brought up to it. I—I am born to it, born to wonderful, unheard-of greatness ; and you shall be, or I will hang you, Natty—ay, hang you up with my own hands, as unfit to live, to bear the part and character of a son of mine and of a man. Their place is war, their nature is war, the world is war, and all things in it, devouring one another. To strive, to struggle, to over-reach, to get all they can for themselves and trample on others, is their birthright and instinct. There is not a man who gets on in the world, and is fit to live in it, who does not do this and ten times worse for success, which covers all his sins, be they legion ! Boy, your green hand offends, it is not clean ! Flesh it in crime, wash it in knavery and blood, it will grow strong and smell sweet ! See how they will stretch forth their eager arms to grasp it, as a trusty friend! Are you assured? Be so, and what I promise is within your reach."

" I will do what you bid me."

" That is all I require. The taste and longing will come by-and-by. Hear me now! You know those Germans, Wolfstein and Schnapps?"

" Of course I do. 'Twas I who introduced them to you."

" And I found out their talents; I know them better than your father or you. They are amazingly clever men; the Germans are all intellectual, and to be dreaded when their super-subtile brains turn to roguery. I will use those men, but watch them too; or do better, put nothing tangible in their power. They have a pair of friends, Swivel and Son, the great city jewellers."

" I know them too."

" Of course you do, and so does your father; but I know them as they are, and not as fair-spoken tradesmen, bidding high for corporate honours. They are sharp, useful men, up to business; but Schnapps is originally clever. Now, I have a grand project in my head. No danger attends my scheme, for the whole is here, and will remain here, locked in my brain; and the parts, the separate instruments—you among the rest—cannot betray one another; certainly not me. All I require is thorough and utter obedience and submission to my supreme will. No talk, no inquiries, but simple action, not even a look or a whisper in the strictest confidence; for the time comes with us all when what is told in confidence ceases to be a secret. I want nothing needless; we are to live, and move, and do—*do*, mind, as if this thing existed not, had no action, knowledge, or being. The business will work itself through on this system without peril to the six partners."

"Who are they?"

"Myself president, or grand operator, and five instruments—Wolfstein, Schnapps, the two Swivels, and you, Natty."

"Thank you, mother."

"You will have reason to thank me, rogue, when you enjoy the fruits."

"Well, as to the fruits, how are they to be divided?"

"Of course each can work for himself; but whatever is done in the partnership, the profits will be equally divided, fair share and share alike, no superiority here or preference."

"Well, so far so good; but what is it, mother— what is the business?"

"To obey, to do, and make no inquiries; that is the secret. When you come to the work, you will never know more than what you yourself perform for legal purpose; you shall never be able, nor they, to trace the deed home to its source. Do you see this page of ciphers? Go and study them. When you know them pat, I will examine you. Now you have had your lesson, guard your tongue, lay the wisdom you have learnt to heart; not a breath or a sign to anyone; study the cipher, it is very simple; practice your imitation. Go, child, retire to your own room; I have done with you."

Jonathan Cubborn slunk away to his chamber.

The bell rang to admit Trapper. The solicitrix was buried in the pages of a brief. "Oh, is that you, Trapper? I want you, sit down. I was on this case of Scoppins *versus* Squibbers; but I am glad you are here. This ugly affair of the fire at Spells annoys me. We are not friends, you know, with those people; we never shall be, my boy's wound still rankles in my heart. This has given them a kind of malicious handle; they are busy all about circulating scandal, the vilest reports. By-the-by, has anything tangible reached you?"

"No, nothing that we could use. I am, however, on the look out; but if nods, and hints, and looks, and shrugs are a language, 'tis as plain as if old Tolland cried it in the market-place, that Jonathan is put down as the incendiary."

"Hush, Trapper; this must not even be spoken. I have had my suspicions that some calumny of the kind was afloat; but we must check it, Trapper. I want you to place the real truth before the public."

"Yes."

"Well, I have certain information——information from an undoubted source——" Mrs. Cubborn paused, and fixed her large eyes full on the clerk.

"Yes, ma'am."

Trapper opened his mouth as if about to swallow a whale——the undoubted information——looking a model of surprise and wonderment.

"I see you are attentive. Well, I have ascertained from an undoubted source, that for a long time before the fire, that fellow Spell was discontented with his poem, and had more than once threatened to commit it to the flames—the flames! Do you heed me?"

"Yes."

"Well, he met with a whole host of disappointments from the magazines, and all that; in fact, he was sick of the thing and of what he had done. He is only a poor-brained fellow after all, and he has overworked himself. But he had been puffing-up this identical poem, and his mother never ceased talking about it, also that scamp Dove, though his daughter, Iris, really wished the whole farrago anywhere out of her ears, made deaf and dazed from her father's continual boring. Well, coupling all these established facts with the snug insurance money, is it not clear to you how the fire occurred—eh?"

"I must own I do not see it in that light, ma'am."

"You do not see it?——But you must see it, Trapper. You must, I say!—you grow dull. I want you to work it. 'Tis a part of your duty. By-the-by, how does that affair of the *Flam* get on? I wish to lay hold of that paper for you, Trapper; we must be no longer dependent; we must be proprietors, man. What is doing?"

"Oh, Frogget is going a-head swimmingly. He will soon be out of his depth. I expect we shall have him in Spinsterton Towers soon. Then the paper, ma'am, is our own."

"Very well, Trapper, very well. Don't spare the writs. You know my bargain about that. But you must not be so stupid; you must do your duty."

Trapper saw determination in Mrs. Cubborn's eye. He was not prepared to throw up his situation, and he took out his note-book, and said—

"Of course, ma'am; I am always ready to take instructions."

"I should think so, when I state nothing but facts; I like to have the truth where I can to go upon. I did not make that last rise in your salary, Trapper, for nothing,—I had an object in view."—(Mrs. Cubborn had a way of insinuating a meaning.)—"But however, now to business. I want you to put the undoubted facts of this case before the public. It is to be, mind you, an extract from an American paper. Go, now, and let me have a nice spicy morceau ready for the *Flam,* or any other paper, in half an hour,—a neat paragraph, well pointed, and not too long."

Mr. Trapper had got a habit of obeying his mistress according to her own blameless, common-sense way whenever he perceived that his interest was clearly concerned; otherwise he was rather dogged and slow to apprehend. He saw clean through and through his prompter now, but looked as unknowing as if the whole scheme was quite legitimate and innocent. Mrs. Cubborn understood her man, she knew he was thoroughly sordid and selfish at heart, but he was indispensable to her movements; what she most dreaded was his marriage, or too intimate connexion with anyone who might one day master his secrets ; she had, therefore, a knack of conveying the hint, that if Cubborn, senior, should hang or drown himself, or get out of the way in any final direction, he, Gilbert Trapper, would become lord and master. " Then," he would say to himself, " wont I pay her off for many a slight now and shabby trick!   I have only to bide my time, that will right and steady everything." We are all, one way or other, biding our time in this world, till eternity slips in, and proves that not the future, but the present is alone in our power.

We have given the vernacular of the managing clerk's thoughts, which for the present were locked up in his own snug breast.   He retired to his room, took up his pen, and speedily put together his story.   Quickly returning, he found that this time the lady required no reminder; his knock was immediately answered by the well-known tingle of his bell, and forthwith Mrs. Cubborn addressed him :—
" Sit down—go on—I am attending.   How slow you are ! Do get forward, Trapper."

" Yes, ma'am."   Notwithstanding the pressure he hemmed his usual " hem," three times to clear his throat, and then began :—

" INGENIOUS METHOD OF MAKING A LITERARY REPUTATION.—A luckless scribe, weary of continual rejection from the pages of our magazines, and other foremost periodicals, resolved upon establishing a name, not for what he had done, but what he had left undone.   He caused it to be given out among his friends that he had been long engaged in the production of a poem which his critical admirers,

who, he said, had read the MS., pronounced a work
of the true stamp and ringing metal, in fact, a
genuine epic of sustained merit and character
throughout. This panegyric was made to find its
way into the newspapers and other journals, and at
length a series of advertisements appeared announcing that the *chef d'œuvre* would soon be published.
The world of letters was kept on the tiptoe of ex-
pectation, when all of a sudden came the melancholy and calamitous intelligence that the glorious
poem, already in a state of completion, a mass of
valuable MSS., and a rare and extensive library,
were all consumed by an accidental fire. Fortu-
nately for the gifted author the property was insured, but the world had lost by this a transcendent
work of genius. Such was one side of the ingenious
story. Rumour, however, always busy, suggests
that the poem destroyed was purely a feat of the
imagination, and that the sterling ore of the insurance office was the most solid and enduring part
of the work. The fire is believed to be the result
of spontaneous combustion, and the enkindling art
of the poet still continues to enjoy the fruits of his
creative fancy. His fortune is enhanced, his effusions
are inserted, and he has earned an imperishable
name for a work which never had an existence beyond his own inventive faculty."—*American Paper*.

"No, do not say American paper; quote the
New York Herald at once boldly."

" But they might blow upon it."

" Let them ; 'tis true, you know it is true. Why,

you stupid, if it were the biggest lie ever invented, you might safely cite to support it even the authority of the *Times* itself."

"What, without being found out?"

"Unquestionably. Do you think the owls who conduct a paper know every line that goes into it when once it sees the light? So far from that, no one knows less about the journal of the day than the very hands that produced it; they are busy upon the next issue. You ought to be aware of that."

"Wonderful! There, I have put *New York Herald*. Well, ma'am, what do you think of it as a whole?"

"It drags, Trapper—it drags; it is decidedly heavy, not at all up to the mark; but it must do, I suppose. You will get it into the *Flam* first, then work it into the dailies, the weeklies, and the leading provincials. Remember, a shilling a line for every time you can produce it to me in a public journal. Be prompt. I am very busy, you know, with this great chancery suit."

Mr. Trapper disappeared, and the plotter continued her thoughts.

"I do not think this will bring the fire home to the pair; but people will get the clue,—the way will be open for the train when laid. Ill-nature will do the rest. I will take care the insurance-offices get the papers; they are rather too lively in smelling out arson. Ah! it will do, I see it will. I will sweep them from the face of the earth, I will. People will read, and laugh, and babble, and listen

and believe. We shall not be idle; no, no, my revenge is with that sure devil,

> ' Whose hoof is on the road,
> A treading-out the face of God.' "

Saying this, Mrs. Cubborn drew her brief before
her, and was soon buried and lost in the depths of
the Rolls Court.

She might have been some half hour engaged in
this way when her husband's well-known rap disturbed her. She raised her head, and rang the bell
assigned him. He entered.

"Well, what do you want of me? Do sit down,
I am not going to eat you. Well——"

"I came about that poor boy Natty."

"Oh, leave Natty alone; he is busy for me."

"Busy! why he is shut up in his room, and no
one can get to him. I want him to attend to the
business."

"My instructions were that he should not be
disturbed."

"Pretty, indeed. And what about this fire? I
must speak; he is my son,—he is the heir to a fair
property and a transmitted profession."

"Well, what is all this bother about—what do
you mean?"

"I mean that you are leading my child to destruction!"

"Your child!—your child, forsooth!—who told
you he is your child, nincompoop? He is my child."

"Everybody says he caused this fire."

"Everybody tells a lie; I know its authors."

"You do? — Then pray make the villains public."

"That is just as I choose. I am in possession of the facts; but it may not suit me to be so open-mouthed. However, the boy's fair fame must be vindicated; leave all that to me."

"I fear I have left too much to you, woman."

"Who is a woman? Have a care; be more cautious and respectful."

"I will be plain and candid, so take it as you will. You are ruining my son, you are ruining my profession, you are driving everything to destruction; our name is already infamous, a by-word everywhere. I tell you what it is, if you do not change, and conduct yourself more like a woman, I will quit you altogether and go."

"You may go—to———, if you like; but, remember, I will follow you thither; ay, and rake up the burning devils around you! Do not menace me, fellow. Know who I am and who you are. I could hang you any day!"

"Not me. I am not to be alarmed by your threats, I can tell you."

"Alarmed! I don't want to alarm you. But have you not abetted and suggested perjury over and over, and done worse, ay, worse?"

"I own, to my bitter shame and sorrow, there were times when, listening to your evil counsel, I did not not set a proper value on the sacredness of an oath; but catch me stumbling again, and I will thank you. No; I am cured!—I have had my lesson! And to be candid with you, I know those who will share their fortunes with me, if you do not mend——"

"Monster! dare to utter that threat again and your life pays for it! Well, suppose—oh, do sit down, pray, I will not touch you, you are too contemptible for my hands—well, suppose you went away to-morrow, think you I would not be after you, and pursue you to the end of the earth, till I saw you hanging?"

"You are an awful woman!"

"I am awful did you fully know me. I am awful. I am in a bad, competing world, and I will not be put down or trampled on, though all the fiends of hell were about me. Well, go, Andy Cubborn—go, denounce or renounce me, and see how far I shall be from you and from your trull the next day! Your career here has not been so immaculate! You had better keep a still tongue in your head!"

"With those exceptional cases I have mentioned, I have done nothing to be ashamed of."

"Nothing! why we all, the best of us, practising attorneys, do deeds the sun dare not look upon; often for ourselves, often not to lose a cause when a trick, or an oath, or an act of oppression will save what may be a just cause. But you, Cubborn, your crimes stink in my nostrils and in the face of Heaven!"

"Mercy, woman, what can you mean?"

"Go, leave me; try and break up this business, and you will find out."

"I suppose so; for you stand at nothing."

"True; you speak the exact truth now. If you

budged I would tell a tale, concoct a tale, if you will, prove a tale on oath, on veritable oath of undoubted witnesses, that would soon break your long neck in a halter!"

" You would?"

" I would. So no more threats of separation; and do leave the boy to me, he is in safe hands; no one cares for him half so much as his mother. The profession requires development. We do not make half enough of it, and I have determined that to be an attorney is really to be at the head of the commonwealth. You laugh. I wonder you can laugh after all that you have heard. But I shall live to make good my words; so there is nothing for you but quiet obedience and submission. Pray, what is doing in regard to the election? You know it is coming round, and it is my policy to return Wheatley for the county."

" Then, I fear you will be disappointed. Hilary Dove has ruined his prospects. The home-truths that fellow speaks sink deep in people's minds, however superficial he may appear."

" We should never have lost him only for you. If the county goes before I want it to go, look out —look out, I say, for my malediction! My plans are large, and I want this item of success at the election to bring matters home. It will not do to lose the Wheatley connexion. Go; I am upon this affair of Scoppins. I will let you have my notes upon it in the course of the day. Let not Natty be disturbed."

Husband and wife separated, each to follow some

worldly pursuit, differing in dishonesty only by the heart of boldness and courage, and the peculiar intellect possessed by the operator, resolved to be busy to make money anyhow and any-through. Did the Cubborns' practice disagree with that of the rest of our commercial world? Only in intensity, not in principle. It is this sordid principle of constant gain-seeking which we wish to see rooted out of society.

CHAPTER XX.

THE OLD TRUNK.

HE Spells were still in the Edelstone lodging-house. Myrtle Cottage was being rebuilt, and they were undecided whether they should reoccupy it, or let it and settle in London. Many things invited to this latter step. It was necessary that Oberon should actively pursue the attainment of his profession. Literature with him was dead since the loss of his MSS. He could scarcely bear to look at a poem, and he entirely ceased to write for the public press. A life in chambers would be lonely apart from his mother, and somehow he did not like the idea of going to town and returning daily to the village. The Wheatleys were expected at the Priory, and it would not be prudent or honourable in him to remain on the spot, continually liable to come into the presence and conversation of Ernestine. This had to be avoided. Iris Dove, too, he understood would soon be back, and for one reason or another he did not desire to be in too close proximity to her. His plans of marriage, if he had any, were at present vague and undecided. He had no settled calling, and until this should be determined on, and he was on the road to fortune, and able to maintain a wife and family, he thought it would be

unwise to encourage a passion which perhaps after all might never lead to a legitimate and satisfactory conclusion.

He therefore set to, and began to arrange the few papers left him from the fire, with the resolution of fixing at least for some years in the metropolis. He consulted his mother on his views, so far as a profession and residence were concerned, and these met with her heartiest sanction. They were but two; and for the present eligible lodgings would answer all their requirements. Deborah could still wait on her mistress. A suitable place being found in Upper Gower-street, Bedford-square, the little family were to settle there in the course of the following week. Rummaging through and turning over his papers, Oberon came upon the old trunk which he had rescued from the conflagration, simply because access to the cellar where it stood was not precluded by the smoke and flame. The accumulation of MSS. in a literary house is endless. If the abode be at all neatly kept—and we all know how Myrtle Cottage was managed—the removal of some of the papers now and then to an out-of-the-way place becomes necessary. The box of documents saved from the devouring element had never so much as been previously examined. It was known to contain some letters of Oberon's paternal grandfather, Henry, or Heinrich, Spell, for he was a German; and as these had been rendered unimportant by the death of Bertram, Oberon's father— they had been thrown by in the trunk we have mentioned to rest in the cellar with other lumber

which only some such sweeping visitation as a
fire could disturb or suddenly destroy. The writer
of the letters and his correspondents had long been
gathered to their fathers, and as they left no imposing name behind them, their memorials, if any,
were forgotten. But as Oberon was now really at
a loss for something to do, he opened the box,
which he found to be well secured, and seriously
set to work to decipher the various documents it
contained. As he advanced in his task, he got interested in the materials thus strangely disentombed.
When he had accomplished his labour in a student-
like manner, made a brief abstract of the subject
of each letter and document of any importance,
noting the whole, and arranging them according to
their matter and dates, he sought his mother, who
herself had become anxious to learn the contents of
that singular relic, alone saved from out a mass of
such valuable papers.

"My dear mother, somehow I find that we have
never taken a family interest in our ancestors. Do
you know, my curiosity this way was first actively
excited during my short stay in Vienna, where I
saw that the Spells were held in much consideration. On my travels abroad I had an opportunity
of being introduced to some of them, but declined
the honour; for I need not tell you how repugnant
it would be to me to be thought a poor relation.
But now the papers in the old trunk have really
awakened a very natural family concern in me. I
do not wish to stir up painful memories in you, but
I should like to know something about my father,

and his father, and if possible about his father
again, or my great grandfather. So there is a
string of paternals for you to unravel. Then I
have never heard you tell the story of your own
family. I know you were a Miss Erndale—but
what Erndale? Were they of Kent or Sussex?
Or did they come out of that migrating county,
Norfolk, whose inhabitants are to be found all over
England, and, I suppose, the colonies also. Come,
dear mamma, as we both have leisure now, do indulge in a little family gossip. Every gentleman
should know from whom he sprang; for I believe
in the lineage of men as well as of horses."

" Well, really, my dear, genealogy is a subject
which never much interested me; but, as you say,
one ought to know his descent, if only to show that
it was legitimate and honourable. For myself, I
am derived from a race of clergymen. My father,
Dr. Erndale, was rector of Little Plimpton, Devon-
shire, and my grandfather was a poor curate in the
same parish. They married, one into the family of
the Illinghams, my mother's name, and her mother
was *née* L'Estrange, of the Norfolk family, I believe. It was a stolen match, they report, and gave
some umbrage to my grandmother's friends. My
father died early, and my dear mother soon followed
him; and I must own, I was only a poor governess
when I first beheld your father. Oh, Oberon! I
ought not to touch upon this—do excuse me."

Mrs. Spell buried her head in her handkerchief,
overcome with grief. Her tears fell fast and warm;
and so solemn and ghostly did everything become,

that it seemed as if the dead were in that room beside the disconsolate widow. Oberon, deeply affected himself, did all he could to comfort and restore his mother. But he had revived very painful and distressing scenes. He was passing over the grave of a troubled spirit, and it was almost impossible to allay the hovering oppression and sorrow.

Both were silent for a time, overwhelmed with grief. At length the feelings of the mother asserted their superior power, and drying her own eyes, Mrs. Spell endeavoured to console her son.

" 'Tis over, dear; I am well now—do you be well also. What you have requested is only natural and necessary. I will go on, dear, if you will listen to me."

" A moment, dear mother. Proceed now. I am better. But will it distress you?"

" No, not now. I almost think this conversation a duty, a debt I owe to you and, perhaps, to the dead. We may not be always together, dear child. We come of a short-lived family; on both sides the destroying angel visited us soon—too soon for this earth's happiness. Well, dear, to continue :—Your father and his sister Frederica, our Mrs. Lever, who had been a few years married, came as young friends on a visit to the family where my lot was placed. They were amiable people where I lived, and almost regarded me as a daughter, certainly they treated me with marked kindness and affection. Bertram Spell was then a merchant, in partnership with his father. We had frequent opportunities of meeting.

A mutual passion sprang up between us. He very soon proposed for me, and was accepted. His mother was dead, but his surviving parent, Heinrich Spell, was very fond of me, and immediately gave his sanction. We were married, Oberon; and if ever there was a union of hearts, it was ours. Well —yes—in one month from that—for our bliss was very short—we lost your dear grandfather. He met with a fatal accident in one of the crowded thoroughfares of the city. That to us was a terrible bereavement. We felt very lonely in the world; but a more solitary hour came. He—he, my precious, noble husband—oh, Oberon, he was a glorious being, so good, so generous, so affectionate, so brave, so handsome—he was snatched from me. My God! —my God! how I have suffered! He was always averse to commerce; traffic of any kind he abhorred. He was ill suited, dear, to a city life. Somehow he one day got into a quarrel with a French merchant, his senior, a son of the revolution. I believe it was about a matter of principle. Your father was rigidly honest, and the Frenchman was a man of the world, and so they seriously differed. There were sharp words and quick blows. The angry Frenchman sent his defiance. It was accepted. They met, as they should not have met, with swords. My beautiful beloved was murdered by a hoary rebel. His bleeding and mangled corpse was all I ever saw of him since that fatal morning. He was still alive when borne home, but they would not allow me to see him. Oh, dear Oberon! no wonder that I should shudder at violence of any kind! It was only three months after your poor grandfather's sad and painful death, and a bare four from our marriage, that he fell, and I was left a desolate widow. 'Tis marvellous how I survived; but you came not many months after to comfort me. Since then you have been my only solace, you, and poor Deborah, who nursed you. Oh! my dear child, I hope you will never do anything to break in upon the happiness you have brought upon me since the hour I saw your dear father's image in you! Promise me, Oberon!"

"Never, mother, so help me Heaven, never! All through life shall I be and remain your fond and dutiful son, now as heretofore, and hereafter as now."

The ratification was tender and solemn; and if ever the angel of affection registers human vows, here was one worthy of his crystal pen. Mrs. Spell, when she had somewhat composed herself, briefly resumed.

"You know all the rest, dear child. But have you found any papers which really interest you?"

"Well, dear mother, I must own that I have. They take the shape of correspondence, and are nearly all in German. There are some letters from a Wilhelm Spell, the uncle of my grandfather, which are really entertaining. It appears he was much attached to his sister, my great-grandmother, Margherita Spell, who was married to her own cousin—one of the Spells—and who, strange to say, also lost her husband a very short time after her marriage, I cannot exactly make out how; but she gave birth to Heinrich some few months subsequent to the decease of her husband."

"A very strange coincidence indeed! But sometimes these singular occurrences do happen in families."

"There is a mass of fragmentary matter which some day might be of use. I will lay the papers carefully by, and when I next go into the city I will call at 39, Old Broad-street, my grandfather and father's offices, and make inquiries there. As I said, the information might prove useful. You know, dear mother, I am now going to work hard at an honourable profession; it might happen that I shall distinguish myself; then family will be of some account. The Erndales, the L'Estranges, the Spells, the present General, who is a count, among the rest, might all be of some importance in working out and sustaining a pedigree."

"You have decided on the chancery bar—is that settled, dear child?"

"Well, ma, I think it is."

"I am glad of it. Do you know I could never be brought to like the common-law bar after what I witnessed at a trial in Westminster Hall long ago with your father, who took me everywhere. A poor gentleman, who had been an officer, was under cross-examination by the then attorney-general, one of the most eminent counsel of the day, and afterwards Lord Chancellor. Well, he did so worry the poor gentleman, and was so common-place and cunning in bolstering up a very bad cause, that I really felt that such a profession must be deteriorating and degrading, quite unworthy of an honourable, pure, and ingenuous mind."

" The license of the common-law bar is indeed to be deplored. Sometimes it is flagitious. The judges are to blame for allowing this species of persecution and torture to run riot in cross-examination and attack. It often happens that the meanest artifice is tried in order to make an impression on a jury or to prop up a rotten cause. Matters, 'tis true, are not so bad in these days as in former years; but liberty of speech is still much abused, and I think with you, incompatible with what ought to be an elevated and honourable profession. At the chancery-bar, dear mother, I shall have the judges and my legal brethren—all superior men—alone to please; and I hope by due diligence I shall succeed in winning their respect and esteem. They shall never find me touting to either clients or attorneys. I enter, please God, next week, the chambers of Mr. Vigilly, the eminent conveyancer and equity draughtsman, as his pupil: and I shall all along endeavour to keep within the strict line of honour enjoined by the profession."

True to his new plans of life, Oberon Spell took a ground-floor office in Lincoln's Inn, and entered seriously and methodically on his legal studies, joining his mother every evening in Upper Gower-street. He thus bade fair in the opinion of all competent persons to work his way up to distinction, wealth, and eminence as a chancery barrister.

CHAPTER XXI.

IR ROGER WHEATLEY, his lady, and daughter returned to Edelstone. The elections were approaching, and it was necessary that the sitting member should be on the spot. His prospects had been seriously impaired by the indefatigable and unscrupulous exertions of Hilary Dove and his myrmidons, for the agitator had gathered around him a host of political followers. He was still on his travels, plying his mingled avocations of Hygienic Food agent and Radical lecturer. But his electioneering work was pushed forward for him by a band of sturdy and zealous adherents and admirers. Iris also was away on a visit to one of her father's numerous friends. She was the object of many earnest suitors, some of them men of wealth and commercial position ; but the heedless girl only laughed at her lovers, and her father did not press the suit of any one of them. Her affections, if anywhere fixed, were at home in Edelstone, and thither her parent's sanction went with them. The law student was in London, deep in fathoming the various mysteries connected with the rights of real property, and in genial endeavours to make his mother happy. He was soon made aware that Ernestine was once more

in her and his native village. This debarred him
from the enjoyment of some relaxation and pleasure.
It had been his delight, since the commencement of
his legal career, to run down to Edelstone, visit his
friends there, and stroll for hours in the park, not
an idle or unfruitful spectator of its noble scenery.
He had now deemed it prudent to discontinue his
rambles. He came at rare intervals to the village;
but Oberon Spell, the handsome, was no more seen
straying in Priory Park. His abstinence here was
not in harmony with the secret inclinations of his
mother, who with feminine tenacity still clung to
the brilliant prospects designed them, she thought,
by Heaven : but she admired her son's strength of
resistance, kept silent, and left events to their
natural course.

As to Ernestine Wheatley, the noble domain surrounding her mansion became the scene of her constant daily walks. She never tired of flitting into
every nook and corner with her maid. She was
anxious and moody, evidently in search of something.
How her heart beat and her colour went and came
when anybody approached; and then, her sigh and
blank look of disappointment! No ! she would try
again; she might have missed him, he was so fond
of hiding away in the lonely places. He was not here
—he was not there—he was nowhere. Her picture
was hope and despair—anxiety, nervous, pining
anxiety. How she longed to come upon him; and
yet, if she had she would have wished herself miles
away, or buried in the seclusion of her own chamber.
Her visits were renewed from day to day, and at all

hours, whenever she could snatch a moment from her studies.

But morning, noon, evening, and sometimes night with its dancing moonlit beams came, they found the accomplished and beautiful lady a wanderer—but vain her search—vain her eager, prying looks—vain her longings! He came not. He had deserted the park. He was a stranger in Edelstone. It was too clear he had taken up a fixed resolution to avoid her. This did not deaden her love, while it strengthened her obstinacy and pride. Should a miserable adventurer's daughter, and her father's enemy, baffle her and win from her that noble heart—the object of her choice? Him whom she could make at one turn so exalted and happy! Were riches, power, accomplishments, and beauty on one side, and form, genius, learning, and principle on the other, to give way to the machinations of an artful girl and her unworthy, low-minded, ill-conditioned parents? Ernestine had a firm, unconquerable will—she had unbounded influence over her own father and mother—she resolved to save Oberon Spell—and to make him her husband if possible—but at all events to deliver him from the snares of the siren.

Withal the lady was practical, cunning too, as young hearts will be; but as she reviewed and examined her schemes one after another, they faded away before her commonsense and sagacity, as dreams—the visions of a very sick fancy. The realities were terrible. Granted all other obstacles overcome, could she conquer to herself his love? A double victory—root out a set passion—and fix her own image unalterably in his heart? Could she make herself the sole object of his affection? He was high-minded and noble, resistant and constant —how then could she subdue him? tame down that lofty nature to her will? She was but a woman—no, not a woman—not yet out of her teens; and though strong and mighty in love, alas! in her sex and years she was weak. What means could she employ to obtain a recognition—a return? Had she not tried?—cunningly, prudently, adroitly tried?—her Cupid's arrow had sped in vain. He was cased in triple panoply—his love for another— his natural independence—and his total disregard of herself. How penetrate these, and reach his bosom? A thousand plans haunted her by day and by night. But they came and went, and went and came—were cherished and were gone, without leaving any tangible result behind. Their only effect was on her own brain and bosom. She looked the picture of an exhausted, weary spirit. The sunken eye—the fevered cheek—the parched tongue —the nervous frame that started at everything— the sleepless nights—the anxious days—the one incessant palpitating death-watch at her heart—these told the story of hopeless, unrequited, concealed love. In the language of her own darling Oberon,—

> " Joys and sorrows rise like days of sun and storm,
>   But who can count the fond heart's sleepless vigils?"

At one moment she thought of confiding everything to that meekest and most loveable of women, Martha Spell. But then she saw at a glance that this honourable lady would not sanction a clandestine passion, and would insist on the knowledge and co-operation of her parents. And would all this circumbendibus bring her nearer to the centre of his heart? She instinctively felt it would repel his free and noble nature. No, she would not trample on delicacy.

Should she confide all to her mother? That mother had been her instructress and guide. She had grown up more as her companion than daughter. The interchange of thoughts between them—all save on one subject—was most generous and perfect. Still her mother was a lady of noble birth and fixed and haughty ideas and bearing on every matter connected with her own station. She was too naturally dignified to be merely proud; but her sense of family honour—what she owed to her ancestors and to posterity—precluded altogether any notion that she would ever give her consent to a *mésalliance*. But even here there might be some hope, some shadow of excuse, if Oberon returned her love. Ah! would there, indeed! only let her be sure of that, and she would elope with him— the thought—the crime—did come into her bosom —and she would leave the reconcilement to time and affection. But he, the man—he, the lover— the prompter and supporter made no sign. He was cold and silent as a statue, or if he moved, it was away from her in repulsion. He shunned her. This it was which made her lot terrible.

Her father was pliant and sensible; a man conscious of his wealth and rank it is true, but too conversant with our modern world not to know that a suitor of respectable family, youth, health, handsome person, accomplished, gentlemanly, of admitted learning and ability, and pursuing one of our foremost professions, might be considered an eligible match even for an heiress, the daughter of a baronet and ex-minister. This liberal and enlightened sentiment of her father's Ernestine had long ago ascertained during one of those indiscreet conversations which parents sometimes indulge in before their too susceptible and observant children. The arguments of her father referred to a young barrister of their acquaintance, on a matter which had no family connexion with them whatever. But they made a deep and lasting impression on Ernestine, who at a very early age became capable of entertaining her own opinions and convictions; nor were these always in unison with what she conceived to be the mere prejudices of a haughty aristocracy.

Should she confide in that father? She felt with feminine instinct that her reception would be far more encouraging than the cold and formal audience she would be sure to experience from her mother. But then the idea was altogether preposterous—untenable. How could she tell her father that she loved a man, and that man the village youth—Oberon Spell?

Should she make a confidant of Martin? The woman was only her maid it is true, and not educated beyond the average of persons of her condition. But then, as Oberon Spell said, for she loved to form her thoughts and actions by his divine words,—

> " There is a soul of wisdom in the world,
> Beyond our written knowledge; broad and clear,
> Germane to every mind, which shines on all,
> And makes men's genius equal,"

words which, as we have seen, Iris Dove could turn to account.

Martin had sound, natural understanding and sense, much experience, and was withal very kind, good, and faithful. Moreover, she knew that Oberon Spell was a favourite, and Iris Dove and her mother odious to her feelings. Should she confide in her? It would be something to have one being on earth to whom she could unburden her overloaded heart. Then her maid was ever with her, and there would be no strangeness or formality in whispering her secret to her, and this was half the battle. But against this rapid trust she had been trained by her mother never to communicate family matters to domestics, and above all things never to put herself in their power. How could she disobey a solemn and wise parental injunction? And after all, what good could Martin do her? Would it not be a desecration to impart her holy and mysterious thought—the very jewel of her heart—to a servant's keeping? and this against the express family commandment. No, Ernestine could not bring herself to this depth of disobedience and folly. So she re-

mained as she was, pent up in her own grief, till in
the words of her own poet,

> " Sorrow pluck'd the rosebud from her cheek,
>   And planted the pale lily."

The heiress of Edelstone was seriously ill. Nobody knew what was the matter with her. But
she was visibly pining, wasting to a skeleton. The
anxious eye of an affectionate mother was upon her;
the fond regards of an observant father; all the servants were concerned, and friends saw the change
in the lovely girl with regret. She was questioned
as to her symptoms and sufferings. Her answers
were not satisfactory. All she could say was that
she did not sleep well, and that she did not care
for food, or for study, or for anything, but to ramble
all over the park, often wearying herself.

The doctor was called in, or rather the young
lady visited the great man in town; for the very
first and foremost advice was sought. Sir Ulysses
Kennard made a very careful examination of his
patient. He pronounced no definite opinion. But
he hinted that the physician required was the
confidence of a mother. He thought the girl's
mind was troubled, and her feelings possibly in
some degree affected. In fact, the experienced and
unerring eye of the aged doctor soon discovered
Ernestine's real malady. But practice had taught him
that it would be unwise to be too explicit on the
subject. He therefore spoke generally, and left an
opening for the explanation to come to him. He
prescribed some sedatives, and above all things the

confidence of her parents, and requested to see his patient again that day week.

From the cautious communication made by the physician, Sir Roger Wheatley and his lady could only infer that Ernestine had some secret cause of grief which was preying on her tender nature. Her mother rebuked herself for not perceiving the cause of her illness sooner. As to sharing her inmost confidence, she had no doubt about immediately obtaining that, and her only wonder was that any secret should exist without her knowledge. She dared not doubt Sir Ulysses Kennard's great authority, but she owned to her husband that she had her misgivings here. However, the matter would speedily be set at rest.

For two or three days subsequently nothing was said to Ernestine to induce her to open her mind to her mother. Both her parents watched over her most tenderly, even with more than their usual affectionate vigilance and care. She partook of the medicine prescribed for her, and diligently obeyed, as far as she was able, the directions given with respect to her food, exercise, and studies. In no particular was the docile and obedient child found wanting.

One evening as Lady Wheatley sat alone in Ernestine's room, after some general observations, the mother addressed her daughter in the following terms :—

" Ernestine, my dear, I think it my duty, as your mother, to say something special to you."

" Yes, mamma."

"Well, my dear, may I conclude that I have your perfect esteem and love ?"

" Oh ! yes, indeed you have, my dearest mother."

" And that now as ever I share your entire confidence ?"

Ernestine did not immediately reply. Lady Wheatley continued, not failing to observe the deep blush which tinged her daughter's pallid face.

" I mean, dear, that now as heretofore you keep no secrets from your mother."

Ernestine well knew whither the inquiry was tending. Her heart beat violently, but she remained silent.

" My dearest child, I would not annoy you for worlds, or be the cause of giving you a moment's anxiety or pain. But, in truth, your papa and I have become, as you know, very uneasy about your health ; and somehow I have begun to think that of late I have not had your usual confidence—that you are intensely troubled about something which is a mystery to us all. But do not agitate yourself, love. I will pursue the conversation no further now. Only think upon what I have been saying ; and remember I have never violated your confidence in any particular ; and that I am your friend and companion — nay, your confidant as well as mother."

The daughter still sat mute, her beautiful head bowed down. There was a pause of a few moments, during which her colour went and came. At length a flood of burning tears seemed to relieve her.

"My dear child, I fear I have pained you. Oh! Ernestine, forget what I have said if it afflicts you."

"No, mamma—no, my dearest mother, 'tis I am in fault. I will speak to you. I will tell you all. I should be wronging you to break the sweet link of united affection and trust between us. I will unburden this poor heart to you."

"Presently, dear Ernestine, presently. Just take your medicine—that will relieve you. Ah! there is no glass. I will go for one myself that Williams may not see you."

The judicious mother purposely left the room for a few moments that her daughter might collect her scattered thoughts, and whilst alone somewhat re-assure herself. In about ten minutes she returned with the wineglass, and administered the restorative.

"Thank you, dear mamma, I feel much better now. I will—I will try and bring myself to tell you my story; only you must not blame me, or be angry whatever it may be."

"It would be cruel to be angry with you, my love. Ernestine, I have not often in my life been angry with you."

"Oh! I know you have not; and that is the reason why I shrink from giving you any cause of offence now."

The anxious parent thought this an ominous introduction, but she said nothing, smiling compassionately on her child as before.

"Well, dear mamma, I suppose you are waiting till I fulfil my promise, though I scarcely know how to begin."

Now it was that Lady Wheatley showed her feminine tact. She did not wish to press her delicate and nervous child to an abrupt disclosure. She was not quite certain, but she strongly suspected some affair of the heart. She therefore thought it most prudent to beat about the bush for awhile. She said quite innocently :

" Is it my dear, any scruple of religion ? These things will sometimes occur in the course of our reading. I have heard your papa say so. For my own part, I must own I never had any such frivolous thoughts. Is it anything that way ?"

" No, dear mamma."

" Or the sufferings of any of our poor pensioners ; old Watkins, for instance. But we do our best for him, and indeed for them all. They begin to think it a right, and are never grateful. But do tell me, dear. Ah, perhaps, for I wish to help you on, it is grief for the political annoyance your papa now and then suffers. This kind of thing, dear, is the life of gentlemen. I believe they would pine and die without party excitement, commotion, and opposition. So I would not take that seriously to heart."

" I do not, mamma ; though I own I take a great interest in politics. But it is not that."

" Now I am fairly puzzled. Do tell me in one word, my sweet dear child, what it is which afflicts you, and is our affliction also ? Only think of your papa's anguish and mine."

" Well, mamma, I am coming to it. I have a heart, my dear mother."

"Ah, a heart! Why, dear Ernestine, am I right —are your affections engaged?"

"That is it." She bowed her head and wept once more, this time hysterically.

"Nay, my dear, be comforted. What you have revealed is not so terrible. We women are not strangers to such feelings. Why were you so foolish as to make a secret of the matter to me? Do you know, child, I feel quite interested now, and long to learn the whole story. Who is it, Ernestine?"

"Spare me, mamma—spare me a moment."

"Ah, I see—I see. So that lady-killer, your cousin, young Summers, has bewitched you during his recent visit at the Ravines. Why, there is no crime in that, my lady. Everybody says he himself is fixed at last—smitten. Only you are so young."

"Eighteen, mamma," said Ernestine, half revived by the playfulness of her mother.

"Have I guessed right, truant?"

"No, indeed, mamma. Lord Summers is a libertine."

"Well, my dear, these are not matters for ladies to enter on. But in the name of the blind god, Cupid himself, who is the happy man? I could run over a long list of your admirers, but I own none pleases me better than my kinsman Summers. He is a little gay or so, they say, but we must not listen to such things, or mention them. What is more serious, your papa does not like him."

"I suppose he has good reasons for his dislike, mamma?"

"Perhaps; but Ernestine dear, you are forgetting.

Do tell it out at once, and ease my curiosity. Who is it?"

"Oberon Spell, mamma." She said this in a low, deep whisper, and then buried her head in her hands.

Lady Wheatley sat still a moment perfectly bewildered; then perceiving her child's bitter agony, she arose and once more persuaded her to revive herself with the cordial medicine prescribed for her.

"I fear, dear mamma, it will not do me any good; but I will take it as you wish. There—and now I will swallow no more physic; I do not like it. I have told you all, mother; I have broken my secret to you, and I have your promise that you would not be angry."

"Neither am I, my love; only a little surprised —a very little surprised. I suppose this is natural.

"Oh, quite so; I expected it."

"But, my dear Ernestine, there is nothing serious. You understand me—that is, arranged— concluded—or anything that way?"

"I love him! that is all."

"Oh, as for that matter, child, you know I am no trifler; but I could not count my various loves, or likings rather, coming and going, and coming and going again, when I was of your age. But when I saw your dear papa, my love was fixed."

"Mine is fixed, my dearest mother. It will live and die with me."

"My child, what you say now is serious indeed. I did not think that young man and his mother had so much cunning and dishonour in them—pardon the terms—as to seduce your affections."

"You wrong them, mamma, indeed you wrong them—him! They do not know anything about it; or if they do, if he does, my feelings are not returned. He loves another! You now see the abyss of my misery."

"Oh!" said Lady Wheatley, drawing a deep breath, and inwardly congratulating herself that all was not so bad as she had expected.

"I see, my dear Ernestine, I have wronged those good people. Well, he is a pleasing-looking young man, and has fine intellectual qualities, so your papa says; but, my dear, if he is engaged, there's an end of it. You would not love a man whom you must regard as already married."

"Such is my crime, mamma."

"Well, my dear, we will say no more on the subject at present. Remember it is now in my hands—in the hands of your friend, your companion, your confidant and mother. Feel assured that whatever is best for you shall be done. So be comforted, my child."

"And you give me hopes, oh! my dearest mother, do you?"

"The hopes of a Christian, Ernestine—courage and fortitude. We were sent into this world to bear our trials, to take up our cross; but, as I said, we will not dwell on the matter now, I must go to the drawing-room. Retire to your chamber, Ernestine, and Martin will prepare you to join us. God bless you, darling!" Kissing her child, Lady Wheatley descended to the drawing-room, where she expected company. Ernestine went to her own room to prepare to mingle in a gay assembly.

CHAPTER XXII.

LADY WHEATLEY did not return to the subject of her last conversation with Ernestine, but she skilfully endeavoured to occupy her attention, so as to leave her but little time for moping reflection. Everything too was done to improve the patient's health, but that evidently did not amend; Ernestine remained wasted and careworn. The long nights were passed in those contemplations denied her in the day. The heiress to the Ravines and Priory was fast gathering to her fathers. The whole house—parents, friends, domestics—were concerned and afflicted.

The deliberations of the baronet and his lady on the state of their adored child were constant and prolonged. In the estimation of the proud dame such a solution of the difficulty as a marriage between her daughter and Oberon Spell, the poor author, or barrister, or whatever else he might choose to be called, was altogether out of the question. She pooh-poohed that view of the case as wholly inadmissible; the antidote was worse than the poison. Health might come back, and would most likely come back; but marriage is a life gone for now and posterity. That would never answer, even if encouraged on the young man's side; and of this there were strong doubts. Her mind was made up that no issue whatever, not death itself, would drive her to sanction so miserable an alliance. She would be true to her pure blood, no matter what the sacrifice; nor did she despair of being able to recover her child's health in her own dexterous way, and aided by Sir Ulysses Kennard's experienced advice. She was a woman herself—she understood her own feelings; she remembered that she had no fewer than nine quondam adorers seated at her own wedding breakfast. She looked forward to time and circumstance as the great restorers; but time and circumstance are the harbingers of disease and death where the heart-wound is deep and incurable.

Sir Roger Wheatley was not of the same frame of mind as his lady; the pride of aristocracy was not uppermost in him; he rather regarded family distinction from the side of wealth than of mere hereditary rank. Not that he did not feel the dignity and consequence of a noble pedigree; he was himself of very ancient lineage, and could boast of some time-honoured national achievements to illustrate his scutcheon. But he lived in a practical age; he breathed the free, democratic air of the House of Commons, and although a Conservative in politics, he could not well shut his eyes to the real influence of money in a great commercial nation. He saw many distinguished and some great men around him who had sprung from the people, and he could not but perceive how very little the want of family honours and high and remote descent really affected their position. It all depended on the man himself—if the aristocrat was in him he must rise, and would be ever equal to his station. He thought it possible for a man of true nobility—no matter how lowly his lot at the outset—to ascend to the loftiest elevation and fortune in our free and encouraging country. Nor did he know of any profession so suitable to a well-sustained ambition as that of a barrister. There was in this young man, Oberon Spell, a commanding exterior, a lofty and independent bearing united to good manners and great learning and ability, which might raise him one day to the supreme honours of the Chancery Bar, if only his powers should be well directed. No question but so severe and profound a student would become a consummate pleader and learned lawyer. Then he was of a good family: the Spells were of gentle blood—the Vienna Spells; one branch of them having turned from some unaccountable whim to commerce. He had heard the old Marquis of Lorndale talk very highly and somewhat mysteriously too, of this family. He knew everybody and almost everything, and no doubt had good reason for his eulogy. Mrs. Spell was the daughter of Dr. Erndale, a very erudite divine, and his mother was a L'Estrange, a remote connexion of Lady Wheatley's paternal grandfather. These were not such bad antecedents and recommendations. Lord Summers was the cousin of Ernestine, a relationship in a husband he did not approve. He was no special favourite of his; he knew a great deal about him, and should be sorry to give him his daughter, unless indeed a great reformation became perceptible. But he could decide nothing hastily; all he wanted was to combat Lady Wheatley's stiff and unapproachable exclusiveness and ancestral pride, and to make his daughter's health and happiness the sole study of both her parents. But he would now, however, abide the opinion and advice of Sir Ulysses Kennard, and be a great deal guided by his conclusion.

But before the day came for a renewal of the visit to the physician, he thought it only an act of kindness and prudence to interrogate his child himself on the delicate subject affecting her; he therefore took the first favourable opportunity to introduce the matter to her.

"Ernestine, my love, your mamma has deemed it to be a duty to communicate to me the ideas you entertain in regard to our friend, Oberon Spell. I do assure you I am by no means insensible to his excellent qualities. But, my dear, there are many things in this life which we must be content to admire without allowing our feelings to go further. Otherwise society would be intolerable. The relations of father and mother, brother and sister, children, husband and wife, kindred, friends, master and servant, superior and inferior—all necessary to order and morality—can only be maintained by an observance of this essential rule—one that commends itself to the pure and delicate heart, as well as the informed and disciplined judgment. I hope I am not distressing you, my child."

"Oh no, indeed, papa! I am so much obliged to you for all you say. I feel and comprehend you,

and honour a father's instruction and advice.
Only——"

" Well, what, my dear ?"

" I fear you do not understand me, that is
all."

" How, dear Ernestine, explain."

" Think not, dearest papa, since I am permitted
to speak to you on the subject—and I respect you
too much not to speak out plainly now that you
have been kind enough to give me the opportunity
— think not that my regard for him is mixed up
with any concern for myself, or to gratify any wish
or feeling of my own.   Oh no! my sole concern is
for his happiness.   He is about to sacrifice that to
a most preposterous passion, to a liking for a young
person who cannot but make him miserable."

" You allude to the daughter of that man Hilary
Dove."

" The same.   A forward, uncultivated person ;
from all I hear, resembling her father in boldness
and want of principle, and her mother in cunning
and dishonesty. Married to such a creature as that
he must be wretched !"

" Really, my dear, these are matters which
scarcely concern our house, and which, least of all,
should concern a young lady like you. We must
not forget ourselves, Ernestine.   I fear you do not
exactly apprehend the awkward position they place
you in. We have nothing to do with the manner
of regulating the affections of these young people.
It is a rule of life not to meddle in the domestic
affairs of others."

"I knew you would not understand me; and I have done."

"No; I want to comprehend it all. Speak out, Ernestine; your father will not blame you, child."

"I will speak out, for my heart is ready to burst. Know then, I hate—I do intensely hate Iris Dove! Nay, start not, papa, but hear me,—I do hate her from the deepest depths of my nature. You gave me permission to speak: I tell you the very air she breathes is suffocation to me! I speak for his sake —for his dear sake; not my own, heaven is my witness!"

"My dear, these are terrible thoughts—dreadful admissions!"

"I know they are. But I want to go to sleep, my father, to get a long deep sleep, and forget it all."

"You do indeed, my love, for these feelings and expressions demand oblivion."

"They do; I said I knew you would not understand me. I shall be silent."

"No, no, Ernestine; that would be doing me an injustice. I want to get at your whole soul, to meet your difficulty in full. I hope your father is worthy of your confidence."

"Of my utmost confidence and trust, dear papa, and I will be plain and open with you, because I want a guide and friend—a confessor; and you know how I reverence you as my all, as my earthly protector and comforter."

"Ernestine, my love, my only desire on earth is to promote your happiness; so that be secured I

would go so far as to say, I would not be too particular in regard to any honourable means."

"There spoke my dear papa. Ah! I knew you
would take an enlarged and enlightened view of my
agonized feelings. Well then, dearest papa, I have
such a deep, a settled, and eternal interest in the
welfare of Oberon Spell, that I would sacrifice my
life rather than she should have him. You must
not ask me why this is; you must only know that
it is, my father."

"Dear child, be calm; it is dreadful to see your
excitement and suffering. Now, dear, I must tell
you that from the feelings you express, it is you that
would be likely to make Oberon miserable."

"I, pa—I?"

"You—a woman capable of these paroxysms of
jealousy—for this is the passion you are suffering
under, Ernestine, would be sure to render the life
of a husband wretched. The never-closing evil eye
would for ever watch him—the eager presence would
ever haunt him—the suspicious feeling would ever
torture him—the causeless incessant anger would
make his house a pandemonium."

"Oh, pa! and should I ever become that monster?"

"Unquestionably, my child. I know you have
reason clear enough to draw conclusions inevitable.
You must see whither all this blind passion—for it
is not love—must ultimately tend."

"You are right! you are right! I am saved
from a precipice. I must not be unworthy of him.
This were still a lower depth of misery. My dearest

papa, I humbly acknowledge my sin, and I stand corrected for ever."

"Thank God! But dearest Ernestine, as I wish to make the best use of my time, I must ask you one more question: If Mr. Spell is engaged to this young lady, as we all have reason to believe,—nay, you must bear it—your affection for him is irregular. You must know that. Have you tried to overcome it?"

"Oh, yes, papa! Tried!—look at me. I could tell you much of my endeavours—struggles—pangs! but, see me! Am I not changed?—very much changed? Read my efforts in my broken health and spirits."

"I do, my love. You have suffered—you are altered; but a matter like this must be treated reasonably, calmly, kindly, not by impulses of passion. It is all very serious, and cannot be undone by explanations which may tend to aggravate. Feel this, however, Ernestine, that I thoroughly understand and appreciate all your motives and feelings. I sympathize with you, and with God's help will aid you, Ernestine, my beloved daughter, my only child, the sole remain of my house. Nay, nay, be comforted. Perhaps there is a way out of it all."

"There is, papa—one."

"Come, Ernestine, put away all wayward, sinful thoughts. These are temptations. 'Cease to do evil; learn to do well.' Prove yourself worthy of an honourable man's love. I have a very high opinion of Spell; he is a noble young fellow."

"Oh, he is glorious, did you but know him!"

"Well, I think I understand *him* at least. But, young lady, how came your knowledge of him to be so far superior to mine?"

"To yours, papa? How should you know Oberon Spell? Why, I was almost brought up with him. Every day in the park, when I was a wee little child, I played with him. He used to run and fetch my ball, and I used to fling it archly away that he might throw it at me; and I used to run at him with my hoop in my mad romps, and he used to catch me. Oh, hundreds of times have I hung round his neck as a little child, and twined my fingers in his brown locks till they tingled. I loved him as a child, pa, and he loved me too, he did, till she came —the evil one!"

"Nay, Ernestine, forbear! Oberon Spell was always more intimate with Iris Dove than he possibly could have been with you."

"It may be—it was, and I correct myself; he never did love me! I never knew a thought from his lips that was not good and pure, or an action of his that a saint might not witness. 'Twas all my fault. I should not have played with a handsome boy; I did wrong, very wrong, even as an unsuspecting child, and I suffer."

"One more word, before I forget it, Ernestine."

"Yes, papa; I am attending."

"Iris Dove is not the inferior mortal you would make her. I have seen her, conversed with her, and I think I understand her. Trust me, such a face and form, such open and undesigning speech and manners cannot be associated with cunning, want of principle, or dishonesty. That affair of the brooch was mysterious; but the fault, if it rests with them at all, does not affect the child, but the mother. I would not have you think meanly of the young lady, Ernestine. She might make a very good wife for a sensible, plodding man."

"But not for Oberon Spell!"

"Providence might even will that, my dear. We ourselves must be honest; we must not invade the property or covet the loves or husbands of others; we must not be revolutionists and anarchs, Ernestine, or violate the Commandment."

"Oh, my dear, dear father! how you do speak home to my understanding and soul. I appreciate and feel every word you utter; still, excuse me, dear papa, for the thought—a presumption, perhaps —she is not, and cannot be, what I am; I who have treasured every scrap of his verse, every page of his composition. There is not a published poem of his, or a fine saying or passage that I cannot quote from memory; and if you were to hear how she under-values—despises them."

"They will settle all these little matters between themselves."

"I know I detain you, dear papa, but I will do my best to save him. Remember, Hilary Dove, her father, is your worst enemy. Save him—my Oberon, dear papa—from that vile connexion, and I will live to bless you. Mamma is coming up the long avenue; she will be here. I must not appear thus agitated before her. Do you forgive me, dear papa?"

"From my heart, Ernestine. May God forgive

you ; for 'tis him you have offended. Retire to your room, my child."

The father kissed his weeping daughter, and was soon joined by his wife, to whom, as matters stood, he could offer but little consolation.

All now depended on the doctor. But, no ! there was one hope left, still one solitary hope. That proud father would try it. He would do anything rather than risk the life of his darling child, the sole heir of his house and fortunes.

Sir Ulysses Kennard saw his patient the next day. He had previously heard from her father a full account of the real state of affairs ; he had thus been enabled to make, as it were, a thorough diagnosis of the disease. The physician was a bland, gentlemanly man, and soon placed the young sufferer quite at her ease, and even interested her by his pleasing conversation. But he saw no improvement, rather deterioration.

"You may try change of scene and air, if you like, and I advise it. But guided by my experience in many similar cases, there is only one safe remedy for these rooted affections. Offer no opposition. Let things take their course. The disease will often in this way cure itself, especially if there is repulsion on one side. I have met this young fellow, Spell, at the house of his uncle, in Eaton Place. He is a very fine young man ; one could make anything out of such materials. His college course was highly distinguished ; and at the bar, trust me, he is sure to make his way to eminence. He is a very remarkable person, and has my warmest well wishes."

" You anticipate many of my own conclusions, Sir Ulysses. It would not be difficult to place him in a position which would justify an alliance with my daughter."

Lady Wheatley looked astonishment, but was too well-bred to express dissent from her husband.

" I think your choice would not be misplaced, Sir Roger, and we must not only hope the best but try the best; for I ought not to conceal from you, that the case is serious. There is a glitter in the eye which I do not like. I would at first see the effects of change of scene and constant occupation, as far as possible in your ladyship's company. If this should fail, and our patient should become worse, I candidly advise you, as a friend, since you have done me the honour to ask my opinion, to see Mrs. Spell. She is a very sensible, superior lady, and earnestly devoted to her son. She will, no doubt, do much to raise his fortunes, and save him from what may be—though I do not understand the circumstance—a *mésalliance ;* but I refer to the young person, Dove."

" We will follow your excellent counsel, Sir Ulysses. Meanwhile, I should observe that young Spell's family, on both mother and father's side, are of gentle blood, so to speak. The young man himself has certainly the unerring stamp of a gentleman, in person, in manners, and bearing."

" I ought, perhaps, to mention," said the physician, " for there has heretofore been no secret in the matter, that Spell's cousin, Miss Lever, a wealthy heiress too, has long been designed for him."

" Such was the case, I believe," said Lady Wheatley, " but Mr. Lever himself now, I understand, entertains quite different views. That engagement, if ever there was one, has been off some time."

" Indeed ! I have not visited the family of late ; but you know your course. Our charming young patient must be saved !"

With this, the friendly and professional interview ended.

CHAPTER XXIII.

THE ELECTION.*

IT did not suit Sir Roger Wheatley's political plans, interest, or position to be absent from the county at that moment. The elections were pending. Hilary Dove was once more on the spot, and a most active and, let us add, able opposition was got up against the Conservative candidate. The great object was to carry two Liberals for Riverside, thereby giving it a real party voice in the affairs of the nation, instead of the present tame balance of neutrality. Sir Felix Sackville's seat was safe. He and his father and grandfather before him had been the stock Whig members. He was a good landlord and a great sportsman, a thick and thin supporter of the Liberal government, and very wealthy withal. He was, therefore, very popular with men of all parties. Those who differed from him in politics liked his consistency. They could calculate upon the man, although his vote might be sure to clash with their own special views. Decided politicians, like decided characters of every kind, are esteemed in England.

Sir Roger Wheatley belonged to the old school

* It will be seen by the context that this election took place before the Reform Bill of 1867-68 became law.

of members of parliament, among whom there pre-
vailed the notion of a description of divine right in
the great owners of the soil to rule the people.
With them the feudal idea had not died out with
the advance of individual liberty. They held the
largest stake in the nation, and had therefore, so
they thought, the best title to make its laws and
govern it. They sometimes forgot that it was men
they had to rule and not broad acres, or they really
believed that the masses in every population were
incapable of thinking for themselves or of independent action, and that the select few must always
govern the aggregate many. Hence hero-worship,
the domination of kings, the sway of priests, and
the reverence claimed by title and property. These
were necessary elements of a compact and powerful
society. The imperial and aristocratic principle
developed itself naturally in the constitution of
communities, and Toryism was but the regular consequence of ambition among a people—a sure sign
of healthy action and due subordination in all the
members. There must be a head—there must be
a centre to approach whither the efforts of all will
tend ; and in proportion to the stability and authority of the supreme direction, the well-being of the
inferior agents and their vigour and most productive
energy will be established. Let Liberalism do what
it would it could not shake these innate and
universal principles of the union of human kind.
Sir Roger Wheatley and others of his class indeed
felt that the very circumstance of an election of
legislators in itself ignored the prerogatives of riches

and station. This was a fact which could not be got over. But notwithstanding, he and his party would do their utmost to conserve as much as possible of the aristocratic element in the democratic portion of the government; because if allowed its full scope, the popular branch, overwhelming in numbers, would weigh down the others and bring all to the ground. The Conservative candidate was also an excellent landlord, an enlightened social reformer, and if anything wealthier than his friend and colleague, Sir Felix Sackville. By all who knew him he was beloved. The agricultural party were entirely with him, and the most affluent and settled inhabitants of the boroughs. His natural fears were from the threatened opposition votes of the numerous new towns and extensions which had sprung up everywhere in the county. These, if not won over to his side, must swamp his supporters.

Mr. Nutmeg, the Radical candidate, was altogether of a different stamp from the two sitting members. He was literally a man of the people. He had sprouted from nothing—a pure city mushroom. He began as an errand-boy in the very warehouse where he was now magnate and principal. He commenced life as a beggar and became a millionaire. This he owed neither to great industry, wonderful perseverance, superior attainments, nor enlarged mind. How then did he rise? By the exercise of two arts: he always made the most of opportunities, and cuffed down where he could everybody before him. There never was a man who could show what he did to greater advan-

tage, or more skilful in making little of and undermining others. He was great in keeping both
superiors and inferiors in their places. In fact,
Gregory Nutmeg was a natural aristocrat, and
people soon began to feel it. He rose almost
miraculously, and had actually to learn to read and
write in order to fill the posts offered to him. Spell
he never could, but got over this rather necessary
acquirement by employing a secretary in after years,
and by seldom putting his pen to paper, except in
matters of pure business, for which he was entirely
capable. But then, in assumption he was always
equal to his position, never abashed, no matter
what his defects. He readily and summarily put
down all signs of opposition. He was dreaded in
the warehouse. For that he cared little. The
chiefs thought him a useful and able man, and
when a junior was introduced among them he
always undertook to patronise and direct him. In
time these became the heads, and the heads had
long ago acknowledged him for their master.
Where he could he ground down everybody. Under
him they had no chance to rise. But Mr. Nutmeg
practised one peculiar art; he always made it a
point to assist unfortunate city men when in the
very depths of distress. His custom was first to
ruin, then to aid; taking care that he secured ample
protestations of gratitude from those he had most
injured. The abject letters of thanks he received
this way would fill a large range of volumes. The
smaller the trifle given to the miserable applicants
the more fervent and extreme the acknowledge-

ment. With all his shortcomings Mr. Nutmeg was not a vulgar man, not naturally vulgar. His tongue and his appetites were under control, and no one with this power of restraint can be said to be coarse. Manners, in the conventional sense, he had none beyond those of a shopboy; but these are matters which result from long training and imitation, till custom becomes a habit. His most uncouth displays were in the dining and drawing-rooms. There, though he kept a very grand house, he made sad mistakes, and was truly uncomfortable. But in the city and his warehouse Mr. Nutmeg was quite the gentleman—quite so. Didn't he know how to silence intruders, and to keep snobs and upstarts in their places, and to awe wretched creditors to the earth! He had been over and over again solicited to become a common councilman. It would have been easy for him to rise to an alderman and to be lord mayor, but he left these paltry Gog and Magog honours to small men and shopkeepers. When elected to serve as sheriff, he paid the fine like a man of substance and position, and delegated the summoning of juries, the incarceration of debtors, and the hanging of felons to persons of an inferior stamp who coveted the office. He would not be Jack Ketch with a silver collar.

This was the veritable man of the people selected by the Reform Club to contest the county of Riverside with the distinguished Conservative member, Sir Roger Wheatley. The train was laid well. At first Mr. Nutmeg was by no means prominent. He was known to live in a very fine mansion in Tipton,

that convenient suburban amphitheatre of villas.
His name appeared largely in the city subscriptions.
This was the modern benevolent way of claiming
oppidan honours. The higher the figure the greater
the man. The worshipful the aldermen, the
sheriffs in their gilded carriages, and the right
honourable the lord mayor himself, could not cope
with the man whose least subscription to a *public*
charity was a hundred guineas. This it was which
gave Gregory Nutmeg a true place among city
magnates. But beyond this he was scarcely known
in the county. However, Hilary Dove soon bruited
his fame far and wide. He had taken up the
grocer's cause, and it would not be his fault if he
was not soon the most popular man in Riverside or
the kingdom. Iris, the beautiful and showy Iris,
accompanied her father. She was his select and
holiday companion, his foil for any plebeian shortcomings he might exhibit. He was proud of her,
and the very earth she trod seemed, too, to be proud
of her, so lovely had she become, so grand and imposing in appearance. As tall as her father (Hilary
was of a good size), but though young, more
stately in her carriage, with her open sunny countenance, and, let us add, with the best costume of
the day, the daughter of the agitator, arm-in-arm
with him, passed through the streets and public
parks and promenades, an object of universal attrac-
tion, and in many instances of admiration, homage,
and tender regard. She did not, indeed, mix up
with the political meetings. That would have been
unseemly; but she was present at most of them

when the gathering-place was of suitable importance and respectability; and her affability and extraordinary beauty not only won personal admirers, but conciliated for the advocate and his cause attention and consideration, where otherwise he might not have been listened to or well received.

A specimen one from the stock speeches of the demagogue, the other from an address of Andrew Cubborn's, will each best explain the tack and course cleared for the rival candidates by their respective pioneers. The scenes lie in the pair of competing hotels, The Innerman and The Comforter, which graced the capital of the county. There was scarcely a pin to choose in the accommodation afforded by each of these showy houses of entertainment. The Innerman depended on the public and drew all it could from each customer, and the Comforter depended on customers and squeezed as much as could be squeezed out of the public. Their system was identically the same, the only difference being in what was a customer and what the public. Both were good to fleece, which was the sole object of the innkeepers. Mr. Dove and the Liberal party took up their quarters at the Innerman, while Mr. Cubborn and the Conservatives were housed in the Comforter.

The large room of the Innerman was densely crowded, to hear the address of Mr. Hilary Dove in favour of the liberal candidate, Gregory Nutmeg, Esq. There was a raised platform, on which some ladies were seated, the wives and daughters of Mr. Nutmeg's committee; among these Iris Dove, foremost in personal beauty and grace and richness of attire, had the place of honour. Several gentlemen immediately surrounded the chair, which was filled by Mr. Alderman Dips, late Lord Mayor of London. There was immense cheering when the orator appeared, the gentlemen shouting and clapping their hands, and the ladies waving their handkerchiefs. At length, silence being obtained, the chairman duly coughed, and then proceeded in a neat speech to introduce that great bulwark of the liberal cause, Mr. Hilary Dove, to the respectable meeting, who in reality needed no introduction. " He is here to speak for himself," said Alderman Dips, and sat down.

" Mr. Chairman, ladies and gentlemen," began Hilary Dove, " I am not here to interest your feelings, my business is to arouse your patriotism, to convince your judgment. The time will soon come when the voters present will have a great constitutional right in their hands. For once in your lives you will be kings, and have the destinies of this great empire confided to you. Not alone the existing generation, but remote posterity will feel how you exercise this great privilege. The future, gentlemen, is built upon the present. The foundation is to be your work ; and as you lay it, so will the superstructure be. The inhabitants of this town and county, the kingdom at large, the whole British empire, to our most distant colonies, are truly and virtually concerned in your choice of a member of the legislature. The mighty stake at your disposal may be given some of you only this time, to exercise at the election to come. It will be the grandest moment of your lives, and it behoves us all to employ it in a manner worthy of the occasion. Our forefathers have vindicated for us this right; they have fought and bled, and counselled and watched to obtain it; they are our eager witnesses. To your safe keeping they have confided *Magna Charta*, the Bill of Rights, the *Habeas Corpus*, this present prerogative of free voters, and all our dearly bought, cherished liberties. Let us beware how we use a trust so sacred. It belongs not to ourselves alone, but to the illustrious chiefs of the past and to Englishmen yet unborn. There are two great parties in this country—the Liberal party and the Tories. Now, what I want to ask is, why should there be party views at all as respects the House of Commons? It is the assembly of the people—their representatives. Ours is a mixed constitution, and there is the seat of the democracy. What right, I demand, has aristocracy to intrude itself there? The people do not invade the prerogative of the Queen : God forbid ! They don't meddle with the privileges of the Peers. Oh, if they did, how loud would be the outcry ! Why, then, I require, in the name of all that is constitutional, just, and fair, should the Tories, representatives, not of the popular interest, but of the imperial and aristocratic branches of the State, interfere with the third division, which belongs wholly and solely to the people? I know it is assumed that the action of party is good for the nation ; that it works well for pure administration and wholesome legislation. There never was a more fatal fallacy, gentlemen.

Party turns the House of Commons into an arena
of contention for office.   The struggle of members
is not for the public weal, but for private, selfish,
and corrupt ends.   The whippers-in, and not principle, knowledge, or justice, decide the great
questions of government.   Now, were there no
parties, did these abnormal divisions not exist in our
portion of the legislature—were the members all
Liberals—that is, all wholly and solely devoted to
the cause of the people—you would no longer have
the sad experience of the greatest and most important public questions postponed from year to year
for want of a sufficient majority to carry them.   A
house divided against itself, proverbially, cannot
stand; and, trust me, that the day will come, if this
state of things be not altered, when it will be acknowledged that party has been the ruin of our free
government.   When I speak of a lower assembly
all composed of Liberals, do not mistake me; I do
not mean to say men all of one opinion; no, that
would be unattainable; but what I do mean to say
is, that no member of the popular house should
declare himself to be there to represent the aristocratic elements of the constitution.   What can be
more absurd and inconsistent than to hinder a peer
from interfering in elections and, nevertheless, allow
the nominees of peers, their representatives and tools,
to stand up before you and claim your suffrages?
I repeat, party government is the bane of our House
of Commons.   For this reason alone time is frittered
away, the business of the nation is neglected; and,
instead of the lower chamber presenting any of the

grave and regular features of a senate, it often becomes a mere debating club, or the scene of conversations which would discredit a lady's tea-table. So much then for the party of resistance, which is only a resistance to all sound, practical, and progressive legislation. I should like to know why an organized opposition should be so beneficial in the House of Commons, and so distracting and disastrous in all other councils? Decide, then, this moment, gentlemen, so far as you are concerned, that this baneful antagonism shall cease. And do not be led away with the idea that the difference between the Liberals and the Tories is small. It is great, gentlemen, very great. It reaches the heart of the constitution itself; it is a pure contradiction—the distinction between motion and rest—progress and inaction. The Conservative cry has ever been, ' we have gone far enough ;' ' further advance will place liberty itself in danger.' This is their watchword, their master argument. Let us go back a little, my friends, and inquire who are those Tories? There was a time when the government of this country was purely regal and aristocratic. The king reigned and ruled, calling the lords spiritual and temporal and the knights of the shires occasionally into one great assembly—for they all sat together—to vote supplies and to consult upon the affairs of the nation. Such was the anti-popular origin of most of our laws ; in fact there was no people. Well, it is very hard to forego any privilege; and the barons and landholders had gone on from age to age believing themselves, with the Sovereign, the rulers of the kingdom. In

time the masses, who had been the serfs and clients
of the king and barons, obtained power, and a House
of Commons, much as it is now, was formed.   But
some of the old leaven remained, and legislation was
mainly carried on to secure or extend the interests
of the landlords.   It was only natural that a body
of wealthy and powerful men, owners of the soil,
and in later days, of large funded property, should
support their own order, and ignore or forget the
rights of the people.   I defy any one to examine
our laws and to say that this evidence of an exclusive aristocratic and patrician spirit, intention, and
endeavour, is not to be found throughout all our
statutes down to the present half-century.   Self-
preservation is the first law of nature; and the
Tories, long before they got that name, took good
care of themselves.   I scarcely blame them ; knowing our common inclinations and tendencies, I am
willing to excuse them. They looked to themselves.
I am here, gentlemen, simply to ask you to do the
same.   Do you look to yourselves and your own
interests.

" But how was this state of things amended ?
There was generally but one great party in the times
to which I am alluding—the party of the king and
nobles.   The first great break-down towards democracy was the quarrel of Henry the Seventh with
the barons.   Then came another and mightier popular movement—the Reformation.   After that we
had the Revolution.   The people, you see, were all
along gaining, while the powers that swayed had
some reason to exclaim that Church and State were

in danger. But they did make the outcry, and continued it all through, down to the Reform Bill and up to the present hour. There arose two parties then; the wealthy and powerful holding what they had, grasping it firmly, and the people, that is, the Liberals, under whatever name they were called, resisting the oppressions and encroachments of tyranny. This went on, gentlemen, until the democratic element of opposition became the staple of the House of Commons; and it now happened, that the Tories, driven from their former high ground by repeated manly assaults, became in their turn to be regarded as the party of resistance. This is their condition at the present moment. The people, that is, again I say, the Liberals, have gone on enforcing the concession of their rights; and now they are in a position, if they will only see their own interests and exert the power, to extirpate the aristocratic element altogether from the lower assembly. God forbid that you should think I mean by this, that the real respectability, knowledge, and justice of the House of Commons should be excluded. No. What I desire is to see the Constitution on its normal basis—the inferior chamber solely for the people, the aristocratic element being amply represented by the Sovereign and Peers. When this is effected we shall have able and progressive legislation.

"And only see what we Liberals have done! I forbear to go back to what some of the barons, the regular clergy, and at a later period the Puritans and other champions of liberty, have wrested from the tyrants who ruled over the destinies of this country. I would only remind you that within your own memories, we have carried the repeal of the Test and Corporation Acts, Catholic Emancipation, the Reform Bill, the Amendment of the Navigation Laws, the improvement of our Criminal Code, and last, not least, our glorious triumph—Free Trade! The Tories say that some of these were their measures; but if they were we extorted them, they could not help themselves, and yielded rather than throw up office or cause a revolution. Let the good work go on then, and we shall clear the House of Commons of those miserable party quarrels, those disgraceful manœuvres which now distract its counsels and hinder useful legislation. Only see, gentlemen, the baleful effect of this spirit of division in our own county. For the last five parliaments you have returned two members as usual ; but where, I ask, has been your voice in the councils of the nation ? Our worthy and consistent representative Sir Felix Sackville, was always ranged on the right side in questions of great moment. But up started Sir Roger Wheatley from the opposition benches, and rendered his vote—your vote—a nullity. Here, then, is a palpable result of party government. Let us do away with this anomaly, gentlemen, in the name of common sense, just, right, and honourable patriotism.

"And who is it you are bound to reject, gentlemen? A man who says, 'there shall be no more reform, we have gone far enough ;' 'There shall be no abolition of Church-rates, the sacred institution is in danger ;' 'There shall be no Ballot, the landlords must know their enemies;' ' There shall be no further retrenchment, the army and navy must be supported.' In a word, encroachment must be staid, the *status quo* preserved, the rights of property respected ; that is, the old tyranny must be enforced as far as possible. Oh, how I abhor such despotism ! It is not what we are, gentlemen, but what we should be, if the Tories all along had their own way. We should be as other enslaved peoples, not the freemen we are here, deliberating on the highest functions of government, which so soon we shall have the power to exercise. I urge nothing personal against Sir Roger Wheatley. It ought to be enough that I proclaim he is a Tory ; he will neutralize your vote in the House of Commons, disfranchising the county. But I could tell you a tale, gentlemen, ay, one that would rouse your manly indignation, as husbands, as brothers, and as fathers. It is now some years ago since a fair girl, a near and dear relation of mine, she was then a mere child, a playful little thing, yet with great intelligence and the best of feelings. Well, this wee maiden was in Edelstone Park, the seat of the great Sir Roger Wheatley ; and what was the young lady doing, think you? She was not plucking flowers, or destroying the fences, or chasing the deer, or scaring the wild fowl, or even disturbing the gravel ; she was simply reciting a poem written by a friend of her childhood who was present, Oberon Spell, and in company with another little boy, now a rising artist, Hugh Graff, when who should sweep by but the baronet's proud daughter, and ordered my child—ay, my child, ladies and gentlemen, to be expelled from the grounds, and never again to enter them. I knew I should enkindle your anger, and I have done so purposely, that if any supporter of Sir Roger Wheatley is here he should do now as I did at that moment. I vowed no vengeance, I left that to a Higher Power; but I said within my heart, there must be an innate and rooted feeling and principle of tyranny here to induce a mere child—as this daughter of the baronet was then—to issue a peremptory command to an inoffensive damsel, merely entertaining her two juvenile companions in a quiet intellectual manner. The effect was that I gave my almost undivided attention to politics; and, gentlemen, you pretty well understand how strong was the force of my enlightenment and conviction: from a blind and ignorant Tory I became what I am, thank Heaven! a foremost disciple and advocate of the great and glorious Liberal cause—a cause with which is identified the progress of the entire human race. I could also narrate another deed of cruelty and oppression perpetrated by Sir Roger Wheatley himself. A certain brooch belonging to this same imperious daughter, was lost, ladies and gentlemen; I had the good fortune to find it in an assembly almost as numerous as the one I have the honour of addressing: and what did I do? Only what every honest man should, and for this I ask no praise. I proclaimed my treasure-trove and fastened it on my coat publicly where the loser might see and own it. This was done, as some of you may remember, in the sight of all. Well, the article was afterwards claimed by a person who represented herself as Miss Wheatley's maid. And what did my wife, in whose possession the brooch then was, gentlemen; well, what did Mrs. Dove do, ladies and gentlemen? why she did what every worthy woman here would do, she gave it to the person so lawfully and authoritatively claiming it. This person happened to be an impostor and a thief. But now learn how our enlightened and merciful Tory member acted. During my absence from my home—Proscenium Villa—he sent in two detectives, and a policeman's wife to search Mrs. Dove, my child Iris, and every cranny and corner of my house. Of course no brooch was found; and this was the reward that honesty and honour got from the sitting Tory member for Riverside. 'Tis true I made him smart for his rashness and oppression: he paid a heavy pecuniary fine rather than go to a public trial. But no amount of gold could heal my wounded feelings. I have never been the same man since that hour, ladies and gentlemen. However, the ordeal and suffering did me good; they converted me to the cause of the people. From a slave—the servile political supporter of this man, I became a thinking being, a freeman, a staunch, unswerving, determined Liberal. And now, gentlemen, you have a duty to perform, and I have one. We must, then, on our side expel this principle of despotism and party spirit, represented so faithfully by Sir Roger Wheatley. The man who does not aid in the good work, is, I say, an enemy to his country.

" Happily for your choice, gentlemen, Mr. Nutmeg

seeks to represent this great county in parliament. He is exactly the description of candidate I would recommend to your selection. He is a man of the people, sprung from the people. I know the city well, and I know how highly Mr. Nutmeg is respected. His career has been that of a foremost citizen. He must have had rare and original qualities to rise to the eminence he has attained. He must have combined ability, perseverance, extensive knowledge of trade and commerce, great public liberality united to private economy, a habit of conciliating his inferiors and studying their interests, and of commanding the recognition of those above him by his superior powers, sterling integrity, and consistent and manly conduct. In a word, he must possess the art of governing. Such is the candidate for your choice, gentlemen—such the representative to be the exponent of your opinions and the supporter of your interests in the House of Commons. We are a nation of shopkeepers, Mr. Nutmeg is a shopkeeper on a large scale. His concerns are yours. He desires cheap tea, so do you; sugar, coffee; the ladies will join us in declaring that such is their wish also—quite a feminine, domestic ambition. But rising higher, gentlemen, to the great argument of the State, I am instructed to say, that Mr. Nutmeg is a staunch advocate of an extension of the Suffrage, of the Ballot, of the total and uncompromising Abolition of Church-rates, of Free-Trade in its widest and best acceptation, of Civil and Religious Liberty, of Peace and Retrenchment, of the diffusion of Education, and the protection

and amelioration of the condition of the Poor all
over the kingdom. Above all, gentlemen, he is
opposed to the evils of party government, and will
go into the House of Commons, should you elect
him, for the sole purpose of studying the welfare of
the people, and advancing the greatness and glory
of the nation, confirming and establishing its institutions, and handing it down improved, strengthened
and elevated to his successors. But it is for you,
gentlemen, to unite and combine with these noble
and patriotic resolves. The power is in your hands.
You are now disfranchised, or misrepresented;
secure two good Liberal votes, and thus do your
part and duty in asserting those rights without the
possession of which life would be insupportable, and
this great kingdom, like some foreign countries, a
mere fastness of corruption and tyranny."

Mr. Dove sat down amid thunders of applause.
He had agreeably disappointed his audience; they
came to be amused, they went away convinced.
Many of those present dated their Liberalism from
that night. The truth is, as the contest approached,
the deeply wounded husband and father became
serious and earnest. For upwards of six years had
he cherished his resentment—had he studied his
cause; and now that the moment was at hand to
give effect to his feelings, all his soul and energy
were concentrated in the battle. He would rout
Sir Roger Wheatley! he would crush the Cubborns!

Turn we next to the agent of the Conservative
candidate. He, too, had his cause at heart. So
much of his own personal success and interest de-

pended on the election of Sir Roger Wheatley for the county. He dreaded his wife's anger; he feared that the loss of the battle would cost him the Priory connexion. It must be said, moreover, that at bottom Andrew Cubborn was a good Conservative. He never shone to greater advantage than in these heated political contentions; he felt it to be his interest as well as duty to present every obstacle he could to the schemes and efforts of Hilary Dove. He remembered with some bitterness that he himself, or rather his termagant wife, was the cause of the break between the commission agent and the baronet. He wisely kept his forbidden son out of the way, leaving him to stay at home or in his London chambers, to concoct plots with his mother. But Trapper accompanied his principal; he was of sovereign use as manager and ostensible proprietor of the *Flam.* The Tory journal had fallen into the lawyer's hands by one of those nefarious plans through which so many newspapers and literary records change their owners. The unfortunate possessor was supplied with money to effect improvements, at an enormous interest and on the security of the property. When he could not repay the advances, Mr., or rather Mrs. Cubborn, claimed the whole for the clerk and secretary, the real acting proprietor being the lady in crimson in the central office at Edelstone. About this time, too, the strong suspicions excited against the Cubborns on account of the fire, began to die out. By a piece of machiavellian cunning the tables were turned. The newspaper paragraph had been placed and circulated.

Whispers and innuendos got rife. There was another and more probable cause for the conflagration; Oberon Spell's fair fame suffered in proportion to the general acquittal of the real incendiaries. This was pretty well the state of things when Mr. Andrew Cubborn took his stand on the "Comforter" platform.

"Gentlemen, I am proud to see you assembled in such numbers. It shows the deep interest you take in the present contest and the cause of your country. This unpaid devotion to public affairs is a national virtue. There are no people who dedicate so much time, attention, and money to the general good as we English. If ever there was a moment when the patriotic sentiment should be encouraged and practised, it is now, gentlemen. We are at a crisis. All our old landmarks are threatened. This is an hour for self-sacrifice and self-oblivion. Every impulse and energy in us should be called out to save the country. We are menaced with a Radical assault on the State, an organic change in the constitution, and if you and other Conservatives do not stand forward and resist the attack, as sure as there is a sun in the heavens the' kingdom will fall. The salvation of your country is in your hands, and you are expected to do your duty.

"Before I proceed to examine the more weighty questions before us, I will clear away the rubbish cast up in another place, to obstruct, confound, and alarm you. We have heard much talk of party government, and it has been described as an unmitigated evil. Now, gentlemen, I do not assert that if the business of the nation could be conducted without differences of opinion, the result would not be satisfactory; but so long as those differences exist and there is no means of preventing them, their reduction to order and discipline must be an advantage. We do not want a parliament of crotchets where everyone will have his say, and the whole assembly, like congresses I could name, is a Babel. I say, then, if differences must continue, let us manage them with the least possible inconvenience and damage to the public service. This alone can be done by the recognition of two great parties in the State. These regularly constituted bodies have their prescribed rules, their parliamentary usages. They acknowledge their chiefs, they follow them, they suppress their own upstart notions for the permanent success of a cause, and in this way not only the strongest united force is given to the Opposition; but, on the other side, the most powerful incentive is applied to good government. In actual practice the party contentions in both chambers are rare, occurring, perhaps, only once or twice in a session. On all other occasions the business of the House goes on, helped forward, I am happy to say, by Oppositionists without distinction. It is surprising what an amount of legislation is got through which never strikes the public eye.

" A great deal of nonsense has been spoken about freeing the House of Commons from its aristocratic element. Can our new magician change human nature ? The patrician sentiment prevailing in the lower assembly of our legislature is only an expression of feeling and opinion inseparable from certain forms of thought and action. It is most probable that a great landholder or owner of other large property, will regard legislation from the side of possession, mastery, or dominion. But have we no such interests to represent in the kingdom? Is England a nation of slaves and paupers? What are laws for, if not for the protection of life and property? While there is such a thing as owner-ship in the country, I contend that the prior and original right is to maintain it, and that it should be first defended. I hope you at least, gentlemen, have something to own and to protect. I am sure it is not your interest to send into parliament a body of tribunes and agrarian levellers. The same, thank heaven, applies at present to every voter in the United Kingdom. The barons and early kings have been assailed for the character of their legisla-tion. 'Tis true, they had not the advantage of political economy, or the prices current, or money-market to guide them. They had no leading articles in the newspapers. There was no public opinion then, gentlemen. But notwithstanding, the foun-dation of all our liberties was laid by them and the conservation of our religion. For my own part, I look back with a feeling of gratitude and reverence on those great men who fought and bled for our freedom—father and son often stretched dead or dying on the same plain in defence of their pos-sessions and country, not always against external enemies, but in opposition to the oppressive acts of individual tyrants. I am pained and annoyed at the ingratitude displayed by upstarts profaning the noblest names and epochs of our history. If we are a people, if we are a nation, if there is liberty, religion, prosperity, I say we mainly owe them to the counsels, the struggles, and the battles of our baronial forefathers ; for the country may well claim kindred with those to whom it owes its very existence. Sweep their influence out of the House of Commons indeed ! sweep human nature, faith, freedom, honour, gratitude, memory, history, property —all we live for, revere, and love—and then, and then only, will you succeed in extinguishing the aristocratic feeling and tendency in our popular assembly. But instead of the patrician sentiment being too strong in the lower chamber, it is, I contend, far too feeble, as is evidenced by the ultimate constitution of the house. Chosen by the people, it holds the public purse, it virtually elects or rejects the ministers. In fact, the real power of the kingdom is in its hands, and only by shifts and contrivances, by fictions and ingenious compensations, but more than all by a courteous understanding and forbearance, can we stave off the despotic effects of republican domination.

" The speaker I am alluding to confined his observations to the House of Commons. He forgot that in the chamber of peers there is often a very strong Liberal sentiment and party, ay, and on the throne itself, or, which is the same thing in effect, among the responsible advisers of the Crown. Surely this is an ample set-off for any prevalence of an oligarchic feeling or action in the lower assembly. The truth is, the same self-willed human nature prevails everywhere; and as we have ascendency in the Commons, we have democracy among the Lords. Party feelings and interests are pretty fairly divided and distributed in the three branches of the legislature, only unfortunately we have a too frequent display of Radicalism from the throne in the presence amongst us of a *quasi* Whig government. But the whole theory about parties is as ignorant as it is false. The House of Commons is intended to represent the entire population—men, women, and children, poor and rich, electors and non-electors, the rights of the Queen on her throne, as well as those of the meanest cottier in his cabin. It was never intended to represent any special class or interest—certainly not the unpropertied masses alone, not any particular holding or corner, any exclusive division, borough, or county, but the whole British empire. And it is to be hoped there is as much aristocracy and property in the country to represent as there is plebeianism and pauperism. I trust I have disposed of the elaborate essay on party government, gentlemen.

" I come now to the real issue we have to try at the forthcoming election. It is the question between Conservatism and Liberalism, which is the better calculated, under existing circumstances, to advance the permanent interests of the country. I take it for granted, that if the extreme Liberals win their way in the House of Commons, we shall have a ten-pound county and a six-pound borough franchise as the law of the land; that is, the whole legislation and government of the country will be in the hands of the uneducated and impoverished many—the multitude—the mob—the lowest class in the kingdom. I am speaking to sensible and practical men, and I ask you in your experience what you are to expect from electors paying for their cottages 3s. 10d. a week to entitle them to a county vote, and 2s. 3½d. a week to a borough vote? They will naturally cleave to their own order. They will follow demagogues who will profess to study and carry out their clients' immediate views. Remember, they are strong enough in numbers to out-vote all the other classes taken together. As society advances, as the community becomes richer, rents increase, and the men occupying six pound, ten pound, ay, and fifty pound houses in these days are not to be classed with the tenants paying the same amount twenty years ago. They are of an inferior grade. So that the humblest rank of labourers, costermongers, sweeps, and other roughs, may be expected to occupy the 2s. 3d. cabins—a choice body to erect into an electoral constituency. The 3s. 10d. occupants in town and rural districts are to swamp and annul the votes of you, gentlemen, as if this were not done sufficiently now by the new order of fifty-pound electors found in houses of this moderate value in the suburbs springing up everywhere around London.

"Well, when the rights of property and intelligence are ignored and abolished, and the ten-pound and six-pound men have the laws in their own hands, their first operation will be to extend the franchise to its consistent and normal limits. We shall have universal suffrage—it may be that not male adults alone, but women and children—the strong household of your family-man—will each have a vote. This I say is the correct conclusion from premises so disastrous and absurd, from the adoption of a qualification so immoderately low. They may stop short of anarchy, though I am not so sure of that, but it is quite clear that they will covet a redistribution of property. When once you let loose the three-and-tenpenny and two-and-threepenny roughs on society and make them your political masters, you must expect an agrarian revolution—the England of present and past generations will be gone for ever. We shall have a new era—the era of democracy—where the servants will be the superiors, the unpropertied classes will rule the owners of property, and where respectable men will stand aloof and give up government and legislation to incapable and unprincipled agitators. Such, gentlemen, will be the sure effect of electing men of Mr. Nutmeg's stamp as the nation's representatives in parliament.

"But it is said that the working classes would not abuse their power, that they would strive for the glory and greatness of the country, and seek equal right and justice for all. I know not where it is found that working men so nobly and heroically differ from other men and from human nature. They would be an overwhelming and overpowering majority, not composed of various grades balanced one against the other, as the electors are now, but a

compact class, the sole arbiters of the House of
Commons.   I say, then, they would study their
own interests.   They would stand by their order.
They would, perhaps, seek for nothing that did not
look honest and fair.   They would consult their
immediate advantage—direct taxation, a volunteer
army and navy, a paid House of Commons, laws to
subdivide lands, and compel a more equal distribu-
tion of property, the abolition of a State church,
the abrogation of the peerage, the annulment of
hereditary rank, the destruction of the throne, and
the creation of a free republic.   There would be in
all these extremes a show of right and justice, an
abundant display of common sense, reason, and
argument; but its real force would be revolution
and confiscation.   There is in the theory of a pure
democracy a certain simplicity and beauty; the
best of men in all ages have been captivated by the
appearance; but the experience, like many a marriage, is anarchy or an ultimate tyranny.   Such, I
contend, would be the result in this country of further lowering the qualification.   I have watched
the trades unions, I have observed the conduct and
learnt the aspirations of some of our young city
men.   I know the feeling of the real producers of
the country—how eager they are to clutch a share
of their employers' profits.   I have carefully studied
the opinions of their organs, and I declare it as
my most matured judgment and conviction, that if
by deteriorating the franchise you lodge the electoral
power of the nation in their hands, a revolution is
inevitable.   And remember, gentlemen, we should

not have to deal with our own sex alone. There might be—there are—ambitious women, even among the meek and docile daughters of England; and Heaven help the State that shall be left to their tender mercy and justice.

"Where is to be the limit? Have we not descended low enough already? Consider that the increase of rents has made the qualification less than it was when the Reform Bill became law. You must draw a boundary line somewhere. If you remove the present humble barriers, the floods of democracy, ever pressing to rush in, will overwhelm the kingdom.

"A great deal has been urged about the people's right to the franchise. There can be no right here but expediency—the good of the greatest number. And here, as elsewhere in our social and political order, it is better that men should earn the privilege, and show some stake, consideration and security for its proper exercise. You do not make foremen or partners of the labourers or apprentices of your establishments. They must, as journeymen or able hands, first display competency and merit. The same safe rule, feel assured, holds good of the electoral body, who are *bonâ fide* partners in the great firm of the nation.

"After all, what is required is a competent and incorrupt legislature. You want an able and pure body of law-givers. So long as you secure that, the mere manner of choice—the number of the electors is not of such prime importance. I leave you to judge whether a beggarly mob, hounded on

by demagogues, is more likely to select the fitting
men, than voters who hold the property of the
county, and who are blessed with its largest share
of enlightenment and principle.

"But we shall have the ballot to protect the
voters! The ballot, gentlemen, can only mean a
cover for deception. No man wishes to hide what
he is not ashamed to do. Take away from your
Englishman the public exhibition of the hustings
and polling-booth, and you destroy his interest in
the election. Voting, as you know, is attended
with some trouble, and if the virtue of the man is
to lie concealed, I very much fear he will not act
for conscience sake or patriotism. But the ballot
would be a robbery—the perversion and confiscation
of a right belonging as much to the non-elector as
the elector. The franchise is a trust conferred on
certain propertied men for the good of the nation.
The two pound a year cottier, as well as the great
landlord, are equally represented at the poll. To
satisfy this indefeasible claim you must have universal suffrage in its extremest exercise, or there
ought to be open voting. But it will indeed be a
sad day, gentlemen, for the interest, the freedom,
and independence of election, when the overt and
manly competition at the polling-booth is trans-
formed into a secret and irresponsible system.
Already you have many more electors than will
trouble themselves, even when under the stimulus
of their fellow voters and the public eye, to use
their privilege. Only let the operation be hidden,
and you will find how few will put themselves out

of the way to record a vote which nobody can see
or recognise. I could go into an examination of
all the other blessings which Liberalism is to confer
on us. But this would be tedious, and our time is
limited. One thing must strike you in comparing
it with our principles—that no government is possible under its direction. The cabinet must be
Conservative in act, whatever they are in profession.
It may be said that this concedes the whole question ; for if ministers must be constitutionalists, it
matters little to what section of politicians they
nominally belong. No, gentlemen, the difference
is very serious indeed—it is whether you will
encourage hypocrisy or not. It ought not to be
tolerated, that men should squeeze themselves into
office by adapting their views to the crotchet-
mongers of the House of Commons, and then expand into statesmen when enthroned in Downing-
street. But the concession to conservatism is not
a little remarkable, and should decide any waverer
at once. What, then, shall we say that a Whig
administration and Tory administration are the
same ? No, I repeat again. The Liberal ministry
is too often forced along by their pledges and their
friends to adopt counsels which they would shrink
·from and reject were they unshackled. They must
please their party in doors and out of doors. This
is the real danger of giving them the predominance.

" The triumph of Radical principles will altogether disfranchise you, gentlemen. The moment
the constituency shall decide to elect Mr. Nutmeg,
it will proclaim an opinion, which, prevailing, must

swamp or annul your suffrage. You may go to the poll, indeed, but only to have your total and overwhelming defeat by the masses recorded. You have, then, simply to determine whether you will give away your votes to your servants and labourers making them your political masters. But I put the matter on the higher national ground. Is it wise or expedient to risk our present state of peace, order, and prosperity, to introduce a degree of popular licence unknown to our fathers? Ask yourselves how it happens that the nation is great and free, while so many states around us are either in a backward condition or enslaved? You will remember that all our liberties were achieved without this extreme extension of the franchise—achieved, in fact and truth, under the sway and principles of the old Toryism. On you and your co-electors throughout the kingdom it depends whether these blessings shall continue. To you, voters, God has confided the power to save or destroy the British nation—a nation, bear in mind, which has colonized and civilized more than half the globe. With you it rests whether we shall have a Queen—who may be said to be under your manly English protection ; whether we shall have a church for the poor as well as the rich ; whether steadfast and comely Christianity shall hallow the land ; whether the rights of property shall be maintained ; whether those honours to which we all, one way or other, aspire, shall be transmissible by the illustrious and heroic holders to their children as their lawful acquisitions ; whether we shall have the gravity and the efficacy of a senate in the House of Lords, balancing and composing the two extreme parties in the state; and finally, whether the House of Commons shall be an assembly of gentlemen comprising the wealth, intelligence, and respectability of the land, or whether these shall be driven from it and have to give place to adventurers and demagogues. These, gentlemen, are the mighty issues to be decided at the forthcoming elections.

" I am almost ashamed to compare the two candidates set before you for your choice. On the one side you have a baronet of ancient lineage, many of whose ancestors have fought and bled for their country, many more of whom have sat in public council for its good. You have an able statesman, an experienced politician, a man who has represented you in the House of Commons for upwards of thirty years, who knows the rules and usages of that assembly well, and the business of government and legislation. You have a large landholder and owner of funded property—pledges of his steadfast and conservative administration. You have a kind and considerate landlord, personally known to most of you, and from whom many have received acts of courtesy, favour, and liberality. You have a perfect gentleman, of whom the House of Commons is proud, and a man of the highest enlightenment and education. Above all, you have a candidate who will defend the Constitution in Church and State from the assaults of demagogues—men without property or principle—whose aim is to found a selfish republic on the ruins of this great and glorious nation. This is the experienced, tried, able, affable, wealthy, generous, and meritorious statesman, whom I am to place in comparison with Mr. Nutmeg, the grocer. No wonder, gentlemen, I should shrink from the invidious task. There are acts which in themselves are a satire, without penning a line or uttering a word.

"Mr. Nutmeg is almost a stranger to us all, gentlemen. He is a successful tradesman, who has advanced from very small beginnings in the metropolis. This may be to his credit. But I know something of city life; and my experience teaches me that not all men should be proud of their rise from humble circumstances. The tricks of trade are proverbial; and many a shabby trick may have been played, many a deed of oppression done, and of false pretence assumed, before a moneyless adventurer could mount to opulence and station in the city of London. I wish these observations to be regarded as general, not personal; for though I know this county well, of Mr. Nutmeg I know very little. We see his name to advantage in public subscriptions; but this kind of charity has now become a species of rivalry in great city houses—the badge and test of their respectability. I should be sorry to found my idea of any man's real benevolence or private bounty from these prominent and popular displays of his munificence. I shall, therefore, not dwell on this point, as a special merit and recommendation in the Radical candidate. I prefer considering the public qualities of business-men for the work of legislation. Why, gentlemen, the ablest of them are found to be either bores or non-entities in the

House of Commons. They are generally men of one idea, who never received any high training or regular education, who smell of the desk or the counter in all their proceedings, and are wholly unused and unfitted for the intellectual task of generalization. We seldom hear of statesmen or orators emanating from that class of members. As a case in point, who does the premier select for his Chancellor of the Exchequer—the business-man *par excellence* of the government? Not the merchant or trader, you may be sure; but the poet, the orator, the novelist, the philosopher, the thinker and statesman, who can comprehend a large and deep fiscal question, and administer the finances of a great nation in an enlightened spirit, involving practical results as well as recondite principles. You may be sure that such a man as Mr. Nutmeg, with all his boasted knowledge of commerce, would never be appointed by the Prime Minister to construct a budget, and explain its details to a full, eager, and expectant House of Commons. On the contrary, Sir Roger Wheatley was formerly in the Cabinet, and from his able and luminous financial views, which his speeches in the House amply testify, might not inappropriately be the object of the first-lord's choice for so important a department of administration; and this without having served a city apprenticeship to business. The truth is, gentlemen, very poor faculties are sufficient to conduct trade successfully. The operations are seldom of an intellectual order. Take a boy who from dulness has failed at everything else, and let him plod in a shop, warehouse, or counting-house, and you will find he gets on very well. In fact, it is only mediocrity that can rise in business; talent or genius would spurn its trammels, practices, and usages. The highest recommendation Mr. Nutmeg can have for the novel position he aspires to is that he has had the art of stepping before others, and must be supposed to possess some kind of pretension to sit in the presence of the natural leaders of his country. This forward virtue I willingly allow him.

"I do not wish to indulge in any loud and alarming cry—that the throne is in danger, the church is in danger, and the peerage is in danger. I have, nevertheless, proved that all three are in actual jeopardy, if not peril. Let only the three-and-tenpenny and two-and-threepenny franchise become law, and they will bring down these great institutions to the dust. I leave you, gentlemen, and your friends to judge how you should act in this situation. You are to decide whether hereafter men of your stamp shall be a nullity in the country, or that bulwark of the State which England has ever found in her sturdy yeomen. If you return Sir Roger Wheatley, unquestionably you neutralize your voice in the House of Commons on certain occasions; but is not this better than doubling the evil. Besides, the equal balance of votes will not happen often, and assuredly it will be a less inconvenience and obstruction than trailing Mr. Nutmeg at the heels of Sir Felix Sackville into the lobby on all great party divisions, to have him in most other instances an obstinate Radical, in mischievous, independent opposition.

"In a very few days, gentlemen, parliament will be dissolved; the Lord Chancellor will issue the Queen's writ, summoning a new parliament. It behoves us all on that unique and great occasion to do our duty, so that the illustrious dead who have confided to us this free and happy England shall have no cause of rebuke of us to trouble their spirits, and that distant posterity, enjoying the blessings of peace and liberty in a powerful and prosperous nation, shall hallow and honour the age which offered a timely resistance to the inroads of democracy, and transmitted to them, improved and consolidated, the liberal and beneficent institutions of our common country."

Mr. Cubborn evidently produced a deep impression on his hearers, and in the course of his speech elicited frequent long and loud applause. But somehow his success was not equal to the orator of the antagonist party. The lawyer was not personally popular, and his style of delivery and appearance were far inferior to those commanding recommendations in Hilary Dove. Besides, it must be admitted that the Liberals are the heartier class; they have generally something to gain by the movement; while the Conservatives in actual possession are slow to believe in existing danger. Moreover, in our opinion, the solicitor's address had not the vigour, strength, terseness, and logical point evinced in his rival's discourse. It was truer and more practical, more too in the vein of ordinary English speeches, but it went less home to the enthusiasm and expectations of the meeting. However, it had the honour of being printed in a pamphlet from the columns of the *Flam* at Sir Roger Wheatley's expense, who was so well pleased with the entire argument, that immediately on its perusal he forwarded a very handsome letter of thanks to Mr. Cubborn, enclosing a draft for a hundred pounds, for that gentleman's acceptance. Mr. Nutmeg thought it would be wiser not to make too much of his agent's efforts. In fact, he was somewhat jealous of his popularity; and on this occasion flew to his old practice—to kick the steps by which he rose from under him. Of course, he left this genial process till the struggle was over. For the present he was simply depreciatory. Neither candidate had much reason to be proud of the personal qualities of his representative. But they very well answered the heats and broils of a contested election.

At length the great day came. The writ had been issued, the hustings erected, the polling-places demarcated. The most systematic exertions had been employed on both sides. The excitement was very great all over Riverside and elsewhere in the kingdom. There were men in both camps who would have cheerfully laid down their lives to win the battle. Say that the public takes no interest in these struggles. But only witness any well-contested election. Hoary old fellows with one foot in the grave, fathers and sons, husbands, wives, and even children, were all fiery enthusiasts for victory. Nothing but the election was thought of or talked of; and many was the poor woman, trapseing one child by the hand with another in arms, and perhaps a pair before her who hurried to the scene, and only regretted her man had not a vote to make

" Summat on it, if it wor on'y a drop o' drink to comfort one." There were bands of music before the hotels and principal committee-rooms. Flags flaunting everywhere, ribbons to constitute an elec· toral order, beer, gin, and brandy-and-water in rivers. Who paid for it all our chronicler doth not record, but no doubt there was an arrangement. Hilary Dove kept up a regular army of roughs. They had strict orders only to make a noise, to roar and shout, cheer and groan, but to keep down fists and cudgels. A number of sturdy farmers undertook to guard the approaches to the hustings for Sir Roger Wheatley, Sir Felix Sackville, and their friends, and to groan lustily when little Nutmeg appeared. Clamour and hubbub were triumphant. The nomination somehow proceeded, but all was uproar and confusion. Nobody could hear anybody, though the vociferation from everybody was incessant and alarming. It was in vain that " Order, order !" was bawled, disorder reigned supreme. After a great deal of action and display, the show of hands was obtained. The old members, Sir Felix Sackville and Sir Roger Wheatley, were declared to have the majority. Upon this a shout was raised which rent the heavens, answered by a roar which seemed to

" Bellow from the vast and boundless deep."

A poll was demanded for Mr. Nutmeg ; and the days of real business quickly succeeded—anxious days and sleepless nights for the two contending candidates ; almost equally so for the electors. Not a voter in the county but was roused and stimulated. Mr. Nutmeg was resolved to win. Sir Roger Wheatley on his side had good reason to rely on the pluck and earnestness of his agricultural and propertied supporters. The numbers at first were entirely in his favour, and his return was considered sure. Sir Felix Sackville was safe. He had a help from both parties. When the contest was drawing towards its close, a large accession of Radical voters was collected together from the new towns, and rode in a train of omnibuses and cabs to the polling-place in the county capital. These advanced in a continuous stream with bands playing and colours flying, Hilary Dove heading the procession in an open carriage with Alderman Dips and the leading members of Mr. Nutmeg's chief committee. The triumphant approach of this jovial company decided the waverers, who were in great force in the town. Waifs and strays, they were holding back for their " commons," as they facetiously termed the electoral sugar. The whole move was consummately arranged, and decided the contest. When all the returns were counted up and had passed through a scrutiny, it was found that Sir Roger Wheatley was defeated by a majority of forty votes.

In the very midst of his chagrin, disappointment, and bustle, Mr. Cubborn dispatched a letter to his wife announcing the disaster. He attributed the loss to its proper cause—bribery. The lady replied by the same messenger, with her accustomed promptitude and energy :—

" And why the d—l didn't you bribe bigger ? If

the thing had to be done, it ought to have been done bravely. Ah! Andy Cubborn, you are a poor, paltry, sneaking creature, not worth your salt. Hilary Dove is the man for the occasion. It will not be your fault if a fine scheme of business be not ruined. At bottom I am not sorry that the bashaws have had a snubbing. Now is the time to bleed Wheatley while he is down. By-and-bye he will be himself again, kick, and grow saucy. Do make as much of the thing as you can, and come home. Bring that sot of a clerk of yours with you. I want him at my elbow for other business."

Such was the consolation Mrs. Cubborn thought fit to administer to her husband—the rub on the grazed skin in the way of domestic friction.

The only other incident worth recording in this heated contest was the appearance of Ernestine Wheatley and her mother in a private room in the Merry Thought, from which they could see all that was passing at the Edelstone polling-place.

"Oh! mamma, look! look! he is coming. Hugh Graff is with him. But they separate. Oberon on our side. Hurrah! hurrah! my life upon him. He is faithful. How grand he looks; but I think he is paler. That traitor, Graff, has actually gone and voted for old Nutmeg. I wonder where he could have got the property."

"My dear, pray do not be so excited. Young Graff has lately bought some houses in the village, and I understand he has just painted the portrait of Mr. Nutmeg. This may account for the vote. Besides, his father has always been a Radical.

Mr. Spell, I believe, is now the registered proprietor of the new Myrtle Cottage."

" I think pa's victory is sure since Oberon has voted for him. Oh ! I verily believe I should have died if he had gone against us."

But notwithstanding all this youthful enthusiasm, the news of the baronet's defeat came that evening. This was felt as a great blow in the · family. Ernestine, who entered fully into the political situation and spirit of the contest, was inconsolable. The whole party was dashed by a defeat as unmerited as it was unexpected. Sir Roger Wheatley, that able and useful member of the Conservative phalanx, was out of parliament.

END OF VOL. I.

www.ingramcontent.com/pod-product-compliance
Lightning Source LLC
Chambersburg PA
CBHW031043120726
47905CB00007B/2283